The Cure for Lonely

The Cure for Lonely

by

Jessica Thummel

FREIGHT BOOKS

First published 2017

Freight Books
49–53 Virginia Street
Glasgow, G1 1TS
www.freightbooks.co.uk

ISBN 978-1-911332-39-8
eISBN 978-1-911332-40-4

Typeset by Freight in Plantin
Printed and bound by Hussar Books, Poland

Jessica Thummel is a writer from Dodge City, Kansas.
Currently she lives in Denver, Colorado.

For Mike

1

It was 1989, and in the four years since my best friend Eddie died, his girlfriend Gwen had been shipped off to gay-reform camp (my fault, she'd say), I had finished nursing school, a heart attack had put my father in the ground, my younger sister Sally had lost her virginity, my mother had bought a sports car, and life had just whatevered along with the same boring people doing the same boring things until I started to think, hell, maybe Eddie had the right idea, putting the barrel of a gun up to his chin. I'd been itching to leave Lawrence for years, but who's to say when I actually would've left if it weren't for one day in June when I got fired just hours before Gwen came back into my life, quick as a twister and only a little less destructive.

No one from my family had lived outside of Kansas since the Gavin clan, a mix-breed of German-Irish immigrants, settled in the area around the same time Sherman was setting fire to the South. We were pioneers, my father liked to brag, rough-and-tough outlaws who hunkered down and held tight no matter what. Loyal, too, he'd argue, showing anyone who'd sit still his copy of a microslide of a newspaper he'd got from the archives at the Lawrence Public Library, the headline: *Gavins Hiding Pa Bender?* As if stowing a serial-killing innkeeper back in the frontier days was a source of family pride.

For twenty-one years, I had lived in that same spot as Rosie Gavin, an oval-faced wimpy-looking kid, wearing slacks most days, ties sometimes. I kept my haircut short like Rob Lowe and my nails bitten down to a nub. The year after my father died, I legally changed my name at the county courthouse, not really having a clear plan for what I would do next, what I *could* do really. I was only doing what felt right, and being called Rosie never had. Now there's another slide in the archives, but this one my father would've kept secret. A listing on page seventeen, column four, before the obituaries and just past the classifieds in the June 17, 1988 issue: *Rosie Samantha Gavin (June 21, 1966), daughter of Molly (1943-) and Bruno Gavin (1937-1987) will hereby be recognized, by the state of Kansas, as Sam Ro Gavin as requested by the aforementioned.*

My mother wouldn't speak to me for weeks after I did it. She said it was stupid. Rosie was a family name, and Sam was a boy's name. Why did I always want to confuse people? But it didn't matter. Kansans were stubborn; half the people in Lawrence still called me Rosie, no matter how often I asked them to stop.

Anyway, the day I got fired, my shift started out with a troublesome new patient, or as we were supposed to call them, 'resident' who took it upon himself to act up the same afternoon a bigwig from corporate came down to check on us. The visit was unusual. People from corporate typically kept to their carpeted cubicles, avoiding the ammonia-and-oatmeal odor of the front lines. The new patient, Howard, had dementia, but he was tall and fat despite his old age, and he'd forgotten where he was when I went to help him into his wheelchair. The old man panicked when I touched him, and he up and socked me in the eye. Stung like hell. Started swelling almost immediately. Now, I'm not the type to hit a patient, no way, but I didn't set him down gently in the chair, either – Christ, he was three hundred pounds; he couldn't go down gently into anything – but just as his massive ass slammed down in the chair, the fucking thing collapsed around him like a cardboard box because it hadn't been locked properly, and Howard started wailing, and, my stupid luck, the bigwig walked past the doorway at that precise moment and had enough sense to stop and investigate the commotion.

He fired me right then and there as Cara ran off to call an ambulance.

I spat on the tile and went out to my car. I thought about running over the sign for *Spring Meadow Assisted Living* on my way out, but what would that have done besides fuck up my front end? No, I thought, this was a good thing. It was providence. I knew I could find another job at another nursing home with similar malfunctions, but I was done with catering to old hags like Betty always shouting for her slippers, and Maynard with his perpetual foreskin infection. I wasn't really sure what my other options were, but at least now I had the time in my schedule to find out.

As I pulled out of the parking lot, I thought about how Eddie, in his most metaphysical marijuana funks, used to yap on and on about the probability of an infinite universe. He used it as an excuse to follow his own code of ethics: *man, just do what you feel like; don't wait for one of the other yous to get it right*, he would say. And in that moment, making amends with Gwen, who I'd heard was back in town, seemed like the first reasonable and realistic thing to do.

I came to an empty four-way stop where I pulled a roach from the ashtray and touched it to the Zippo flame. I puffed on the joint while I drove a square around town and listened to *Madness* on the tape deck, and thought about exactly what I would say to her.

After a few songs, I stopped for a forty-ounce bottle of liquid courage, and I drove toward Gwen's parents' house. I parked a block away and finished the beer while watching a flock of starlings swirl like smoke in the sky. Finally, I decided to say:

Fuck what these people think. Run away with me, Gwen.

Gag. It was a dumb idea. The last time I'd seen her we were seniors in high school and she was sitting on the edge of the bathtub, naked beneath a towel, looking all shameful while her mother yelled through the door, *I hear you two*! But still, running away was something we'd done at least a dozen times before, back when Eddie and her and me would take off to Kansas City or Topeka or a party in Hays, just because (little use it was) it felt like escaping.

I hadn't seen her in so long, not because I didn't want to, but because we were both too stubborn or proud to call first. Though seeing as her fiancé Bobby was no longer a factor, or so I'd heard, I saw my opportunity to finally swoop in and tell her how I felt.

I pulled the car up a block, got out, and strutted up the sidewalk, hoping she was watching from the window, that she might be excited by the sight of me and come running out, squealing *I've missed you!* I prayed her mother wouldn't answer.

I looked down at the doormat – *Unless you can walk on water, wipe your feet here* – and realized I was numb-faced drunk. I rang the doorbell, heard footsteps approach, and watched the peephole go black before the latch unlocked. Gwen's mother, Joan, opened the door and pushed her makeup-slathered face up close to the screen.

'Roooosieeeee,' she said. It was a tense sound, as if someone had a gun to the back of her head.

I considered correcting her about my name, but I knew she'd probably just shut the door.

'I'm here to get Sally,' I said. My sister had been best friends with Rachel, Gwen's sister, since middle school.

'Sally's not here.' She focused on the bruise starting to appear around my eye, compliments of my demented assailant, as if waiting for an explanation, and I decided to give her one.

'She didn't tell you, did she?'

'Tell me what?'

I paused. 'Yeah, that makes sense. She probably didn't want the attention. Tough kid, Sally.'

Joan looked suspicious. 'What is it?'

I gave her a lie I assumed might be tragic enough to get invited into the house, or, at the very least, get Gwen's attention if Joan mentioned it later, maybe over dinner, all of them sitting around the table. 'I'm sick,' I said. 'I got dizzy yesterday, fell, and hit the corner of the kitchen counter.'

Joan narrowed her eyes, studying, searching for hollowness in my face or weight loss anywhere, anything that might indicate I was terminal, but she didn't invite me in; she only stood there while the smell of their house, still the soft mix of spices and lacquered wood, drifted out through the thin slit in the door.

She turned her head and hollered out, 'Rachel! Rachel, come here.' A second passed, and a layer of sweat started to bead up over my body just as Gwen's sister came into view. She gave me a weak smile but didn't speak until Joan asked her if she knew anything about me being sick, and Rachel shook her head and said she hadn't heard. I could feel my heart pumping up in my throat.

'Nothing? Sally didn't say a thing?' Joan asked, and Rachel shrugged. 'That's hard to believe. Such a talkative girl.'

'I don't remember,' she groaned in that petulant-teenager tone.

Joan turned back to me. 'Well, Rosie Gavin, we'll pray for your speedy recovery.' She smiled like she'd done all she could and shut the door.

Halfway to the car, I looked up at the second-floor window where the curtains were pulled open and someone sat in the darkened window staring down at me. It was hard to make out more than the silhouette until the person leaned forward and her face emerged from the shadows and suddenly I felt long and gangly and awkward as I moved across the grass. I raised my hand to wave. Gwen raised hers too, slow, controlled, like she had a question. I put mine up to my ear like 'call me.'

She didn't call. I waited. Watched *Unsolved Mysteries* and *Night Court* with Sally, ate leftover tuna salad, and thought about gassing up the car and driving somewhere like Oregon, to that gloomy town where the kids from *The Goonies* lived. I wanted grey skies too. I wanted a treasure hunt.

My mother came home from work around eight still wearing her apron from the grocery store. 'Idiots,' she said to neither of us. 'Spend all day trying to be civil to a bunch of idiots, and now Larry' – she sighed – 'he has the flu so I have to go cover his ten to ten. He'd only scheduled *himself*. Who's that stupid?' She scratched her fat arm with an acrylic nail and looked over at me. 'What the fuck happened to your eye?'

'Bird flew in my car,' I said. I couldn't tell her I'd lost my job.

Ever since my father died, she'd been laying the guilt on full-spread, and she'd probably ask for *more* rent instead of giving me a break.

She narrowed her eyes like she didn't buy it. 'You need more iron. That bruise looks anemic.'

'In what aisle of Dillons did you get your medical license?'

Sally, who was curled on the corner of the couch pretending to read some giant book while she waited for her boyfriend Paul to come over with a bottle of Seagram's 7, shifted uncomfortably. She'd never been any good with confrontation, and it annoyed the hell out of our mother.

'Take off that goddamn sweatshirt, Sally, and stop touching the A/C. I'm not made of dollar bills.'

Without a word, Sally got up and turned the dial on the thermostat.

'It's because she's getting fat,' I said. 'I know you ate all my doughnuts, Sally; I saw you.'

Sally gave me a nasty look, and I shot her a smile, and she flipped me the bird.

'Asshole,' she said.

My mother lit a cigarette and changed the channel on the TV without asking. She sat down next to me, smelling like the canned air in the grocery store: sour potato skins and butchered meat, dried milk with a touch of cinnamon gum.

I got up and went to my room to spark a joint. I blew the smoke out the open window and turned on my tape player at low volume and while Freddy Mercury belted that we, he and I, were such champions, I lifted and lowered a set of twenty-pound weights until my biceps felt like splintered wood.

2

Gwen was a flake. I knew this. When she moved to Lawrence our freshman year of high school she'd blown through various bubbles of friends, fracturing each group until she was the leader. I wasn't part of any one clique – Eddie was my only real friend – but she still managed to splinter our friendship when she decided she wanted a boyfriend a few months in, and Eddie started spending all his free time with her. It wouldn't have mattered so much, except that I already had a giant crush on Gwen and she'd taken all kinds of advantage, pretending she wanted to be my friend until Eddie came around and then twirling her hair and falling into Eddie's chest anytime he said something resembling funny. The real annoying part: once she had him, of course, she'd decide that she didn't want him (citing some bullshit about her parents' rules or God's watchful eye) until Eddie was seen on the Smokers' Corner across from school, making out with Kelly Owen instead of learning to change a tire in Driver's Ed, and then all of a sudden she'd want him like his dick was twelve inches and it pissed diamonds. So he'd go back to her, but nothing would change. If she got a bad grade or heard the wrong sermon or just felt a whimsy, she'd leave him again, and Eddie would be at my window, drunk and heartbroken and swearing never again.

To be honest, I always had mixed feelings whenever they broke up. On one hand, I felt horrible seeing my best friend in pieces over a girl, but every single moment I spent with him while he had the girl I wanted was torture. I felt like smashing his head. I felt like Cain. Seeing him sad was a binary experience for me: hard to watch, and yet it filled me with hope, every time, which is something I will always regret.

Still, Gwen's pussy was the only one I'd ever poked around with, and for some reason the only way I could get off, like *get off*, was if I thought about her in the shower: her skin slippery with bar soap, her tangle of hair spread against her tits, the white-tiled wall behind her back, her eyes closed, lips parted, the squishy suction of my middle and index fingers pumping. Her moan, god.

It wasn't that my material for arousal was small, either. Hell, my dad had a thirty-year subscription to *Playboy*. It was as common as *Cabela's* on the back of the toilet. I'd studied hundreds of different women, all types: hairy-bushed and clean-shaven, small-tittied and udder-sized, and more recently the implant chicks who look as hard as gourds. I'd seen all races and ages and imagined fucking these women from all different angles and still, when I got close, I heard Gwen moaning, felt her spaz around my fingers, followed by the pounding at the door, her mother's voice alight with righteous panic.

There was also another emotion that compelled me toward her, deeper than lust, some primal tug frayed out and elongated by Gwen never calling, never writing. I hated her and yet all I wanted to do was scoop her up and carry her away to a place where we could coexist, where she would love me. That was what Gwen did to me. She splintered my emotions until sadness and anger and hope popped up in the most unusual ways, like desiring her and wanting her dead all at once, which was the feeling that hit me full and square in the chest when I heard a knock at my bedroom window a little past midnight, and I went to lift the blinds, assuming it was Eddie's brother, Marcus, and instead I saw Gwen's face behind the glass.

I lifted the window, and Gwen stepped back to see me better.

'I hope you had a tetanus shot because that screen is jagged and rusty as hell,' I said.

'That's the first thing you pick to say?'

'I just don't want you dying of lockjaw.'

'Speaking of dying…' Her face opened to a moon-white smile. 'My mom made us pray for Rosie Gavin at dinner tonight. Said you might be moving on to heaven soon, and I wanted to see if I could come with you.' She reached down and lifted a hatbox from the dirt, pulled back the lid. A wad of green bills bobbled – all twenties – and a few gained air and sailed out with a draft. She clamped the lid shut, and I knew she was serious about something, I just wasn't sure what.

Sally's light turned on, throwing a yellow square into the backyard.

'So are you dying or not?' she said.

'I just wanted to see you.'

'Can I come in?'

'Sally'll tell Rachel.'

'I don't care,' she said. 'We're fucking adults.'

I wondered if she'd made all the money in that hatbox herself or if she'd stolen it from her parents. I didn't ask.

I went to the front door and let her inside. As we came through the living room, Sally was leaving the kitchen with a glass of water and she looked at us both with a wild sheen. The only reason there'd even been the whole lesbian scandal with Gwen and me was because Sally and Rachel had spread the story, making sure everyone knew they weren't dykes like we were. Middle school girls, I've noticed, are a lot like evangelical Christians – they just won't shut the fuck up about what they think they know.

'Hi Sally,' Gwen said in a sweet, intimidating tone.

Sally smiled and looked down at a hole in her sock and hurried back to her room. She slammed her door behind her and started chattering to Paul.

Gwen had been to my mother's house at least a hundred times and so she charged down the hallway to my bedroom where she pulled open my closet and started ripping T-shirts from hangers. 'Bobby is on his way to my house. Right now. My mom said he could stay in the guest room. Can you believe that bitch? Can you believe her? Like the sanctity of being engaged outweighs the fact that he's a cheater. So I'm leaving. We're going to see the ocean. You and me. Just like we planned before. We're doing it now.'

I liked this Gwen. The madcap Gwen. The other side of her

was lethargic and self-doubting and full of venom, but right now I could let that one slip into the background. I could focus on this one, the girl who would streak down a busy street, or call up Pizza Hut and pretend to have an orgasm while she ordered a hand-tossed pepperoni, or decide to run away from home lickety-split. I knew she was using me, trying to find the best possible way to twist the knife a full circle in Bobby's (and probably her mom's) heart, so I didn't want to submit too easily, especially given how casually she assumed I'd drop everything and go at her command.

'I have a life, Gwen. What makes you think I can just leave?'

'You said we'd go to the ocean and I could ride a dolphin—'

'Like a horse?'

'Or maybe pet it—'

'With a saddle and a bridle and—'

'Okay, maybe there's no dolphins, but there was definitely an ocean promised.'

There had been a lot of promises we hadn't kept, and I wanted to tell her that, but I looked off and pretended I was weighing my options while I counted to eight. 'So you're just going to leave Bobby?'

'We're so over.'

'Then why's he coming to Lawrence?'

Gwen collapsed her shoulders and let out a long breath. 'I'm sure Sally's already told you the whole embarrassing story about how he screwed his academic advisor, and his coming here doesn't change shit.'

I already knew, sure, but hearing her say it gave me a little thrill. 'Maybe I have a girlfriend,' I said. 'Maybe she wouldn't like me leaving with you.'

'Sally already spilled everything to Rachel. I know you're single, and your only friend is Marcus—'

'That's not true.'

'—and you go to the movies almost every Friday night. Alone.' She started rooting around in my dresser drawer and pulled out a pair of plaid boxers. 'This is your underwear?'

I grabbed the boxers from her hand and wadded them up in my fist. 'There are a lot of things you don't know about me.'

She blinked. 'There are plenty of things you don't know about me, either,' she said, play-seductive.

I imagined all the opportunities I'd have to see Gwen naked if we made it to the coast together: after a shower, or when she'd slip into her nightclothes, or out in the water when a wave pushed off her top, or after a few bottles of wine and a good coaxing with my hand above her pants. I thought about the two of us sitting on a little balcony, right outside our new coastal paradise hotel, looking off at the fog or the sunset, telling jokes and stories and having, not the time of our lives, but perpetual good days. I thought of her and me starting new somewhere without our histories.

'Which ocean?' I asked, and her eyes and lips and cheeks all reached for the ceiling.

Just then, we heard some drunk shouting outside my window. 'Gavin! Gavin!' It was Eddie's brother, Marcus, and he started banging on the screen. It wasn't unusual, the window visits; my father, when he was alive, almost shot three of my friends, some more than once. It was just a part of the routine. No one who knew me and came over on the regular would ever knock on the front door.

Gwen asked who it was and I shushed her and moved her toward the closet. 'It's Marcus.'

She tried to shrug me off, but I opened the closet door and shoved her in. 'He'll flip if he sees you here.'

She actually looked offended. 'Why? What did I do?'

'Seriously,' I said, and she folded her arms.

'He doesn't still blame me. C'mon. That's retarded.' Innocent as she claimed to be, she knew I was referring to Eddie.

'Just disappear for a second.'

'Like I held the gun to his head.'

No, you just fucked another dude, I should've said. Instead, I told her, 'If I have to defuse him cause he sees you, we're not leaving tonight. We'll be lucky to get out of here by next week,' and I shut the closet door.

I went to the window, lifted the blinds, and casually asked Marcus what he wanted.

'Dude, what happened to your face?' he asked.

I told him I got punched at work. He squinted to see through the screen. 'Knuckles,' he said, diagnosing the source. 'What did I tell you, Gavin? Bob and weave, man.'

I asked him, again, what he needed.

He said he was next door, shooting the shit with old Bill. He smelled like hamburger grease and beer, and he blew a wet burp out of the side of his mouth and asked if I wanted to come over and get high.

'Why do you hang out with old farts?' I asked.

Bill, my mother's neighbor, was a skinny, bow-backed, wily, old man who went from stone still to animated whenever his passions were riled. Sometimes when he got to talking, it was like listening to a canyon speak, all gravelly and bottomless and ancient-seeming. He was famous in some parts of the world as *the* William S. Burroughs who wrote confusing-ass books, *Naked Lunch* and *Junkie* among them. I'd never bothered to read them, and Bill had never mentioned writing once in all the times I'd gone over there with Marcus, but I'd seen the faded bulletin board at the library celebrating 'Lawrence's Most Famous Local Author,' and occasionally people would drive down our block real slow, like they were looking for JFK Jr. or Michael Jackson or something, and they would snap a picture of his red little bungalow before pulling away. Around here, though, he was just known as Bill: collector of cats and weapons and oddballs like Marcus. He and my father had a five-year feud over whether or not it was legal to shoot off a firearm in one's backyard with Bill saying it was. Everyone knew he had accidentally shot his wife in the face a long time ago, which made his position of what-harm-could-come a perilous one.

How Marcus knew Bill had nothing to do with me. Marcus was a slinger around town, sold marijuana and mushrooms mostly, organic things that could supplement his fizzling boxing career (made especially flat whenever he got a shipment of Afghani opiates and decided to take a hiatus from the sport and get junked for weeks instead). He sold to Bill on the regular, and they were friends now, so whatever.

I honestly didn't love their company or the fact that I felt like part of the sofa pattern whenever I sat in Bill's living room with his group of friends, all old enough to be my father or grandfather and completely disinterested in a weird kid like me: not girlish or boyish, just neutral, like a grown-up newborn in three layers of T-shirt.

Marcus burped again. 'Gotta pay the bills, Gavin,' he said. 'So, are you coming or not?' Either way, he needed our stash, which was currently buried in the closet next to the person he hated most in this world, and I told him to give me a second.

I went back to the closet where the light was on, and Gwen was sitting, digging through a box of old photos. She threw it all down like she knew she was in the wrong, snooping, and I asked her to move so I could get to the ShopVac.

'What are you doing?' she asked.

'Getting some weed,' I said. It wasn't my weed, exactly. It was Marcus's weed, and I just happened to be holding on to the vacuum where it was stored. In exchange for holding on to the shit, blocks of schwag smuggled up from Mexico by who-knows-who, I got to smoke up whenever I wanted. And whenever was pretty often.

I jerked a few buds from an open brick and put them in a sandwich bag. Then I put on my shoes and told Gwen I'd be right back.

When I returned, I packed a suitcase while Gwen studied a photo of me and Eddie that she'd found in the box. In the photo, we had our heads poking through the oval holes of a carnival cut-out, which had, on the front, a cartoon painting that made us look like two bodybuilders flexing in their 1930s circus stripes. When I saw it, nostalgia floated through my body like loose cobwebs, sticking to everything.

I asked Gwen if she remembered that trip, how we ran away, all three of us, for an entire weekend at the Kansas State Fair.

She shuddered. 'We had to sleep by the pig pens.'

'Their beds were better than ours,' I said, which was true; the pigs each had their own mass of dry straw and an oval-shaped rubber mattress at one end of their individual pens, and a blanket that I actually saw one use properly. Together, we all slept in the car in the parking lot.

'Where do you think Eddie would go today if we asked him?' Gwen said with a dumb smile across her face, like we could actually, if we wanted, call him up and wonder all together.

I pulled the photo from her hand and put it in the luggage and snapped it shut.

'He'd probably just want to do the same old shit.'

'Worlds of Fun,' she said.

'Well, I'm ready for a new amusement park.'

That seemed to energize her, and she bit my shoulder as we were walking out of the house, and we threw our bags in the back of my car, and buckled ourselves up. Inside, my hands on the wheel, we said nothing as we sat in the dark driveway, silent for over a minute, neither of us brave enough to admit what we were really thinking. Finally, I fished a penny from the door panel and told her, 'Tails: east. Heads: west,' and I tossed the coin and we watched it undulate in the dome light, desperate to know we weren't headed for nowhere.

3

The gap between us and Lawrence widened just as quick as the Dump would go, while I tried to hammer out the logistics: where exactly were we driving and how long would we be gone? Gwen seemed unwilling to make any hard decisions, probably so she could complain later, drop her criticisms about the food or wind or smell. She wanted to escape, but she didn't want to be responsible. Every town I suggested, she'd shrug. *San Diego? Sure. Seattle? Sure. San Francisco? Sure.* I hadn't had the chance to study an atlas, but I knew if I kept following the interstates west we were bound to meet the Pacific someday, and so that became our indefinite plan. Go west.

The minutes bled over into hours as Gwen thumbed through a pile of *People* magazines she'd brought along. She read with a flashlight, while I watched the headlights fan across the highway and prayed a deer or dog or coyote wouldn't cross our path. I listened to the radio, but kept the volume down low – *the situation in Panama is bad and getting worse, students in China protest for democracy in the streets, a man in Boston steals an airplane and shoots rifle fire into neighborhoods* – until I couldn't take the politics shuffled in with Randy Travis and Garth Brooks, and found a cassette. Buddy Holly always had a way of making me feel like nothing mattered.

Every so often Gwen would turn to me and relay a bit of gossip from one issue or another: Prince Charles escaped an avalanche in Switzerland, Robin Williams got married, Glenn Close had a baby, boring news I mostly tuned out until she read something, perfectly, with her bible-school elocution, that sent chills rippling under my skin as if muscle had lifted from bone. 'Billy Tipton's Strange Secret: He was a She.' Gwen started reading the article out loud, describing a popular jazzman, beloved by everyone who knew him, including his sons, his wife, his neighbors, and his fans. 'It wasn't until his death,' Gwen said, 'that most people, including his own children, who were adopted, learned the big secret: Tipton had been born a woman.'

Gwen stopped reading and looked over at me. I tried to make my interest appear even with Gary Coleman turning twenty-one, but I cared a whole hell of a lot more about this story. I'd heard of people in drag, but actually pulling it off, all your neighbors and friends, and kids even, believing, was something I'd imagined but never really considered. It sounded impossible, something that would happen in a sci-fi movie or a fantasy, but not in real life. No way. But if Tipton had pulled it off...

I looked away from the line of endless asphalt and raised an eyebrow. 'Are you done?' I didn't want her to be done. I wanted to know everything about this Tipton guy. Did his wife know? Could he use urinals? Did he take steroids? I ran a hand over my chin, flexed my biceps, wondering. Gwen looked down at the magazine and shook straight the cover, which had a picture of Ronald and Nancy Reagan embracing, and the quotation, *'Don't Worry, They're Happy.'* She continued reading about the stunned community where Tipton had lived and about his wife, who refused to discuss their life or how Tipton had pulled off such a feat for fifty years.

As she finished, the tape stopped playing and the car went quiet. 'Her?' I finally said.

'Hmmm?'

'At the beginning of the article, they called Billy him, and then they called him her.'

'That's what he gets for lying to people all these years.'

'All those years, just erased by one anatomical revelation? Jesus, his kids didn't even know.'

Gwen rolled her eyes and turned the page. 'It's weird,' she said. 'Don't you think it's weird?'

I didn't know what I thought. I wasn't so sure it was weird. I mean it was about the weirdest thing I'd ever heard and yet I got it. All my life I felt more like a boy than not a boy. I'd told my mother this when I was five or six, when they started separating the students by gender in my classroom, and she got so angry she slapped my face, ensuring I never brought it up again. I understood Billy, or thought I did – I *liked* it when people treated me like a guy; preferred it, honestly – but I didn't know how to explain it, or I was worried that understanding Billy made me weird too.

I shrugged and turned the cassette over. 'Peggy Sue' started playing. I thought about what Gwen said, how Billy was lying to people. But, was it a lie? Or, was it the end of one? And whose fucking business was it, anyway? Certainly not Gwen's and probably not mine either.

Gwen folded her arms and laid her head back against the window. After a minute or so, she said, 'What's really weird is being back in this car.' She opened the glove box and started pulling out everything with Eddie's name on it. Before the Dump had been mine, it had been Eddie's and it felt like she was disturbing his tomb. I took the pile from her lap and threw the papers back in.

'Geez,' she said. 'I wasn't looking at that or anything.' She turned off the tape player as revenge. 'I can't believe you still listen to that shit.'

'Buddy Holly is timeless.'

'Only because of people like you and, you know, old people. Don't you have any Madonna?'

'No. I refuse.'

'I should've brought my music.' She bundled her coat and placed it against the window. 'Wake me when we stop for breakfast,' she said and settled in.

'Gwen.'

She opened her eyes. 'Yeah?'

I had the urge to lay it all out, not my feelings about Billy Tipton (because that story was still gaining roots, spreading synapses), but about how happy I was to put the past behind us, both in literal miles and any residual anger we might both have, but what came out instead was this pathetic-sounding question: 'How come you never called?'

Gwen moved her coat from the window and rebundled it, an action, I assumed, that was meant to delay. 'Because I wanted to surprise you.' She was being dense on purpose, her favorite way of wiggling out of an answer. 'Weren't you happy to see me at your window?'

'Every summer you came back and you never called, not once.'

'You had my number too, you know.'

'I didn't, actually.'

'Yeah, well, you could've gotten it.'

'Sure. Hey Joan, I know I finger-fucked your daughter, and that was a little awkward for everyone, but would you mind putting her on the phone?'

'Why are we talking about this?'

'It's been gnawing at me.'

'And you couldn't say something earlier?'

'I didn't want to piss you off.'

'But you want to now? Now that I'm stuck.'

I knew maybe she was right. 'No,' I said. 'I just want to put it behind us, you know. I want to leave that question in Lawrence.'

Gwen sat up straight. 'I'm sorry,' she finally said.

'I'm not asking you to say you're sorry. I want to know why I didn't matter.'

'You did matter.'

'It didn't seem like it.'

'Oh, poor Ro,' she said. 'I suppose I mattered to you so much and that's why you and Marcus were all over town calling me a whore.'

I wasn't quite sure what she was referring to, but a bell was ringing somewhere inside my skull. 'You know my name is Sam now, right?' I said. 'I mean, if Sally's such a talker, I'm sure she mentioned that.' By then it had been over a year since I had changed it at the county courthouse.

'I heard,' she said without looking at me. 'It's just habit.'

We didn't say anything for a good ten seconds, and then she asked me why I had been trash-talking her.

'I don't know what you're talking about,' I said.

Gwen spoke slowly, as if she were explaining to a child. 'Bonnie Allen said you called me a whore.'

'Marcus said that. Not me.'

'Oh, I see. So, I mattered enough to just stand by and let him say that.'

'He's a grown man. He can say what he wants.'

Gwen looked out the window, and then back at me. 'You know what? Fine. You want to have this conversation. Okay. I was pissed at you. Really pissed. You took advantage of me.'

'I what?'

'You did. You knew I was vulnerable over Eddie. You knew I was reeling—'

'We were all reeling.'

'And you got me into the shower with you.'

'You're making it sound like I tricked you.'

'You knew—'

'Like I dangled candy—'

'I was vulnerable.'

'*Here little girl!*'

'And *I* got sent to gay camp. Me. Not you. My life got turned inside out. Not yours.'

I felt a smidge of sympathy for her, but it wasn't my fault her mom was a psychopath, and I sure as shit wasn't going to take the blame. My life had been tipped over, too, and I told her that.

'Fuck you,' she said. 'No. Seriously, fuck you.'

I lit a cigarette and rolled down the window. Gwen twirled a piece of her hair and put all of her focus on a bundle of frizzy split-ends.

'Do you really think I took advantage of you?'

She nodded solemnly. 'I did.'

'Did?'

'Not advantage, necessarily. More like manipulated. And

you sorta did.'

'*Please, please touch me,*' I said, mocking her voice.

She slapped my shoulder.

I laughed. 'Maybe *I* got taken advantage of. Where's my Christian counselor?'

Gwen rolled her eyes. 'Can we just, whatever, drop it? I don't even care anymore.'

'Cool,' I said. 'Neither do I.'

'I'm just going to rest my eyes,' Gwen said, and within a few minutes, she started snoring.

She slept on as the sun chased us in the rearview, as we passed over the state line, as the miles stretched in a blanket of featureless horizon, hardly even one sad little tree or cow to break up the monotony. She slept on as the pixels of the Rocky Mountains pushed their way through the fuzzy atmosphere and became more solid and majestic, as patches of city – webs of exit ramps and houses and cars – became more frequent, as the skyscrapers appeared off in the distance like tiny matchsticks.

It was the first time I'd actually seen the mountains in real life – before then my travels had spanned from Branson to Dodge City, meaning, in my twenty-two years, I'd stood in exactly two states – and the mountains were bigger than I'd imagined, cartoonishly big, and some emotion gripped at my throat. Joy? Humility? I wasn't sure, but I knew I didn't want to see it alone. I looked over at Gwen, her hand thrown limp between her thighs, fingers curled inward toward the shadowed expanse beneath her skirt. I tickled her palm with my fingernail, but she didn't wake. I spoke her name, pushed her shoulder, and she took a deep breath and finally came to. The sun was straight above us now, overexposing the bleach-dry grass between the two sides of the highway, and glaring from every reflective surface at a thousand kilowatts. Gwen covered her eyes and said nothing about the mountains or miles that she'd slept or that she was grateful she didn't have to drive, only that she was starving and that she had to piss.

4

I took the first Denver exit with a promising billboard: a giant coffee pot with the words *Sapp Bros Food and Fuel* painted in red over its metallic surface. The restaurant was just off the interstate, past a few dusty gas pumps where semi-trucks were fueling up. Behind the building, big rigs were parked like cocoons in a row. As I stretched my shoulders and legs, Gwen bolted toward the door yelling that she'd meet me inside.

I followed her across the small parking lot and into the truck-stop that smelled like diesel and sweet sausage grease. In the front area, there was a regular-looking convenience store with a soda machine and a few refrigerated glass cases stocked with drinks and sandwiches, and five or six aisles of junk for sale – magazines and candy and pain meds – and I looked through a pile of clearance cassette tapes while Gwen finished up in the bathroom. She came out a few minutes later, and I asked her if she liked MC Hammer and I did a terrible impression of the Hammer dance and knocked over a display of potato chips. Gwen shook her head, and I threw the tape back in the pile.

Overhead, a speaker shrilled – *number twenty-seven, your shower is ready* – and I saw a fat man lumber out from a dim hallway with a ticket in his hand. Above the hallway a sign just read *Restaurant*, and Gwen and I walked past the man as he was getting his key. I imagined all the miles caked on him, layers of old sweat and dust, cigarette smoke and frothy swamps between his folds, and I felt a little sorry for the shower drain.

We settled into a booth near the cold and empty buffet table. Some pink streamers hung from the ceiling, and a banner read: *Congratulations Tammy! Free pie for newlyweds. This week only.* The sign looked pretty tattered, and I wondered when exactly *this week* was.

A waitress appeared and took our order, never looking up

from her pad.

Gwen unstuck the menu and peeled it open. 'I want a milkshake. Strawberry.'

'For you, sir?'

Gwen giggled, looking over her menu to share the joke, but I wouldn't look at her. Nerves pricked my skin. 'I'll have the steak and eggs,' I said, and the waitress scribbled it down.

'I'll have the same *as him*,' Gwen said, busting up again.

After the waitress walked away, Gwen leaned forward on her elbows and grinned at me. 'She thought you were a boy.'

'She wasn't even looking at me.'

Gwen pointed to the banner for free pie and clapped her hands together. 'I want that.'

'What?'

'Come on. Let's be married. I have a ring to prove it.' She held up her hand, showing off her big square diamond.

'I'll buy you pie.' Free pie seemed like a pretty stupid reason to risk humiliating myself.

'Come on,' she said. 'What fun are you?'

'It's too early for fun.'

Gwen folded her arms. 'Please.'

'All right.' I grabbed her hand. 'But I'd never pick that ring. It's like a giant, sparkly wart.'

'Bobby said it cost two thousand dollars.'

'Well, Bobby's an idiot.'

'Hey. That's my fiancé you're talking about.'

We both laughed.

After we finished our food, Gwen called the waitress over and launched into a story about how we just got hitched in Vegas and were heading home, and we'd really like a free slice of pie, if they were still honoring their deal. She pointed to the banner, and the waitress moved her ferret gaze over to the tattered sign and back to us. 'Looks like someone wasn't too happy about that,' she said. She used her pencil eraser to point at my black eye.

Gwen placated her, not missing a step. 'Daddy wasn't

too happy about the baby, no. We had to leave town for the nuptials.' She put one hand over her flat belly. 'Vegas sure was fun, though. Don't you think, husband? About Vegas?'

'Filthy people,' I said. 'Should've gone to Reno like Elvis said.'

'We only got rhubarb.'

It was the worst pie I'd ever had, bitter and gooey and soggy-crusted, but it also represented something new. For five minutes, I'd pulled off a Billy Tipton and suddenly, I saw how it could work. How the gears in people's minds generally believed what they were shown. It was exhilarating. Immediately, I had the desire to do it again, but for real and forever this time.

Gwen inhaled the slice like she hadn't just had a full meal, stuffing big sloppy mouthfuls in, and maybe it was the sugar, but her eyes went the sort of shimmery that I'd only seen in kleptos with a pocketful of swag and junkies who'd just scored a fix. She got off on getting away with things. After her last bite, she ran her tongue between her teeth and inside her lips before she smiled. 'You're welcome,' she said. She hadn't noticed I'd only had one bite.

Before we left, we both used the restroom. I went into the men's because the waitress stood in sight of the bathroom doors, flirting with a bushy-lipped trucker. When I walked in, there was a father and a small child at the urinal. The boy was perched on his tiptoes, trying to reach the threshold, and the whole room smelled like shit and ammonia. 'Don't get any on your shoes,' the man told his son. I went into the first stall and lowered my pants and stared down at an oval brown-red stain at the center of my underwear. Panicked, I choked out one word, 'No.' I hadn't thought to bring any pads with me – it wasn't like I paid attention to that particular ailment; nearly every month it came as a surprise to me – and I knew I'd have to go out there and buy some without making a big deal of it. I didn't want Gwen to think of me that way. Vulnerable, moody, bleeding.

Problem was, when I came out of the bathroom, Gwen wouldn't stop following me around. When I stood at the magazine rack, she started flipping through a *Vogue*, so I went to the aisle lined with batteries and car oil, but she was on my heels, like a shadow sewn to my backside.

Finally, I passed the feminine products and I pointed to the pads. 'You need any of these?' I said.

She curled her upper lip. 'Gross. I wear tampons.'

'Oh.'

'Do *you* wear pads?'

I supposed it didn't matter, considering she'd already flat out asked the question, and I didn't want to ruin the new briefs I'd bought for five dollars a pack, so I reached down and picked up the thickest kind. I ripped open the package and put a fat pink envelope in my pocket. I gave Gwen a ten-dollar bill and asked her to pay for them while I went back into the men's room and stuffed the fucking thing in my pants.

As I was washing my hands, a dude with a mullet came in and unzipped at the urinal. He was humming a song and as he let his bladder unload, he lifted up his left leg and goosed out a wet fart that smelled like rotten pasta.

I held back a gag and hurried out to the car, where Gwen was already lounged out, ready for the long haul.

As we were driving out of the parking lot, Gwen pulled up her shirt, revealing her flat stomach. 'Do you think I look pregnant?'

I looked over, happy for the invitation. 'Not even a little bit.'

'But that waitress believed me.'

'You wanted her to think you were lying?'

Gwen shook her head and pulled her shirt a little higher, revealing her lace bra. Her nipples were visible beneath the black fabric, and it was like she was taunting me on purpose. Without asking (or thinking, really), I reached over and traced her skin with my fingertips. She didn't stop me, just looked down at me touching her. My thoughts were not on the road or where we were going but on how badly I wanted to touch every last inch of her, until she screamed and I followed her eyes out the windshield and into a big brown van pulling out immediately ahead of us. Through the window I could see two faces inside staring right back at us, unconcerned, bored almost. Out of instinct, I swerved the wheel to avoid hitting them at the last second and we hopped the curb, crashing right into a retaining wall. The Dump crunched up like a can. I hit my lip on the steering wheel, busting it open and spilling blood all over my lap, the seat; it poured into my hands like warm water.

Gwen wasn't so great with blood either, and she damn near fainted when she saw the red puddle I was holding. I tried to tell her that the face bleeds more than other parts of the body – there were so many capillaries – but every time I moved my lips, another tablespoon would gush, and I started to worry that maybe I should be screaming too.

The van pulled over a few yards away from us, and three dudes slowly emerged from its shit-brown shell. I recognized one as the farter at the urinal, and I tried to tell Gwen this as they were approaching, but her face was pale and green-looking, and I could see she hadn't heard a word.

'You two all right?' the farter asked as he got close to the window. Another one of his friends with gelled hair and tight jeans inspected the front left tire.

I got out of the car, and they all got a good look at my face, which was red and wet and sticky by now, and I told Gwen to deal with them while I walked back to the convenience store and tried to wash up.

Turned out I'd bit my tongue at the same time that I'd split my lip and its giant gash was the source of most of the blood. It likely required stitches but I chose to compress it with a wad of paper towels while I bought a giant cup of ice from the fountain machine. The clerk asked if he needed to call the cops or a tow truck, and I could hear him, but my head was buzzing, like there was cotton spiralled from ear to ear inside my brain. A concussion, probably. I signaled that we were fine.

Gwen came running across the pot-holed parking lot just as I came out of the entrance. She had a giant bump across her forehead, all peaked and glowing pink, like she was becoming a unicorn, and her left eye was sloped and half swollen shut, and she was fuming mad.

'Look at my face!' she shouted.

Behind her, the three stooges were watching her skirt bounce.

I pointed to my blood-stained T-shirt. 'Yeah, well. At least you're not anemic at an elevated altitude.'

'The car is broken. Those boys said it was the axle.'

'Yeah, well, if 'those boys' hadn't pulled out in front of me, you wouldn't be looking like fucking Sloth right now.'

She glared with her one good eye.

'Rocky Road,' I said all malformed.

'They said they'd give us a ride.'

'Who? Those assholes in the van?'

As if on cue, the smarmy-looking one next to the Farter waved and started walking toward us.

'Dude. Sorry about your wheels,' he said.

The front end of the Dump came into clear view as I walked over, and I could see the left tire lying flat, folded under the frame, and the whole front fender bent up. If it were a horse, I would've fed it a carrot and rubbed its nose and put a bullet through its skull.

'Damn,' I said and kept thinking. I lifted my hand and gestured with my fistful of bloody paper towels that I wasn't fit to talk unless totally necessary, and I said, 'Your fault, you fuck,' to the Farter, who had been driving. I tasted more blood and spit red in the gutter.

The Farter was uglier in daylight, smallish for a man, about my size, and older than his haircut and tight jeans and high-tops suggested. He said, 'Right-of-way always goes to the car on the right.' He smelled like beer.

'No way. Not in an exit lane.'

'Fuck your exit lane.'

'Christ, Opie, stop talking already,' Smarmy interrupted, pushing the Farter aside to shake my hand. 'I'm Francis.' His grip was overzealous. Compensating. 'It was *definitely* his fault. We can pay you.' He reached into his pocket and started counting twenties. He held out two hundred dollars.

Part of me felt offended by the bullshit offer, but I also knew it was a gamble, trusting a car as unreliable as the Dump to get us across the mountains in the first place. Fixing it was hardly an option now. 'Look at my car,' I said to him. 'Look at my face. What am I supposed to do with two hundred dollars? Eight hundred, or I'm pressing charges.'

'I'm not paying them shit,' Opie said to Francis. 'There wasn't a stop sign.'

'Did you call the cops?' the third, more nervous-looking one asked me.

I considered whether I should lie or not, seeing as the driver was fucked up and it *really was* his fucking fault, but I stalled instead, afraid I might scare them into running. 'I want eight hundred.'

'Look,' Francis said. 'We'll pay you three hundred dollars for the damage, or you can fuck around with insurance and cops and all that bullshit, and who knows how long that will take. Do you live here?' Francis asked as Nervous went around to check my license plate.

'Seven hundred,' I said.

Opie laughed.

'Kansas,' Nervous said.

'Three fifty,' Francis said.

I thought about pushing the haggle further, edging them up to four fifty, but I *hadn't* actually called the cops, and besides, it was possible, given the typical mindset of Gwen's mother, who was something of a catastrophizer, that I was in the company of a legally missing person, which would raise all kinds of red flags when the cops arrived and would surely mean a trip back to Kansas. Never a fool, I put my hand out. 'Fine,' I said. 'Three fifty.'

Francis seemed surprised by my submission and his next words stumbled out. 'Well. I mean. I don't have it all *now*. We have to make it.'

I wanted to punch all three of them. It was involuntary. 'So, what? You just expect us to wait here and trust that you'll come back with the rest of the money?' I pushed my open palm closer to his fistful of bills, indicating that I wanted, at the very least, the stash he had right then, and Francis unenthusiastically handed it over.

He looked Gwen up and down. Besides her jacked-up face, her body still looked fuckable, and I could tell that's exactly what he was thinking with all his dollar-store charm. 'Come with us,' he said. 'I'll give you the rest when we're done.'

'So, you're broke,' I said.

His laugh was like a blunt car horn. 'Come to the concert, and I'll show you how much money I make.'

'Are you three in a band?' I asked.

Francis actually looked offended. 'Hell no,' he said. 'I'm a business man.'

'We're all business,' Nervous echoed.

'Where's your suit?' I asked.

'He wants to see your suit,' Opie said with a dull chuckle.

'She,' Gwen corrected and then hit my shoulder, like we'd done it again. The gender bandits. Of course, now that some real dicks were around, I was back to being a girl to her. I knew the game would eventually end, but it disturbed me how quickly they shifted their demeanor from thinking I was a dude to thinking I was a girl, especially Opie, who seemed particularly disturbed that maybe I'd seen his penis.

'Why the fuck were you in the men's room?' Opie said.

'I didn't see anything, dude. Relax. There was free pie.'

'Yeah, Opie,' Francis said. 'Free pie.'

'Well, karma made things even, I guess,' Opie said as he gestured to the Dump.

'So, what's your business?'

'Are you saying you want to see my business too?' Francis said, and they all laughed, even Gwen.

A truck honked at us, and Nervous and Opie went to move the van from blocking the exit.

'Do you want to go?' I asked Gwen.

She nodded, grinning stupidly. I could see it now, the ocean vanishing, our whole runaway wasted with this douchebag. The entire drive she had been incapable of making even the tiniest decision and suddenly she was calling all the shots. It infuriated me, but I had no other alternative shy of looking like a dick or a killjoy, and besides, I wanted the rest of my money.

I spit another clot of blood in the gutter. 'Fine, whatever,' I said, and I grabbed our stuff from the car. I didn't say anything to Gwen, but I had a feeling it would probably be the last time I ever saw the Dump and I felt responsible somehow, like I was leaving a piece of Eddie out to bake in the sun. Guilt squared. But I told myself that I deserved this, for once in my life, to just walk away like that. To let it all go.

5

Their van looked like a rape-mobile or something a serial killer would use to transport his bodies. The back had no windows or seats, and Francis, Gwen, and I had to sit on the shag carpet amongst a pile of instrument cases and a cooler sloshing with ice and beer. The other two, Opie and Nervous, sat up front, with Nervous behind the wheel now.

As we drove away, Francis reached into his front pocket and pulled out a plastic bag filled with sheets of paper. 'Business,' he said. I opened the cooler and took a beer without asking.

'Is that acid?' Gwen lurched forward to inspect the bag, but Francis yanked it away and high above his head. His armpits were dark with sweat. Musk filled the van.

'It *is*,' he said, teasing, pulling the bag closer to his torso.

'What's the little picture?' Gwen begged, and Francis turned the bag in his hand, studying the blotted paper inside.

'It's the Mona Lisa,' Francis said, and he showed Gwen the bag. 'Cause my stuff is a work of art. You want a hit?' he asked, delicate, like he was offering a child ice cream.

'Now?'

'If you want.'

'Is it any good?' she asked, scooting across the van, tumbling onto Francis's lap as we pulled to a stop. He put his hand on her arm for a moment, stroking it gently, before he let her up.

'I don't waste my time with bullshit,' he said. 'One of these, you'll be in a one-on-one exclusive interview with the creator of the fucking universe.'

Gwen shook her head. 'What does that even mean?'

'It's a one-hundred-percent positive trip or your money back.'

'So, you're going to charge her?' I asked.

'No.' Francis cocked his head. 'It's cool. It's on the house.'

He winked at Gwen. 'Here.' He opened the bag, pulled free a sheet, and took a hit. Gwen's eyes went wide and wicked. Then he lifted one up to her mouth, and her tongue appeared like she was ready for communion. Francis stuck the stamp to her buds, and she sealed her lips. 'Now,' he said in a hushed voice, 'in about thirty minutes, you're going to feel warm. Maybe a little nauseous, but it won't hurt you. Always keep that in your head.' His face turned paternal, as if she were his to keep safe, but his eyes were cold, hungry. 'I got you. Remember that.'

He asked if I wanted one and, of course, I took the stamp but didn't put it in my mouth. Instead, I slipped it in the plastic wrap of my cigarette pack. Francis didn't seem to notice (or didn't care), and he started to tell us how he and Opie and Nervous (whose real name was Dennis) went to different shows every few nights, selling LSD and pot, bribing the parking attendants with a cut of their profits to keep the cops off them. I listened, drank my beer, tasted blood in my mouth.

The van bumped around and our pace seemed to slow. The sounds of loose gravel radiated up from beneath the tires, and I wondered where exactly we were going. I closed my eyes and pictured a different world, one where Gwen and I were still sitting in the Dump, riding over the Rockies together, alone, without these fools, and I wondered what difference it would make in the long run, this detour. What was a detour anyway, with no destination in mind?

When Dennis pulled open the van door, I nearly toppled out onto the ground. It took a moment for my eyes to adjust to the sun, and I expected to see something urban outside – like a city street or at the very least, some buildings – but we were parked in a dirt lot with hundreds of other cars. Dwarfing us were incredibly large, slanted walls of rust-colored rock jutting from the ground. Maybe it was the beer, but the towering slabs made me feel less complicated somehow, like I could live my life, all my little years, and there they'd be, exactly as is, unable to change, uncaring either way. Part of me wanted to stay right there, staring up, forever, but Gwen jabbed my shoulder and pointed off in the distance, at the city, now in miniature.

Francis got out behind us, holding the cooler and a couple of lawn chairs. 'You ladies want to sit?' he asked, and he put the chairs out on the gravel. Gwen did so gleefully, but I refused and stayed standing.

I helped Francis and his friends pull the instrument cases from the back door of the van. When we were finished, I grabbed a beer and listened to Dennis tune his guitar. Opie was sitting in the back of the van now, melting heroin on a spoon, and he hummed along to the scales. Outside, Francis settled in a chair next to Gwen and began tapping a bongo drum. Gwen sat beside him, holding a pair of maracas, which she stared at for a while, mesmerized, and then she shook them like a baby rattle, terribly out of rhythm.

Dennis strummed a few notes and told me about their business model. 'Basically I just go around and play a song – like I'm fucking around – but the lyrics got all the instructions they need to get back to the van. Like a commercial, I guess. And Opie, here, he makes sure they get what they want when they show up.' Opie looked up from his splotchy arm. He had a rubber tourniquet around his bicep, and a few fat veins pulsed beneath his skin. He gave me a yellow grin and looked back down at his arm and stuck a needle in. He let out a long familiar sigh, and all his limbs went slack.

I asked Dennis if I could come along, as a look-out or something, and he told me to change my blood-covered shirt because it was bad for business. I crawled over to my suitcase, turned my back to them and traded one grey T-shirt for another. Dennis shouted to his slack-jawed friend. 'Opie!' – Opie cracked his lids open – 'Stay alive.' He turned, guitar in hand, and we left Opie slumped against the wall like a snowdrift.

As we passed Gwen, she laughed at something Francis said and her eyes bugged out like the sound of her voice had surprised her. She smiled and looked around for confirmation that it was, in fact, strange. 'Baaah!' she said. 'Beep! Boop!' She went on like that until she found a note she liked and she kept singing it over and over while Francis whapped his stupid drum, nodding like they were finding their rhythm in all that noise.

We walked down to the end of the big dirt lot – farthest from the entrance where cars were still trailing in – and Dennis started to play. We walked slowly, and when it seemed like someone was interested, he would linger for a minute so that they could hear his instructions more clearly. 'You lookin' a little placid. Just need a hit of acid. Find the drum if you want to have fun. Find, find, find the drum.' It was a catchy song, all on its own, and one really whacked-out girl just started dancing along, lolling her head back like it was too heavy for her neck. 'Can't sell food to someone that just ate,' Dennis said and motioned that we move on. I looked around to see if anyone had tried making their way down there yet, but it seemed like everyone was still huddled around their cars, drinking beers.

Finally, we closed in on a group of girls who seemed interested.

'But where are the drums?' one said, interrupting Dennis.

He stopped strumming. 'Huh?'

'The drums. You said to find them.'

We all listened for a moment. Radio chatter, a dull wind.

'What the fuck?' He turned and hurried toward the van. 'Bustin' my ass, and these fucks can't even keep the store open.'

I told the girls to follow if they wanted.

We found Dennis pounding against the back window of the van. Gwen and Francis were missing and Opie was slumped in a lawn chair, one foot propped on the drum.

'I'm out here bustin' my ass,' Dennis shouted, pounding the window again.

One girl frowned at Opie, who was drooling. 'He doesn't look like he's having fun,' she said.

I noticed the bag of stamps poking from the top of his shirt pocket, and I reached over and carefully plucked them out. He gave a small snort but didn't stir.

Just then, the side door slid open and out came Francis, his hair damp with sweat at the temples. He had a shit-eater grin and it stretched damn-near comical when he saw the girls behind me. 'You brought friends,' he said.

Gwen came out behind him, her hair tangled to one side, her shirt inside out.

Dennis continued shouting, but Francis calmly reminded him that they had work to do, gesturing to the girls, which I could tell angered Dennis to no end, but he took the bag from me and I was grateful to be rid of it.

As they were talking to the girls, I pulled Gwen over and asked her what they were doing. Were they fooling around? Did she fuck him? She smelled like pot, and her eyes kept darting to my head.

'There's a light coming off of you,' she said, running her palm a few inches from my scalp. She smiled, looked directly at me, and poked her finger against my black eye, and I felt like socking her.

'Jesus, Gwen.' I covered the bruise with my hand. 'What's wrong with you?'

She was a sadist, was the honest truth, and she started laughing and laughing. I could tell we were getting nowhere – she wasn't going to answer the question directly – but I could assume that meant they had probably fucked and I tasted vomit in my throat. I was done letting Gwen's whimsy and her obsession with gaining every man's attention dictate what I did or how I felt.

'I'm leaving tonight,' I said.

Francis came over and interrupted. 'Leaving? No. Why?' he said. 'I have a big pull-out couch. You two could stay the night. I make a rad omelet. Opie will tell ya.' He kicked Opie, who opened his eyes to nod at us once.

'He just said rad,' I said to Gwen. 'And last I checked, there wasn't a fucking beach in Colorado.' I looked at her like *I will leave your ass here*.

'We got the Cherry Creek Reservoir,' Francis sang

optimistically. He bent over and gave the drum a few awkward slaps. 'If you're looking for a large body of water...'

He sounded moronic. 'How much is one stamp, Francis?' I said. 'How much did you just make me?'

His strumming ceased, and a grin traced his lips. 'I got you, joystick,' he said. 'Don't worry. End of the night, we'll settle up.'

'No,' I said. 'We're not staying til the end of the night.'

'You're in Morrison, honey,' Francis said in a tone that made me want to sledgehammer his face. 'How the hell are you going to get back to town?'

I looked at Gwen, who was clearly tripping and having a hard time keeping up. 'I love Jim Morrison,' she said. 'So sexy.'

I took a hold of Gwen's arm and pulled her over to the van door. She bobbled against it, giggling like a feeble mind. I could hear the first act warming up beyond the rock slabs and the sun had already disappeared behind the nearest peak, but I didn't care. 'Stay or come,' I said. 'I'm leaving now.'

Beyond the shiny lacquer of her stoned-ass eyes, I could see her register my sincerity, and she tried to stop me while I gathered my suitcase and her hatbox. 'Let's just stay,' she said. 'Until they drive us back.'

'I don't want to stay.'

'But what about the car?'

'Fuck the car. I'm walking to the first bus stop I see, and I'm getting the fuck out of here.'

'But, where are we even going?' she asked, sounding half-panicked because I was walking off already toward the road down the mountain. She had said 'we,' which I took as a positive sign, but I wasn't too stupid to know she really didn't want to head home yet, not after only one night. What good was that? How would Bobby learn? And she didn't trust these boys all on her own.

Francis called out after us and approached at full speed, but he had to stop a few yards short to catch his breath. He blamed it on asthma, but out-of-shape was probably more accurate. 'Where the hell are you going?' he asked Gwen.

'San Francisco,' I interrupted, deciding for the both of us. My only knowledge of the city had come from movies – *Dirty Harry*, *Invasion of the Body Snatchers*, *Harold and Maude* – stories of heroes and redemption and sordid, unlucky love. It seemed like a place that nurtured transformation, let it all bubble up and mix together until there were so many different types of people that nothing and no one ever really seemed that different at all. That's what I needed. A place to blend in and figure out who I was stripped of all my history and preconceptions. My mother's neighbor, Bill, once said that's why he moved to Kansas – to just be an old man – instead of staying in New York where people used to follow him around, snapping photos. If I could be myself in Kansas, I would. But I would never be just Sam out there; I would always be Sam-who-used-to-be-Rosie.

Francis looked at me with his mouth slacked open and then he said, 'It's like twenty miles to town.'

'I don't care,' I said and kept walking with our shit.

'Just. Let me just drive you,' he said.

I stopped and turned. 'Now? You'll take us now?'

He nodded, and, by god, dick-face Francis must've really felt something for Gwen because he and Dennis packed up their shit and their junked-out friend, Opie, and they drove us down to the Greyhound station only thirty minutes after we parked up at Red Rocks, and we never did see them, or the Dump, ever again.

6

The trip was twenty-seven hours of surface-deep sleep, interspersed with piss breaks and quick cigarettes in the empty parking lots of roadside convenience stores. Gwen put her hand on my leg once and I left it there, and I buzzed with hope that it was on purpose, but then she woke up and snatched it back with all the urgency of an accident. By the time we reached San Francisco, it seemed like I'd spent years bobbing in a sleep stew, simmering, tenderizing. Gwen shook me awake as we crossed a bridge made of steel that seemed to never end and I could see, out over the water of the bay, a misty sketch of the Golden Gate, and directly in front of us the skyline emerged like a metal and concrete pop-up from behind the fog.

The bus dropped us off at the north end of the city, and we gathered our things and departed into a crowd of people – some with cameras around their necks, stopping often to swap their lenses, and others, the unwashed smell of dirt and oil drifting like feedlot from their clothes and hair – and I noticed the noise. The air was thick with city buzz. People talking, people driving. So many people. Too many. And everything was up, buildings and billboards, the sheer number made me feel like a bug dancing between the legs of a giant mob. In every direction there were windows to be watched from, eyes everywhere, every color, eyes that landed on mine for a burning moment, and I thought: *They know I'm not from here. They know and they hate me.* And the smell, exhaust and smog and human skin cells and trash, all coalesced into a distinct odor of decay I would later come to love, but for a full second I considered running back to the bus, slamming my palm against the door, shouting: *Let me go back.*

But I wouldn't dare. Not even if Gwen wasn't there and no one would judge me for being overwhelmed by the bodies – too many to count, so many they sucked up all the air, they filled the space so I couldn't stretch my arms – because I knew back home there would be plenty of people who would turn up their noses, arms folded, who would laugh and say, 'Of course you couldn't make it out there. Of course. Who did you think you were anyway?'

Gwen wanted to look around, explore, and all I wanted was a hot shower and a real bed where I could lie supine in the dark for at least a good hour. It was only morning and already I was anxious we'd be spending the night on a park bench.

Gwen told me to take a chill pill. That we were on an adventure, and if Lewis and Clark were so worried about setting up camp all the time, they would have never made it to the Pacific. I told her it was too bad they didn't have Greyhound, and she rolled her eyes and set her sights on a big building that looked like a cement courthouse, complete with a clock tower and row of arched doorways out front. She had, in her hand, a wad of different brochures she'd taken from a stand outside the bus terminal. Different tourist specials. *Visit Alcatraz! Stay at the Holiday Inn! One Free Denny's breakfast! Bike across the Golden Gate!* I was smart enough to grab a map, which I tried to use to get my bearings, but the sun was behind a wall of clouds, and it was impossible to know which way was north or south. A strong breeze brought in the bitter smell of salt and fish water, and it was colder than I expected California to be. Wet and bone deep.

We stopped at a cafe on the bottom floor of a skyscraper, and I asked our waiter if he could recommend a good place to stay. He took a long look at our busted faces and asked how much we could pay. We were just two kids from Kansas who had never so much as signed a lease, let alone rented in a city before, so I said, 'I don't know. A hundred.'

He whistled. 'A hundred a night, you could stay at the Fairmont.'

I cleared my throat. 'I, uh, meant a week.'

He laughed and then frowned when he realized I was

serious. 'Check out the Tenderloin; just don't be looking when it gets dark,' he said, and he left to put in our order.

I found the Tenderloin on the map.

'One hundred? How did you come up with that number?'

I shrugged. 'I just don't want to spend all my money on a bed and shower. I came here to get fucked up and eat too much food and stay out late, snorting coke from a hooker's ass crack.' This was bullshit, but no joke.

Gwen laughed and scratched absently at her crotch, which I pretended not to notice. 'Do you really like coke?'

'I've done it plenty,' I lied. I'd only ever tried it twice, and both times Marcus and I ended up in a fist-fight. Of course, I was always on the losing end of that brawl, and getting punched in the face was sort of a buzzkill, but otherwise, I felt like I was king of the fucking mountain, until I came down, and then I wanted to sleep in a damp dark hole for about a thousand years.

'My college roommate, sophomore year, she had a coke problem,' Gwen said. 'Once we snorted coke for a whole week straight. I don't know how much, an eight ball maybe, but I would've kept on doing it forever if I hadn't had to come back to Lawrence for the summer. She wasn't at school the next year, so I never tried it again. I like the acid, though. Francis's acid.' She smiled and tried to say it faster. 'Franccissisasssidd.' She paused. 'I want to go to Alcatraz.'

'I'm not doing anything until we find a room.'

After we ate, we walked down Market, toward the area of the map labeled Tenderloin, just south of Chinatown and Union Square, but not too far from where we were, which I had finally deduced was the Financial District. Gwen held tight to her hatbox, which had already been fingered by a frazzle-haired, baggy-eyed woman who was most definitely homeless and had mistaken the box for a cake box. 'Give a hungry lady a slice,' she'd said. 'It's my birthday.'

The city was divided by stratum – the suits in the Financial District; the grinning men, standing outside their businesses, waving us to *come buy* in Chinatown; the stylish trophy wives out shopping in Union Square – but, no matter where we were, on nearly every corner, there was someone with a sign or a cup and a sorrowful, dirty, sun-leathered face, and an awful story, probably. My first instinct was to buy them some food or give a few dollars, but there were too many. The whole time I'd lived in Lawrence, I'd only seen one homeless person, a Vietnam vet who had a stump for a right arm and played the harmonica on the corner of Mass and 6th Avenue. When I was fourteen, I'd given him my allowance for three weeks straight and still, there he'd be, playing his instrument and begging. He never recognized me, not once, so I finally stopped giving him money, and I'd saved up for an Atari instead.

Gwen pulled her sunglasses from the top of her head and covered her eyes as a passive way to ignore them, and I realized it was a mistake to even smoke a cigarette, because instead of money, they all just asked for a smoke, and I ended up giving out half my pack by the time we made it through Union Square. The city teaches lessons quickly.

As we crossed the threshold into the Tenderloin, I swear I felt a literal drop in temperature (though we were also in the shadow of a building) and we passed a woman wearing a matted fur coat. She had greasy brown hair and dry red lips and reeked of uber-sweet perfume and seemed unsteady on her heels. She was also high as fuck, mumbling something under her breath, scratching the back of her neck.

'There's your hooker,' Gwen leaned in to say.

Just down the block, a dude in an oversized, denim jacket stood resting against the side of a building, watching the fur coat with a stern expression. Beyond him, two men were chatting next to a mailbox. One bent down and lit a pipe he had cupped in the palm of his hand, and a puff of bone-white smoke came out of his mouth before he shivered like his whole body had been overpowered by goose pimples. Crackheads, I thought. The Tenderloin was a zoo of rock bottom. Us included.

I figured it was better to save money renting by the week than blowing all our money on a hotel, so we stopped at three different buildings with FOR RENT signs until we found a place we could sort of afford. The room was on the third floor of a slanted and concrete building that had all the character of a military barracks or the most depressing kind of dorm. The room had bunk beds, a small desk in one corner, and a wobbly dresser where we stuffed the few things we had brought. The floor was bare concrete, and our voices echoed from the walls. There was one skinny window along the far wall, paned off in three sections from floor to ceiling, with the middle section opening by a crank wheel. It smelled a little like fresh paint covering a dead body. This was not how I imagined a big-city apartment would look. Only one bathroom on each floor, and we shared ours with two men from Vietnam and a skinny Russian lady, who dressed like a hooker and had a missing finger. Gwen had befriended her by the afternoon.

'She's a stripper,' Gwen told me. 'Her name's Flora. Like the goddess.'

'Like the bacteria,' I said. 'Vaginal Flora. Belly button flora. Intestinal flora—'

'You're an ass.'

'She's recruiting you.'

Apparently, Flora had invited us to some dance club that night but, without reason, Gwen had said we couldn't go. I grilled her – why? – until she got so fed up she stomped her foot and confessed, very loudly, that her crotch felt as dry and itchy as a poison ivy rash. Now that the secret was out, she scratched like she was trying to rip the skin away. Apparently, Flora had already offered her some balm, which wasn't working. Three hours in the city and already she was swapping crotch balm. Oh the people you'll meet. I laughed and laughed, and she shouted at me, 'Shut up! It isn't funny. People get yeast infections, sometimes. Don't lie and say you haven't.'

But I hadn't. 'I'm going to go take a shower,' I said. I gathered my clothes and the one towel we were given when we paid our rent. *People always forget a towel*, the leasing manager said. I certainly hadn't remembered to bring one.

The shower and the toilet were at the opposite end of the hall, and in two separate rooms, with their doors divided by a row of sinks and a big long mirror in the hallway. The smell of orange oil hung like a web around the shower room door, and it clung to me as I passed the sinks and went into the toilet room. It was dark in there, and smelled like a horse stall on a soggy morning. I pulled the string for the overhead light, but the room barely lit up. It was like one candle in there. When I finished, I went back past the sinks and into the shower room, which was completely tiled and still humid from the last user, and I locked the door and began to undress. I had only ever shared a bathroom with my family, but I learned quickly that strangers can be generally disgusting, a point proved when I pulled open the shower curtain and there sat a huge wad of blonde hair coiled around the drain. It looked like a drowned spider. I scanned the bathroom for something to fish it up, but there was nothing. Finally, I used my pinkie finger to hook the slimy-haired creature and tried not to vomit as I flung it toward the trash can but I missed and the hair-spider slapped and stretched against the wall. I cursed the person who thought *not* to put a toilet in with the shower, and then I wondered how many people just peed in the shower to save some time, and my stomach gave another lurch.

I took a scalding hot shower, and went back to the room to roll a joint. Gwen invited Flora over, and we all sat in a circle on the cold floor and talked about how we got there.

Flora twirled a strand of her yellow frizzy hair while I gave the short version. Adventure to the sea, some desire to dance with the dolphins. 'Isn't that right, Gwen?' She frowned at me and said she was running away from her wedding, like Akeem in *Coming to America,* and that she was looking for Mr Right.

'You are not both lesbian zen?' Flora asked with a Russian accent. Gwen laughed in a desperate way.

I thought about how Eddie would say, *just live your life man,* and I looked at Flora and said, 'No. We're not lesbians.'

Gwen honked out a sound like ha! and pointed at me. '*You're* not a lesbian?'

It wasn't that I didn't like girls, but the whole idea of identifying as this thing – a lesbian – it never felt right. I'd always wanted girls to look at me the way they looked at the hero in the movies: with want and lust. Not a want for sex, necessarily, but want for a man. Muscle. Hair. Smell. I didn't want a girl who wanted to finger me and play with my tits. That thought repulsed me.

Before I could answer, Gwen said, 'I'm whatever, you know?' I wondered how long it had been since Gwen had smoked pot because her eyes were red dime-slits on either side of her nose. She rested her crotch on the crook of her heel she started to rock back and forth slowly. She'd pulled her T-shirt down over her knees so we couldn't see, but I knew what she was doing. Fucked up as it was, it turned me on.

I rolled another joint while Flora told us how she arrived in the States three years earlier, with her older sister, Felicia (who now lived, married to a construction worker, in Cincinnati), and that she had spent the first year going to English classes at the City Hall and stripping up in North Beach on the weekends. Twelve hours of work and she made four hundred dollars, easy.

'Four hundred,' I said to Gwen. She had the body. She could do this. 'A whole month's rent.'

Flora asked if we were running from something, on account of our battered faces, and I told her how we had wrecked my car.

'You mean, Eddie's car,' Gwen said.

'Damn it, Gwen. I'm not having this argument again.'

'Who's Eddie?' Flora asked. 'The one you're running from?'

I laughed; the subtext was uncanny, involuted and inverted by all the pot smoke. I told her Eddie was my best friend before he killed himself after losing a fight with a douchebag named Carl Hemlin. Then I turned to Gwen and asked her, 'Remember when Hemlin shit his pants in ninth grade?'

If it was possible, Gwen's eyes narrowed even smaller and she said, in a bitchy tone, 'Eddie was bipolar.'

That was a fact, and one that Gwen wanted to reiterate, not to Flora, but to me, because we both knew that she'd been fucking around with Carl for months before Eddie died.

'He also had a lot of instability in his life,' I said.

Gwen scowled. 'Who fucking doesn't?'

We stared at each other, and even though I knew she had a point, I felt the urge to slap her mouth.

'So what time are you two going out dancing?' I asked, trying to get rid of her.

Flora perked up. 'You vant to come?' she asked Gwen, and I watched Gwen rock back and forth on her heel again, but her face gave away nothing until her lips curled into a smile. 'Only if Sam's coming too.'

I shook my head. 'I'm too tired.'

'I have pick-me-up,' Flora said, and she leaned forward like someone might hear her. 'Cocaine,' she whispered, sounding very un-Tony-Montana-like.

'Oooh,' Gwen said. 'We just need a hooker now.'

'I can get you hooker,' Flora offered, oblivious to the joke.

'Just let me get my shoes,' I said.

We took a cab up toward the bay, to a part of town called the Haight, but at the time, being new to the city, I thought Flora was saying 'the Hate.'

'Zey have straight dancing on weekend,' Flora said.

I imagined a straight line of people. 'You mean line dancing?' I hated line dancing. I hated all dancing.

Flora searched through her purse for something. 'I don't understand.' She retrieved a tiny glass container, untwisted a small wand, and did a bump from its end. She took another white scoop and offered it to Gwen, who didn't hesitate, not even a little.

'Like country music, people dancing all stupid,' I said.

'Ze gay boys dance much better, it's true, but zey never buy me drink.' She readjusted her tits in her bra, making them jiggle momentarily.

'I-Beam is a gay club?' Gwen asked.

'Alvays, no. Zey have bands. 10,000 Maniacs. Duran Duran. Ze Tea Dances are gay, but straight weekend is mostly sailors and girls.' Flora offered me a bump, and I imagined motor-boating her tits as I leaned forward. The coke shot up through my face and down my spine faster than I expected, and I felt chatty and interested all of a sudden.

'Do you go to the club every night?'

She shrugged. 'Not every night, but some. Have not found my construction man yet, so.'

We slowed on a busy street, and out the window, I saw a line of people waiting on the sidewalk. Flora paid the cab driver, and we took our numb faces and inflated sense of ego and walked past the line of people all shivering in the mist and wind, waiting to get in the front door. The bassline of some pop song permeated the front of the building like a heartbeat. Flora stood on her tippy-toes and kissed the bouncer, a big dude wearing the shortest shorts I'd ever seen. The coke was sinking in now, and I felt taller, full of muscle.

The bouncer let us pass, and we opened the door and went into the sensory hellhole – all loud music and strobe lights and stale air – and I weaved through the crowd and went directly to the bar, where I bought us each a shot of tequila. Gwen swallowed hers out of pity, but Flora refused to touch it. 'In my country, vodka and vater are almost ze same vord,' she said.

I guessed we were all allowed at least one cliché. I wondered what mine was. I turned to ask Gwen but she had already gone out to the dance floor. She saw me notice her and waved for me to follow. I was a little worried she wanted to grind on me just to satiate her itch, but I had an itch too, a different kind, a mental kind. I was horny as hell. I wanted to fist-fuck a volleyball team. I wanted to pound my foot on Carl Hemlin's face. I wanted to totally own something.

I drank the other shot and took the whole room in. It was unlike any place I'd ever been. Big and high-ceilinged with two shiny I-beams from end to end. A stage stood off to one side of the dance floor where some dude was spinning pop music and a few giant checkered cubes were scattered around with girls dancing on top of them.

I followed Flora out onto the crowded dance floor, and we met up with Gwen and all did another bump while the bass from Whitney Houston's 'I Wanna Dance with Somebody' pulsed through our bodies. Flora found a sailor and started grinding her body against his. Gwen and I had never danced together before (I was certain because I never danced; I was like a scarecrow, all boneless and straw-brained when it came to rhythm) and I moved one foot and then the other, watching how the guy with Flora moved in a fucking motion, which I could get into. But Gwen wouldn't move within two feet of me. I pulled my arms up like they were on strings. Gwen laughed. I could see she thought I was trying to be funny so I pretended it was true. It was pitiful. She moved closer, and I pressed my body against hers, situating my thigh between her legs, and she started grinding. She was still laughing – oh funny Sam – nothing I did was serious to her, but some lust-filled impulse in me was satisfied. My leg could have been a bike handle, a tree trunk, for all she cared. I was her scratching post.

We danced like that for a few hours, drinking shots until Gwen was totally trashed and hanging off me. I would like to say that I remembered what happened the rest of the night, but I only recall Gwen and Flora and me laughing in a bathroom stall. Gwen's shoe floating in the toilet. A red room with a pool table. A broken cue stick. Flora between two men. A line dance, which may have been part of a later dream, and of course, the long walk from Market to Geary after Gwen threw up in the back of the cab. It was raining, and the wind whipped through us in bursts.

I put Gwen in the bottom bunk when we got home, wiped her mouth with a dirty T-shirt, and turned her sideways, in case she puked again. I undressed to a few layers, and climbed up to the top bunk, but I couldn't manage to keep my eyes closed. Every time my lids touched, I felt strings deep within my forehead pull them open again. I could feel my pulse in my throat, my fingertips, my groin. I wanted an orgasm, but I was still bleeding. Jerking off with this ailment always felt like poking a fresh wound and gross, so no. I kept my hands above the blankets and replayed our wild night. The swarms of people. The drugs and Gwen grinding on my leg. I imagined days of it. Getting drunk and snorting coke and fucking Gwen, lots of fucking. I wasn't stupid enough to believe it would happen or, that if it did, I wouldn't get bored, but on some level I wanted that boredom, that apathy toward Gwen and the city. I wanted a routine; something to make the unfamiliar start to feel like home.

City sounds drifted in from outside: a siren, a saxophone, a group of people shouting. Every so often, I could hear Gwen's nails raking against her skin. I must have dozed off somewhere between four and five, because my last memory was checking the digital clock just after I heard two people arguing in the apartment below.

When I woke up, Gwen was pacing in our one shabby towel, and I couldn't remember who or where I was until it all came rushing back: the dusty summers, Eddie's gap tooth, the smell of my father at the end of a day. I could taste dirt in my mouth. I felt hollow. Fucking coke.

'I have to go to the doctor,' Gwen said. She squirmed her butt as she walked. 'Flora says there's this clinic. Will you go with me?'

I sat up and grated my scalp, and just the sight – like how people yawn when other people yawn – sent Gwen into a fit. She was wearing a pair of mittens (where she got them, I'm still not sure) but she reached up beneath the towel and rubbed with abandon.

'Oh. Kay,' I said.

'This is bad. I might have herpes or syphilis' —she gasped — 'or AIDS.'

'Some two-bit Denver drug dealer driving a rape-van wasn't clean? You're shitting me.'

'Don't be mean to me. Please. This is serious.'

'Did you use a condom?'

She straightened up and put a mitten on either hip. 'I'm not stupid.'

I didn't believe her. 'Then you don't have AIDS.'

'Just come with me.'

'My head already kills and waiting room lights—'

'Please.' She was on her knees, mittens clasped like I was a bleeding Madonna or something. I groaned.

She offered to go to a movie with me afterward. I told her *License to Kill* looked pretty good, and she buried a scowl, said she'd so much rather see the one where that nerd shrinks his whole family and I told her I was going back to sleep.

'Fine,' she said. 'Whatever you want.'

I swung my legs over the side of the bunk and hopped down.

We tried walking the distance to the clinic, but the map (a glossy ass-wipe they hand out to tourists) was packed with ads and nothing seemed to scale. It was like a cartoon of the city and I was about to say this to Gwen when she decided to hail a cab.

Twenty-five dollars later, we were dropped off in front of a row of low, sprawling buildings, a campus of some sort. I followed Gwen toward the building number Flora had written down, and we clicked our way down a wide, bright, tiled hallway and into an office labeled: Women's Health Center. A smaller sign on the door informed patients that the staff consisted of resident doctors and nurses looking to fulfill their floor hours before their state exam. It didn't say the word amateurs, but I told Gwen the subtext. It said, UCSF is a teaching hospital.

Gwen went up to the receptionist's counter, where she explained her situation to the poor woman. 'I just need to know your first name,' the receptionist said. She handed Gwen a clipboard, and I sat down in a hard plastic chair. There were seven other people in the room. All women, three with babies, two more were pregnant, and one looked about nine thousand years old. Against my will, I imagined her vagina coughing dust into a student doctor's face.

Gwen sat next to me and started filling out the form. One of the babies farted, and the room filled with the stench of broccoli. Seeing no causal relation, taking no responsibility at all, the baby proceeded to wail. I told Gwen I was going to go walk around for a while, and I took a tour of the campus.

I wandered over to a bulletin board between the library and another building. Three different textbook pages were stapled over a flyer for a concert. They seemed randomly chosen: the middle of a bibliography for what appeared to be an article on rhinoplasty, a few paragraphs about malaria vaccines in Uruguay, the title page for Milgram's *Obedience to Authority*. Beside the concert flyer was an ad for a job. *AIDS Research Assistant. Be the Change You Want to See In the World.* The bottom had been cut into tear-away fringes with the same handwritten phone number on each strip. Only one was missing.

It seemed sort of cheesy, quoting Gandhi, but the money Gwen and I had wasn't going to last long, and my job prospects back home were next to nothing, so when I saw only one strip missing, it didn't look like a warning; it looked like opportunity. I knew I couldn't go back to the bedsores, and bedpans full of prune shit, and all the foggy cranky ailments of a nursing home (the non-infectious could be so boring), but I also knew I wasn't ready for the frantic attentiveness of trauma care – gunshot wounds and car wrecks and freak accidents that required a clearer head than I was capable of mustering. So it was either twelve-hour shifts in an ICU or maybe an outpatient clinic, but thanks to Reagan, all of them were probably testing for drugs, so I was shit out of luck. I took the whole flyer and stuffed it in my pocket, went back to the Women's Health Center and waited for Gwen.

She came out an hour later, a tube of cream in her palm. She said it was some kind of fungus and that she didn't want to talk about it.

'So I was wrong,' I said. 'Francis was a fun-guy.'

She blinked slowly, annoyed-like. 'Where's the movie?'

I called about the job the next morning and the receptionist asked if I could be there by lunch. Before that, she'd asked me a series of questions: Did I like working alone? Was I trained in weak-vein phlebotomy? And would I be willing to accept ten pennies above minimum wage and no contract beyond the duration of the study, which was set for eight weeks, with zero benefits, no health insurance or profit-sharing or any of that?

I said *sure* to all the questions – hell, *short-term* and *no commitment* sounded like magic words to me – and I examined the yellow bruise around my eye in the chrome surface of the payphone. It wasn't too bad. The swelling had gone down, the upper lid was almost flesh-colored again.

I cleaned up and sifted through my clothes for the most appropriate thing to wear to a job interview. It was hopeless. I finally settled on a pair of black jeans and three layers of white T-shirts. I usually kept my hair short, but it had grown out quite a bit, and I tried to tame the waves with some mousse that Gwen had brought. She woke up when she heard the foamy sound filling my palm and asked what I was doing.

I told her it was scientifically proven that most people glance first at the left side of another person's face before picking a side to focus on. It's why it's so hard to maintain eye contact with someone with a wonky right eye. She looked confused for the longest time, and finally I pointed to the bruise and asked her if she could make it go away.

'Why?' she asked me. 'I thought you liked it.'

'I'm going to a job interview.'

'A job?' She sat up, brushed some hair from her face. 'You want to stay? Like, for good?'

I shrugged. 'Not forever. I'm not married to the place.' I knew Gwen was just playing runaway, but I couldn't really see what I stood to lose by staying. 'It's better than going back to Kansas, don't you think?'

She stared at a long thin crack in the concrete wall. 'Maybe,' she finally said. She didn't ask any more questions or give me any advice, she just got up from the bed and pulled her makeup bag from the dresser. She smeared some concealer over the bruise without delicacy, and when she was finished it didn't look better, it looked like a tumor or some sort of watery blister floating around my eye. She told me that I maybe shouldn't look for a job just yet. I washed my face and worked on my story for when the doctor asked.

The office was by the campus we'd been to the day before, and I hailed a cab and went over the details of my nursing career in my head. A sourness settled in my gut as I arrived at a very modern-looking squat building with thick warped-glass windows and a buzzer at the door. I'd only had three other jobs in my life: baling hay at Seward's Farm all through high school, reeling movies the summer before I started nursing school, and taking care of old folks at the nursing home. And all of them, these jobs, I'd known someone when I got them: Wally Seward had employed my father for twenty-two years before my father lost his foot and went on disability, Marcus had still been fucking the girl at the theater when I turned in my application, and my very own grandmother, Rosie Gavin, had lived at *Spring Meadow Assisted Living* for ten years before she croaked from a cerebral aneurysm three months into my tenure.

I pressed the buzzer.

A woman asked if I had an appointment. I told her I had called earlier about the AIDS study, that I was there to see Dr Dinka. I heard another metallic buzz and the door clicked open. I took the elevator up one floor while I tried to retuck my T-shirts and flatten out my hair at the same time. The door opened to a busy lobby. I walked in and went over to the counter.

'Just fill out the top page, and bring it back over when you're done,' the receptionist said.

Name. Address. Birth date. I stopped when I came to sex: M_____ or F_____ , and I stared at it for a while before I checked the space next to M. It wasn't something I'd planned on doing, but there it was, asking me for a binary answer, and a part of me wanted to finally tell my truth and another part really wondered if it would work, if I could pull off a Billy Tipton for good. The possibility was pulsing. My whole face warmed over, and I looked around to see who noticed. Every waiting patient was looking down into a magazine. I finished the application and gave it back to the receptionist. She glanced over it and said, 'Thank you, Mister Gavin.'

Mister.

Dopamine soaked into every cell as I sat back down.

Eventually, a squat older man, with a turtle chin and a face like a wet paper towel, came down the hallway and introduced himself as Dr Dinka. He kept his gaze on my bruised eye for a little longer than the rest of me, and I apologized for being late.

He did nothing to acknowledge my words, only turned around and started walking back from where he had come. I took it as a sign to follow and we went down the hall, into an office where a giant oak desk faced two comfortable chairs.

He told me to sit, and I followed his order, but he stayed standing. He walked over to the window and looked out. His hands were clasped behind his back, and a light from the ceiling shone down on his head, revealing the pink scalp beneath his white comb-over. As he read over my application and mumbled to himself, I looked over at his fancy bookshelf, filled mostly with framed photos of the doctor posing with mildly familiar faces, politicians probably, and I figured he must be the *real deal*, whatever that meant. Then I thought this was probably the point of the pictures, to get people to think that, and I resented myself for being such a sucker.

Dinka cleared his watery throat and turned from the window, locking eyes with me. 'Tell me why you're here,' he said. His full focus threw me, the intensity of it.

Someone passed in the hallway, sobbing or hyperventilating or both, but Dinka seemed unaffected other than to shut the door.

'I'm here for the job,' I said as he came back to his desk.

He closed his papery eyelids like he was trying to remember what the hell I was talking about. 'There are jobs everywhere. This is America. Economy's booming. Better paying jobs all over the country. I'll ask again: why are you here?'

I tried to keep my foot from tapping against the floor. 'I worked in a nursing home for the last four years, and I thought it might be more interesting to work in research.'

He nodded and nodded. No one was talking but, still, he kept nodding.

'Tell me what happened to your eye.'

I told him about the patient at my last job, and then I made some lame joke about being older now, that I didn't heal like I used to. Dinka didn't even crack a smile. He started pacing.

'And you left that job, why?'

I shrugged. 'I was just ready for something new.'

He nodded, unbuttoned his cuff, and started to roll the sleeve. I wasn't sure what he was doing, but it became apparent once he'd materialized a butterfly syringe and a pair of gloves from his lab coat. He sat down at his desk, rested his elbow on the corner, and asked me to draw his blood. It felt like State Boards all over again, and my voice gave a quiver when I asked him if he wanted me to wash my hands or just use the gloves, since there wasn't a sink in his office.

'You won't have time to wash your hands between patients all the time. You're not allergic to latex, are you? I knew a man once.'

'No.' I stood up and went over the steps in my head as I approached his bare arm. It wasn't like I drew blood every day at the nursing home. It had been several months since I'd done it, and back then I wasn't being judged by a prospective employer – one I was actually sticking, for Christ's sake – and my palms immediately began to sweat, making it difficult to get the gloves on.

Dinka handed me an alcohol packet. I opened it and rubbed the acrid square against the belly of his arm, and I asked him if he had a tourniquet.

He smiled, like maybe not having one out was part of the test, and he pulled one from the middle drawer of his desk. Once I had him roped off, and I'd found a good vein, I stuck him and filled a vial. It was over in a few seconds, and I wiped the wound and covered it with a bandage. I asked where I should put the syringe – there wasn't a sharps container I could see – but now that he knew I could perform the task, he didn't seem bothered by protocol, and he gestured for me to just leave it on top of his desk.

'Are you asking every applicant to draw blood?'

'You're the first to apply, so yes.' He rolled down his sleeve. 'For the last fifteen years, I've partnered with several researchers, and a few corporations, doing pharmaceutical testing through a program at General Hospital. Eighty studies. That's how many we started. Sixty-two went on to the secondary phase, forty-three had positive results, and thirty-four were approved by the FDA. I'm not new to the business of research. I'm not even new to the world of AIDS research. I was on the forefront. Eight years, I've been studying this virus and, let me tell you, it might be one pesky little shit, but I think we've got it cornered.'

He paused, giving space for this awkward moment where I shifted in the leather chair and it sounded like a wet fart. 'That's great,' I said, and I tried shifting again but could not reproduce the sound.

Dinka kept talking, 'This isn't just about the queers, either. A lot of people still think they're the only ones who are affected, but *your* family's at risk, Mister Gavin. Mine too. This virus could end civilization. A cure, that's what we're after. There is no magic pill. There is science. The scientific method. Trial and error. We are on the front lines of an epidemic and I intend to win.'

I nodded because, while I wasn't exactly sure what he was getting at, he had also called me *Mister* and total relief had dulled my response. I pulled the gloves off and wadded them in my fist.

'Can you start on Monday?' he asked.

'Sure.'

He gave me a quick summary of the job duties, which were entry-level tasks: huddling patients, three an hour, through the office, checking blood pressure, drawing blood, handing out pills.

'Come early. Seven a.m. We'll go over procedure before the patients arrive.'

I nodded again.

We hadn't even been in San Francisco a week, and already I had committed to a routine.

Dinka picked up his phone and told his secretary he'd found a match and to make sure we wrapped up all the loose ends before I left the office. He handed me a thick folder, with a contract that I signed right then and there, and a training manual, and some other articles and checklists he said I should familiarize myself with in the following days. Then he shook my hand, patted my back, and ushered me out the door.

The secretary requested a copy of my driver's license, my social security card, and my nursing license. Her face was stern and expectant, and when I told her I hadn't brought any of them, she looked like every teacher I'd ever disappointed.

'Bring them on Monday,' she said. 'It's really important.'

I told her, 'Yes, ma'am,' and I left, but the conflict remained. I hadn't brought my nursing license, and so I'd have to call my mother who might not be in much of a mood to help me out considering how I'd left, considering I was only calling for a favor.

Sure enough, my mother answered and launched immediately into a tirade. She thought I was dead. She'd had a dream. My corpse in an alley. The Denver Police had declared me a missing person after they'd found my abandoned car and blood all over the interior. 'And just where is Gwen?' She growled the words at me. 'Her mother's up my ass. Threatening to sue me. This is your fault.'

Us leaving, it'd grown to scandal fast as fungus.

'Threaten her back. Maybe Gwen forced me, she doesn't know. Can you please send me my nursing license? I found a job.'

'What the hell is wrong with you? Just leaving. Not even a note or nothing. Just up and gone, and believe me, I can handle you gone, but just disappearing and not calling once, *not once*, then the police called at midnight. Almost a week, you've been torturing me. Not knowing if the phone would ring: *we found your daughter's body*. Christ.'

'Mom, I'm fine.'

'That's good to know. A whole week later. And now I have to deal with Sally bitching because Joan won't let her go over and see Rachel until you send Gwen back.'

I imagined Gwen as a wrapped parcel, bitching muffled beneath brown paper, fifty bucks of stamps covering her face. 'Sure, I'll send her back. No problem.'

'You're kidding.'

'I'm not kidding.'

'You left a shit storm here and, par for the course, I have to clean it up.'

'Can you look in the linen closet? I think I might've filed it in the green thing with our birth certificates and junk.'

'No, I will not just mail the license,' she said. 'Don't you care about your sister?'

I heard Sally start shouting in the background. *Is that Sam? Is it?* There was a rustling, like they were fighting for the receiver, and my mother's voice came back into focus.

'I'm turning your room into a workout space if you don't come back now. I'm going to start doing my Jane Fonda tapes where your bed is. I'll throw it out. I'll throw everything out.'

'You're an asshole, Sam!' Sally shouted in the background.

This wasn't going well. 'What happened to the Dump?'

'The police had it impounded. You need to call them and explain the details of the accident, otherwise they'll issue a fine and sell the car at an auction next month. I'll give you the phone number, do you have a pen?'

'No. Can't you do it?'

'Don't put this on me,' she said. 'I have enough things to do. You think you're the only one who has a world?'

'Okay, well, I can't pay the fine if I don't have a job, so just send the license.'

She kept on with her tirade and I felt compelled to set down the phone and walk away, so finally I did.

I'd call Sally later.

I paid an oily-haired teenaged kid three cigarettes to help me figure out the bus route back to the Tenderloin. He was sitting at the stop, listening to a Walkman, ignoring me until I pulled out the cigarettes and then he perked up and showed me a map at the end of the awning. With his fingernail, he trailed a pink line, said to take the six.

Ten minutes later, the bus arrived, and I boarded and sat near the back with my head leaned against the cool glass. I wondered about altering my driver's license. I mean, I'd seen Marcus create whole documents with a photocopier and the right fonts and seals and labels, but he was artistically gifted, and I couldn't even make a competent birthday card.

One thing was certain, I wasn't going to tell Gwen about what I'd done – letting Dinka and his staff know I was a man – because she'd have a shit-fit. *It's weird. Don't you think it's weird?* she'd say, meaning I was weird. That's what she'd say, over and over until I'd start to agree.

8

Gwen had left a note on the desk – *down at shower* – and a horribly rolled joint, half-smoked and falling apart. I lit it, took a puff, and looked on the top bunk where a ball of orange yarn was tethered to a knitting needle and an ugly patch of whatever-Gwen-was-making.

I wondered if this – the joint, the yarn – was really all she'd done that morning. While I rolled a real joint, she came back from the shower humming 'Material Girl' and went right for my blue folder like a bug to something shiny. She pulled it open and started thumbing.

'What is this?' She held up a pamphlet with a picture of a nurse drawing blood from an older man's arm. They were both smiling. Printed in bold above their heads: *Nursing in High Risk Environments: HIV and AIDS.*

'I got the job,' I said, and I held my hand up for a high five. She took the joint from me and set it in the ashtray.

'It can't be safe,' she said.

'It's twelve weeks of handing out pills to sick people, and your hatbox isn't a magic goose, you know.'

She rolled her eyes. 'Do what you want,' she said, 'but I'm going to the beach and I'm going swimming.'

'Right now?'

She turned and dropped her towel and I took in her naked skin, all of it. She started stringing her legs through a bikini bottom. 'I found a thrift shop down the road. They had swimsuits. I got you one too.'

Something like a laugh came out of my mouth, but what filled me was genuine panic. One, I hated swimming – imagine a worm flailing, drowning in any amount of water – and two, I wouldn't be caught dead in a bikini and I told her that.

'It's not a bikini.' She put on her top and then went over

to the bottom bunk, where she retrieved, from a brown paper bag, a black one-piece and a pair of swim trunks with a red-bandana pattern. 'It was all they had in your size,' she said. I looked at the label: S.

'I'm not wearing this.'

'It's like that thing you wear. That seventeenth-century bra.'

'It's not the same.'

She started covering her swimsuit with clothes. 'How? They both squish you flat as a ten-year-old boy. Don't you like your boobs?'

'It's a compression shirt. And no. No, I don't like my boobs, which is why I won't wear this thing.' I threw the one-piece at her, but I put on the swim trunks as a compromise.

She started combing her tangle of wet hair, ripping through knots like she'd lost all feeling in her head.

'You shower before you go swimming?' I asked.

'I had to shave.'

The hair on my legs was an inch long and I showed it to Gwen. She scrunched her face. 'It's on your toes, even!' she squealed.

'I like my toes,' I said.

Gwen seemed preoccupied as we walked through North Beach, while I noticed tiny Italian flags were painted on every light pole and every single street was slanted against a hill.

Still being naive to the ways of women, I asked her what was wrong.

'It's not fair,' she said.

'What's not?'

'We came all this way, and now you're just going to leave me alone while you play doctor.'

'I'm not on vacation.'

'Since when?'

'Since I decided to stay.'

She stopped walking. 'And when was that?' She folded her arms.

I shrugged. 'I don't know. When you were getting your fungal medication.'

She scowled. 'Don't say *fungal*. It makes me sound disgusting.'

'Coochie-remedy... Labial cream...'

She shoved my shoulder. 'Well if you're going to stay, then *I* want to stay.'

I imagined my hands all over her bare wet skin. 'So stay.'

We started down the world's longest hill, so steep that we had to lean back on our heels to keep from falling forward. Gwen named all the things she could do with her Christian-school business degree. 'I could be a clothing store manager or a personal assistant—'

'Or a stripper.'

'Very funny.'

'Flora said it was good cash.'

Gwen made a *pssshhhh* sound with her lips.

'And what about Bobby?' I said.

'Bobby,' she said, 'can suck a donkey dick for all I care. I hope he's sweating right now, worried about what every single person we invited to our wedding is going to say when he has to call them up and say it's cancelled.' She broke into evil laughter, and I knew for certain she had come all the way to San Francisco for the sole purpose of pissing him off. I thought of how I could make this work for me.

'So, you're staying then?'

'I'm staying.'

I lifted her up and spun her once. She danced into the crosswalk and said she'd be happy if she never heard her mother's nagging voice again. She imitated Joan: *is that how a Christian lady speaks?*

She pointed out a bakery, and we went inside, bought two coffees and a loaf of bread. Outside, we found a bench near the water and settled there to eat while looking toward Golden Gate, toward Alcatraz, both woolly in fog and indefinite as a memory.

Swarming all around us were languages I'd never heard,

strange guttural noises and round vowels that seemed, to me, meaningless. I tried to identify some – French, Spanish, Mandarin? – but gave up. Babel had fallen. I felt lost and content.

'If you had one wish in the world,' Gwen said, 'what would it be?'

Several choices flashed through my mind: A million dollars. Eddie's resurrection. A giant cock. The certitude of an afterlife. Gwen's pussy all up in my face. A lifetime of chocolate-chip cookie dough. An orgasm right now. A new car. Real honest love for once. 'A big stack of cash and a corndog,' I said. 'What about you?'

'To swim to that island.' She pointed to Alcatraz.

'It's impossible to swim that far.'

She measured the distance from the island to the shore with her thumb and seemed to be convinced she could make it. 'My swim coach said I had the kick of a sea otter.'

I changed tactics. 'You totally should. Fuck that cold water.'

She kicked off her shoes. 'I'm going to try,' she said and started removing her leggings from beneath her dress. A man and a woman, sitting a few yards away, quit talking and stared as Gwen peeled away her dress and stood there in her yellow swimsuit. She grabbed my hand, and I wanted to pull her close, grip her hair. She was teasing me with her body, like she always did. 'Swim with me,' she begged.

I told her no but let her pull me to the water's edge where I removed my shoes and waded out to my shins in the freezing fishy water. She tried to shame me into coming out farther. 'Don't be such a sissy,' she shouted, but the water was fucking cold. I splashed her with my foot and said she wouldn't get a hundred yards.

She glared and I could see a new level of determination filling her with false confidence. Those who ignore history, I thought.

I watched her wade out until she couldn't touch anymore, and her head bobbed above the surface like a buoy. She started swimming, real swimming, with her face in the water and her arms winding around and around. She swam so far that it was difficult to see her from the sea foam, and I wondered what would happen if she just cramped up or lost energy and sank below the surface. She was too far for me to swim to her, and with no lifeguards nearby she might actually drown out there. It seemed both impossible and possible.

I pictured the walk home, calling her mother, informing the police, and the feeling was neither happy nor sad, but hopeful, which brought me shame. Even more, when I actually spotted her head in among the tidal grey landscape, facing my direction this time and crawling closer and closer to the shore, I felt actual disappointment. It wasn't that I truly wanted her dead, but that a part of me knew I would be better off if she were out of my life. Her company was poison, a direct reminder of every memory I'd ever wanted to forget, and even worse, I knew she'd never love me. Not me-me.

As she came out of the water and shook some water from her ear, I realized that as long as Gwen was around, I might as well still be in Kansas.

'Shit,' I said.

'What?'

'Almost had it.'

9

That Sunday I went out and watched a double feature, got a haircut, and spent a good hour at Kinko's trying to tape a small letter M over the F on my driver's license to produce a believable copy until I discovered a copy of the copy (with white-out on the tape seam) looked mostly legit. I made five, just in case I'd ever need more, and put them in a manila folder. My mother had finally caved and faxed a copy of my nursing license and social security card to the customer service desk, and I brought all three documents with me the next morning to work.

Dinka's research clinic was in a completely different neighborhood than his private practice where I'd been interviewed. I found the office in an old three-storey building on Castro Street. The front lobby had a chemical smell, one that seemed familiar but impossible to place until I saw a pair of women smoking in the waiting area, both with black capes around their shoulders and their hair rolled up with curlers, and I remembered my mother's home-done perms.

The clinic was on the top floor, down a dark hall with sputtering fluorescents. Dr Dinka stood in the waiting room between two wooden chairs and a coffee table, talking with a woman who he introduced as his assistant, Gayla. She was there, he said, to spruce up the place, and she went back to hanging scenic pictures and fake plants from hooks while Dinka gave me a waddling tour of the place.

In addition to the waiting area, there were two other rooms: an exam room and an office. Furniture was sparse, practically nonexistent – the exam room only had two chairs, a skinny table, and a small sink with a counter for implements. The office was equal in size to the exam room and had a large refrigerator to store the pills and a cabinet for filing the charts. Dinka walked over to the fridge, with his hands behind his back, and he gave me a quick run-down of the study.

'I'm funding this myself,' he said. 'But when we see results, and I'm sure we'll see results, we can move to a national study. Once that happens, this drug'll get off the ground. It'll get pushed through the FDA – or as I like to call them, the Feet-Dragging-Assholes – and in a few months…' He paused dramatically, as if I had some vested interest. 'I want the cure for AIDS – I want my name on it – and that starts here. You do your job and you'll be part of that. You'll be in the history books right next to me.'

So full of shit, I thought. Guys like Dinka don't share credit. If his cure came true, I'd be lucky to get a footnote.

He opened the fridge, revealing a grid of plastic shelves filled with rows of waxy disposable cups, and space at the bottom to store the blood vials. Of course, I'd already known about the blood, but seeing that empty space, those hungry vials waiting to be fed, I felt twisted and my heart heaved, knowing I'd be sharing space with a fridge full of virus.

Dinka said there'd be more blood to draw in the first and last week of the study, but the middle weeks, I'd only do it on Fridays. The pills, which the patients would take Monday through Friday, would be sorted out each week when Dinka picked up the blood to take to the lab. He wouldn't mark which pill was which, he said. This was to protect me. Only he could know who was getting the real drug and who was getting the placebo. These patients, he said, would do anything to get the real drug, so it was better I stay ignorant.

He'd already allocated the first week, and he pulled a cup from the shelf and gave me a look inside at six chalky pellets, brown like rabbit turds.

'And they have to take *all* of them while sitting here?' I asked. I imagined the pills, the ones that weren't the placebo, scuttling around the blood cells, scrubbing them clean, because even with the training, the specifics of the virus and how the drug worked were as foreign as the surface of Mars to me.

'Most of these patients are used to taking lots of pills,' Dinka said.

He showed me a number on a chart and the same number in the fridge, explaining that I should call the patients by their first names but that I should make damn sure I knew their number when I pulled their pills from the fridge. 'Getting this wrong, getting mixed up, ruins everything. The study's sunk. We start over and more people die. This,' he overstressed, 'is most important.'

'That and not getting infected, right?' I said, half joking.

'Sure, sure. Of course,' he said, but it was an appeasement. I was just another rung in his ladder.

He kept talking, and I tried to figure out what was so strange about him. Maybe it was the fact that he worried I couldn't match two identical numbers or that he'd hired me after only a short interview or that I was the *only* person he'd hired.

I asked if the patients would take home pills for the weekend, which seemed to fluster him. He started to tell me how resistance was the whole problem with the drugs people were using, but he stopped mid-thought, as if realizing he was sharing a secret. 'Our group,' he said, 'will only take the pills Monday through Friday.'

I asked how we would know if the pill was working.

'It works,' he said. 'The medicine is effective against the virus. I know it is.'

'And if it isn't?'

'If it's not, the liver will speak up,' he said with a weird smile, which could only mean one thing – liver failure – and I got a hollow feeling, thinking about the backbone of medical ethics: *first, do no harm.*

He gave me another copy of the patient procedure: greet, questionnaire, vitals, blood draw (if scheduled), pills, and photo. Before he left, he stayed to supervise the first visit, cherry-picking criticism about how I held the needle or asked a simple fucking question.

Truth: I felt terrified when I came out to greet the first patient, Franklin, who was sitting in a brown suit, down in the waiting room, looking like he might keel forward and break all over the floor. He stood up when I called his name, and he was much taller than I'd guessed. Confident, too. He swaggered up, pretending to tip an invisible hat, and I smiled back but kept the clipboard between us.

After he sat, I asked him all the questions I was supposed to – how are you feeling? how have you slept? how are your bowels? – then I took his vitals, drew his blood (shaking like wheat stalk the whole time), gave him his pills, and took his photo with the Polaroid.

As Franklin's face emerged from the gray square, he patted his hair and said, 'What's that for, anyway?'

I told him it was another way for the doctor to follow his progress, and Franklin seemed confused. 'You ain't the doctor?' he said, and I felt like I shrunk a few inches. I pointed to Dinka and said, 'No, that would be him.'

The hardest part about the job was honestly not the blood draws or the small talk, but the turnstile nature of the appointments. Every twenty minutes a new person came in and I asked the same questions, and gave the same pills, and took the same picture, until their faces all started to blend together, and in the coming weeks, I would keep calling Franklin, Daniel, and Daniel, Paul, and Paul, Lonnie but Maggie... well, Magdalene, I could remember from the very beginning. She was my last appointment of the day, and she was the one with the book.

The cover had a pair of big red lips, and when I came out and called her name, she was holding it up, reading, so that I could only see her eyes and the bridge of her thin nose and then there were those lips – like they were her lips blown way up – until she lowered the book and I saw her real lips, which were much thinner and paler and cracked, and she parted them to say, 'My name is Magdalene, not Maggie.'

I tried to have some fun with her then. 'It says Maggie right here on this form.'

'Your form is ill-informed. Maggie is the name of an ugly girl who's trying to make friends. Do you think I'm ugly?'

I told her the truth. 'No, miss.' A mass of brown hair framed her small face and she looked younger than the twenty years listed on her chart.

She raised her eyebrow and for a moment I forgot what side of the table I was supposed to be sitting on.

'So does that mean you're looking for a friend?' I asked her.

She grinned in a way, like we might share a secret.

'And what's your name?' she asked me.

'Mister Gavin,' I said, just to make absolutely certain who I was within those walls.

'Coy,' she said and I had no idea what that word was. I thought maybe it was some kind of fish. 'What's your first name?'

'Sam,' I said, and she repeated it, making the hairs on my arms stand up. I wanted to hear her say it again, over and over.

'Where'd you grow up?' she asked. 'You have an accent.'

'Uh... Kansas.'

'That's it.' She snapped her fingers. 'Like Dorothy Gale.'

The horror could not evade my face and she tried to correct it. 'Well, not *exactly*. Not high-pitched. But rural.'

I resisted the urge to touch my throat. 'If you think I'm rural, you should hear how the cows talk.'

She smiled, for real this time, and a warmth washed over me. I knew immediately and without question that I would look forward to seeing her each day.

That first night, Dinka returned at five on the dot and asked me loads of questions: Did everyone show up? How were their answers? Their veins? Their attitudes? Did I feel safe alone? He told me to be careful with the chatty ones. 'They like to get into your grey matter,' he said, 'and try to figure you out. No one wants to waste their time with chalk pills but that's the risk of a trial study.' He continued like we were talking about the common cold and not life and death. 'Watch out for sociopaths. Those who would destroy the study to save themselves.' He looked at Magdalene's photo from my last appointment before sliding it back into her folder.

'The wife wants dinner,' he said, throwing on a tweed jacket. 'She said I could come if I brought the gold card.'

I smiled because I was supposed to. After Dinka left, I finished filing the charts, flipped the lights, and left.

10

'Do you think I'm a sociopath?' I asked Gwen that evening. I was holding up a mirror for her so she could powder her nose without going down to the bathroom, and she stopped dabbing her face and leaned back, staring, measuring me before answering.

'Like someone rich?' she said.

'No, not a socialite. A sociopath.'

'Like a psychopath?'

'Never mind.' I put her mirror down and started pacing.

'You're probably a little crazy,' she said. 'Didn't you bite Tony Leland's ear because you were bored?'

'We were playing Gladiator,' I said. 'And how do you even know about that? We were like five.'

'I don't know. I think Eddie told me.' She picked up the mirror to put on some lipstick. It was the color of pale taffy and made her look like a corpse. She smacked her lips and opened an eye shadow case. 'Speaking of psychopaths, guess who I talked to today?'

I didn't need to guess. If it was someone from home, I assumed the most obvious. 'Bobby.'

That fueled her up. 'I tried calling Rachel, you know, to let her know I was okay, and he picked up the phone instead. Sounded perfectly fine.'

I could tell this ate her up. She wanted him in wreckage, a blubbering begging mess.

I tried to imagine Bobby, who he really was, but I could only picture a faceless dude in a suit. 'What'd he want? Besides to have you back under his thumb.'

She didn't answer me straight away. She tried to put some foundation over a pimple on my chin, and I shirked away, so she starting throwing her makeup back into her bag. Finally she said, 'He gave me an ultimatum. He said I had three weeks to come home or he was going to come here and get me himself.'

'That's not an ultimatum.'

'Yes it is. Do this or I'll do that.'

'No, because in both he gets you back.'

She thought this over. 'Well, he said he would come to get his ring first, and I told him, *good luck finding it, buster.* So he said he'd come get me instead.'

She was still his.

I looked at her hand. The ring was gone. 'Did you sell it?'

She shook her head and pointed to the dresser. 'I put it away. I don't want to see it.'

I opened the drawer and saw it there.

'He called me an oath-breaker for saying I'd ever marry him, and this is coming from a man who cheated.'

'You like it, don't you? Him saying he'll come get you?'

She said nothing.

'Is that what you want?'

She pinched her lips. Typical Gwen. While I was settling in, hoping to make a life, she was still waiting to play her cards. She was saved from having to say anything else because Flora arrived, knocking like a six-foot woodpecker.

We left for a party across town in Nob Hill. At some point, the house had been converted into apartments, and we had to take a series of stairs to reach the front door. The din of voices and music heightened with each flight and became deafening once we opened the door and pushed into the crowd.

Every step I took, I walked through another conversation. Pot smoke and body odor fogged the air. Bits of sentences blipped out from the chatter – *They had to use forceps. I fucked him finally. People are starving, and she still threw it out* – as Flora led us to a kitchen, where a group of barely-dressed girls mixed sangria in what looked like a bucket.

Flora introduced us as 'ze couple from down hall', and I wondered if Gwen said we were together or if Flora was just lazy with descriptions. Gwen didn't seem to notice, or if she did, she didn't react, and so I put my arm around her waist and she let it sit there for almost a minute before wiggling free under the pretense of needing to pee. 'Flora,' she said, 'could you come with me?' Out the window, through some trees and over the rooflines, I could see the outline of the Transamerica Pyramid like a big geometric phallus threatening the dim sky.

One of the girls in the kitchen squealed that we should all take shots, and she went around the room, pouring rum into every open mouth. A few passes of the bottle, and I was slurring words with Winnie (or Wanda?) or better known on the stage as Kandy with a K. She was a big-chested gangly thing, probably eighteen and barely a hundred pounds. She wore her stringy blonde hair in two pigtails and had on as many clothes as I assumed she wore to work. Her eyes were not friendly – they were serpentine and skittish – but she had a big bag of coke, and that was all I needed to continue feigning interest. She kept talking to me, but it was impossible to hear, so I just kept nodding, taking cues from her expression for when I should look surprised, or ponderous, or wildly entertained. I just wanted to roll up a bill and do a fucking line.

Kandy gestured with her finger for me to follow her, and we passed Gwen and Flora, who were leaving the bathroom. They immediately turned and followed us back into the tiny room.

Kandy scraped out a few lines on the tile surrounding the sink. With a rolled-up bill, she snorted one.

Gwen gave Kandy a counterfeit smile before she bent over to do her own.

Kandy leaned toward me and said, 'You're cute, you know that?' She rubbed some coke dust against her gums. Her teeth were toppled together and hectic and yellow.

'Is that a professional compliment?' I asked. 'Or an honest one?'

'What makes you think they're different?'

I winked at her because I knew what she was doing and I wanted her to know that I knew. She didn't think I was cute so much as she wanted me to give her a compliment right there in front of Gwen. Jealousy was an economy for women.

'Don't lie. You call Wally Fat-Fuck, who comes in every Friday with his wad of oily bills and his sausage fingers, cute, don't you?' I said.

Kandy seemed confused. 'Wally Fat-Fuck?'

'Or Greasy Joe-Finger, who cares. You know what I mean. Your job is lying. I mean, you wouldn't take your clothes off without getting compensated, would you?' Of course, I asked this knowing full well her sense of self-value would be diminished if she didn't at least remove her top.

Kandy lifted one side of her mouth, and she reached around with one hand to untie her bikini. Her tits bounced out, round and smooth and taunting.

Gwen quickly looked away, but my eyes lingered – they were hemispheric – and by the time I grew enough sense to look up at Kandy's face, I could tell she'd gotten the compliment she was hoping for.

'They paid for themselves in three weeks,' she said. 'You want to touch them?'

I needed no further invitation and I cupped my hand around the left one. It was chilly somehow and firm as a sandbag, but it had been so long since I touched a tit and it stimulated something animal-deep within me. I had the urge to throw her to the floor and force my way between her legs, but instead, I nodded like a good socially-trained human.

Gwen snorted as if she saw through my smile to what I was imagining. She gave me the rolled-up bill, and said she needed to pee again so we would have to get out. Kandy covered up, filling me with profound sadness and the desire to beg, like a dog, for one more morsel.

I did my line while Kandy tied her top. We went back to the kitchen and flirted for a little while longer, until a tall dude came over and kissed her on the lips. She introduced us, but he looked straight over the top of my head, and they went off to talk to someone else. She left her baggie of coke on the counter, and when I realized I was alone, I picked it up and put it in my pocket.

I got a beer from the fridge, went out into the living room, and tried to force my way into a few conversations, but to every new group I brought silence and fracture, and the people splintered off and re-coalesced into other clusters, leaving me to stand alone once again. I worried my voice was high-pitched. I imagined Dorothy singing 'Somewhere Over the Rainbow.'

I finally fell into a conversation with two guys who worked in porn – one was a director, the other a cameraman – and they half-invited me to a shoot they were doing a few weeks later just so I would stop asking questions about the business. I wanted to know how they came up with all the scenarios and how long a shoot took, and if the girls ever actually had an orgasm or if they were generally faking.

'I could write a script,' I said. 'I could write a better fucking script. Ha! Fucking script! Right? Fucking? Script?'

'I'll give Flora the details,' the director told me.

After the invite, the two men scattered, and I stood there, peeling the label from my beer bottle, searching for Gwen. I finally found her in the bedroom, playing a Ouija board with some kid who looked about fifteen.

'Let's go,' I told her. 'I'm bored.' In truth, I wanted to leave before Kandy came asking for the whereabouts of her coke.

'You weren't bored with Kandy's boobs,' Gwen said.

'Kandy's boobs left.'

Gwen rolled her eyes. 'You know she was an A-cup before she bought new ones.'

'You,' I said, maybe shouted, at the boy. 'Tits. Big or small?'

'I like all kinds,' he said to Gwen.

'Whatever,' I said. 'Whatever. Liar. No. I've got it. You.'

'Brian.'

'Brian, would you rather touch fake tits or no tits, ever?'

'Uh. Yeah. Fake ones.'

I raised my arms, victorious.

'What kind of question is that?' Gwen said.

'Just making a point.'

'What's your point?'

'I don't know, Gwen. Why don't you ask the spirit realm?'

I could tell that my presence had withered any sort of mood Gwen and Brian had established as he rose from the bed and slunk out of the room.

'Thanks a lot,' Gwen said. 'I was having a good time.'

'Let's go have a good time somewhere else.'

'We can't just leave her.' Gwen pointed to Flora, who was already passed out drunk on the bed, next to a golden retriever who was licking her empty hand.

'She's fine,' I said, but to be sure I pushed the dog away and put my fingers on her wrist. Flora groaned. She said something in Russian, rolled over to her side, and cuddled up to the dog. I jiggled her shoulder. 'Flora! Wake up. We're leaving.'

She moaned but that was it.

I gave her another shake. 'Come on, get up! Germany's invading!' A low growl emitted from the dog's throat. I pulled my hand away so he wouldn't bite me.

'Leave her alone,' Gwen said. 'We don't have to leave yet.'

'If you want to stay, stay. But I'm leaving.' I pulled the bag of coke from my pocket and dangled it in front of her. 'And this is coming with me.'

She looked down at the Ouija board. 'Take this, too,' she said.

'I don't know where—'

She stood up and tried to hide it in the back of my shirt, but I told her we should just walk out with it, like we had brought it in the first place. So she made me carry it down the hall and out the front door.

It was obvious that Gwen had never stolen a thing in her entire life because she couldn't stop giggling once we made it safely down the stairs and into the cold night. She kept looking through the plastic lens on the pointer-thing and saying, 'I can't believe we did that,' before erupting in another fit of giggles.

Once we made it back to the apartment, Gwen wanted to unbox the damn thing and play. She had it out on the floor when I returned from the bathroom, even had a few candles lit. I chopped a line for her, another for me, between the Yes and No on the board.

'I'm not playing,' I said because I worried she'd want to 'talk' to Eddie and that sounded like the perfect way to demolish my buzz. I'd done my fair share of talking to Eddie when he was alive, and I didn't care to let our subconscious spell out its guilt or try to justify our actions by pretending he was giving us permission from the other side.

'Why not?' she finally asked.

I gave her a look, one that said *don't fucking ask me that again*, and she pouted.

'It's a piece of cardboard,' I said. 'It's not a telephone.'

'You're just scared.'

We'd both heard stories. Messages about imminent death from demons followed by, gasp, fruition and stolen souls. The horror. I hardened my face. Truth was: she was right. I was scared. But not about demons. Not those kinds, anyway.

I asked her how she figured, and she looked down at the board and asked if she had nicer boobs than Kandy. I moved the pointer to spell out 'maybe'. She looked up at me and opened her mouth like she was surprised.

'The board wants to see. Just to compare. Purely scientific empirical whatever,' I said.

'You've already seen me naked.'

'But the board hasn't. The board, Gwen.'

She gave me a sly grin, and I realized she was allowing herself a dirty thought.

I pulled a five-dollar bill from my pocket, rolled it into a straw, and let her do the first line. As she was bent over, I traced my finger down the side of her waist.

'Prove it,' I whispered. She stood up and handed me the bill. Then, as if overcome by heat, she pulled off her dress and dropped it to the floor.

She stood there wearing a pair of yellow-white panties and a pink-flowered bra. She contorted her body in an awkward sexy pose, something Flora must've taught her.

'You're still wearing clothes,' I said.

'Hypocrite.' She unhooked her bra and pulled down her panties. Her knees wobbled as if her nakedness were heavy.

I sat on the bottom bunk. 'Come here,' I told her.

She did, holding her hands above her head, stretching the sleek line of her stomach. She stopped inches from my mouth. I snapped my teeth and she squealed, concaving her belly.

'Shhh.' I reached up and ran my hand along the back of her ass. Her skin pricked and she moaned softly. I kissed her stomach and skimmed my hands up the backs of her knees, up, while my tongue traced the V of her pelvic line, my fingers parted her crease, and a smell, like muted ginger, made me salivate. She widened her stance so that I could dip my finger inside. She trembled and tried to fall away, but I didn't relent. I didn't dare give her a chance to reconsider.

I laid her down and flicked my tongue between her legs and her body bled away its tension. She didn't reach down, didn't caress me, didn't open her eyes even to see me, and I wondered if she was thinking about Bobby or Eddie, but it didn't matter. I found a rhythm and she was grinding against my face. Her moans shifted from compulsory to primal, mindless, and she shouted that she was going to come. I looked up and watched her face and chest and stomach all lurch and shudder: my gold medal. She really did have better tits than Kandy, and I felt like telling her that, but she'd clamped her thighs around my head, and I couldn't move.

Eventually, she let go, and I came up from between her legs and lay down beside her. She laughed and covered her face, embarrassed. I pried her hands away and tried to kiss her, but she turned away.

'Your mouth is dirty,' she said, and I could see, suddenly, how she would feel about my body, in general, if she was that disgusted by her own. I didn't blame her, not then.

'It's fine,' I said, because when I tried to imagine her touching me, I saw her hands on a different body; I imagined my chest scalped flat, a swirl of hair around my navel, an engorged organ protruding between my legs.

We laid in silence until I could feel her body shuddering. She was crying. I got up and lit a cigarette. 'Do you want to tell me what's wrong?' I said.

'It's just… it's going to sound stupid but sometimes…' She looked up, searching the springs of the top bunk. 'Sometimes, I worry that Eddie is watching us.'

'He's not watching us.'

'How do you know?'

'Look,' I told her. 'The way I see it, you punch your own ticket, you forfeit all rights to control the decisions of people who are still here in the world, still trying. Eddie took himself out of our lives. So, fuck him.'

A fat tear rolled down her face and she smeared it away with her palm. 'I feel like he cemented himself in mine.'

I didn't say it but I felt the same. Fucking Eddie. Self-martyr. His tomb took up half of my mind. All the blood. The bits of brain. That warm metallic smell. I had to squash those images, bury them because letting them surface meant remembering, and I was so tired of remembering.

'You've got to get him out of your head.' Smoke came out attached to my words.

She wiped her eyes and reached for her panties. 'I don't know how.'

'It's funny,' I said.

'Funny?'

'Yeah, funny. You cheated on him how many times? Two? Three? But now that he's gone you're, like, committed.'

'Why are you so mean? How the fuck is that supposed to make me feel?'

'I didn't think about it.'

'You didn't think.'

'You're drunk,' I said. I considered telling her something

horrible about Eddie, like how he fucked Mabel Frey behind the dug-out more than once, or how he used to call Gwen *the teeth* behind her back because of her overbite, or how he killed himself, more or less, because she cheated on him with a pants-shitter, but it would've only hurt her, and hurting Gwen was the main reason Eddie blew his face off in the first place. No matter how callous I felt toward Gwen, helping Eddie accomplish his goal from beyond the grave was not something I was willing to do.

'I'm drunk,' Gwen agreed. 'Will you just. Will you hold me?' She lifted the sheet, and wired to oblige a warm body, I threw my cigarette out the window and slid in beside her.

Gwen passed out quick but I stayed awake, thinking about how Eddie, if he could see me, would be doing a slow clap of begrudging acceptance. He knew how much I liked Gwen, and he'd always mocked the idea that she'd ever like me back, and yet there we were: him in a box and me lying thousands of miles away, my lips just millimeters from Gwen's skin. To be honest, I felt no accomplishment in it though. I felt only the numbness of having who I'd always wanted and not caring either way if I kept her.

11

Franklin showed up late to his appointment on Wednesday, his face the texture of wet bean curd, and before I could take his vitals or ask any of the scripted questions, he told me, rather plainly, that he'd been shitting water.

I wrote it down in the notes and told him if his symptoms worsened that he might need to go to the emergency room for some fluids. I gave him a brochure on how to avoid and detect dehydration, took his Polaroid, and he went home to lie in bed.

He wasn't the only one who came in looking a mess. Several others expressed changes in their bowels – runny, sour, violent changes – while others had fevers and an oily, gelatinous shell of sweat covering their entire body.

Magdalene seemed fine, though. Her usual facetious self. By then I'd already come to look forward to her appointments. She was intriguing; a bright light in an otherwise bleak day. When I called her back to the room she ignored me and stayed seated, staring at her book. I thought about saying her name again, maybe even calling her *Maggie*, but then she held up her finger, letting me know her hearing was just fine, but that she was going to make me wait.

So, I waited.

Finally, she placed her bookmark, closed the cover, and followed me in.

'How are you feeling today?' I said with a wide smile.

She narrowed her eyes and threatened me with those tiny slits. 'How am I feeling today? Hmmm.' She bit her bottom lip and put her book beneath the chair. 'That's a little personal, don't you think?'

'It's the same question you answered yesterday.' I tapped the form.

'Yeah, but maybe things have changed since then. Maybe

something monumental happened. Maybe my best friend died.'

My tailbone seemed to curl up inside me. 'Did your best friend die?'

'Not today,' she said. 'But let's say he had, and let's say I was feeling awful about it. Is that how I should answer?'

I looked back down at the form. 'I think it just means bodily. Like health-wise.'

'I have AIDS.'

'Yeah, but, like, how do you feel?'

She grinned, stretching the cracks in her lips. 'Super,' she said, and I noticed her teeth were perfect.

'It's a stupid question,' I said and hoped she'd back off, but also, a little, I hoped she wouldn't. I hoped she'd go right on tearing through all the stupid shit in the world, shredding the whole stupid fucking thing, and doing it all right there in front of me so I could watch.

'It's fine,' she told me.

'Super,' I repeated over-chipper, and I took off my gloves to write down her answer. She reached forward then, put her hand over mine, and kept it there. Her skin felt soft, like worked leather, and I realized it was the first time I'd touched someone in the study without my gloves on.

'Can I ask *you* a personal question?' she said, and she showed me that smile again. I wondered what her laugh was like, and how hard it might be to pull out of her.

'How personal?' I said.

'Very personal. The most personal question I've ever asked anyone in my entire life.'

I leaned toward her like someone might be listening to us.

She leaned in, too, and held me in suspense. I could smell her hair, like flowers or fruit or something sweet and clean. She whispered, 'Are you giving me sugar pills?'

My first reaction was the stupid truth. 'I don't know.'

She squeezed my hand and said, 'You're giving me sugar pills.' She pulled away and wouldn't look me in the eye. I noticed a rash on her arm had opened into a sore, and I wrote it down in the chart like a good little soldier. Afterward, she hurried out and I felt terrible. I wondered if she was right. I looked at the cups in the fridge again. They all looked the same.

Cleaning up, I found her book under the chair, and I flipped through the first few pages and saw that she'd gotten carried away with the pen. Underlining words here and there. Sometimes a whole string of them. There were little notes all around the edges of the story, or sometimes a star or a heart or a frown, or a whole scribbled sentence, '*Not everyone knows French, asshole.*' I flipped to the front page, hoping to find a signature or her full name, some sign of ownership, but instead I found a note written with different ink, in different handwriting: *Para mi Magdalena, Te Quiero, Humberto*

I took the book with me but I didn't go home yet. I needed a drink and to not deal with Gwen, so I decided to stop at a bar just down the road. I'd seen it before: the manliest place in Castro. Outside, a row of Harleys rested askew on their kickstands, and a group of leather-clad dudes stood near the entrance, passing a joint. They gave me a once-over as I walked past, and I flattened my hair and tried to flick my cigarette so hard I almost dropped it.

Inside, the lights were sparse: a few hung over the liquors behind the counter and one straddled the space between a tattered pool table and a dartboard. I took a seat at the bar, and did my best to appear relaxed when the bartender approached. He was a big-ass dude, and not just muscled but fucking Schwarzenegger. His forearms were probably the size of my thigh, and I could see his veins, thick as worms, spread beneath the skin. He looked like the type of person who juiced, and my first thought was if he could get me some.

He asked me what I wanted, and I ordered vodka on the rocks, and he looked down at Magdalene's book sitting on the counter, those giant red lips pointing up at him, like he didn't like me already.

'We don't have any ice,' he said, and he rubbed his mustache flat.

I asked if they had any beer, and he poured me a lager from the tap. Across the way, another dude wearing leather eyed me with what seemed like hostility.

'Are you lost, buddy?' he asked. He sauntered over and plopped down beside me.

I looked at him, trying to seem unaffected by his size – he wasn't muscley like the bartender, but broad and sturdy like a male hog. He only had on a vest up top, and black curly hair carpeted his skin from collarbone to waistband.

'No. Just thirsty,' I said. 'This is a bar, isn't it?'

'Yeah,' he said, and he slapped the wooden counter. '*This is* a bar, but it's not a family joint where any Joe Square can—'

'I look like a family man to you?'

'You got a stupid mouth,' he said.

'And you got a stupid fucking hat on your head, which I assume you picked out, so. Cheers.' I lifted my beer and he readjusted the leather newsboy on his scalp.

'Are you even a queer?' he asked me.

I sipped my beer. 'What's it matter?'

'Dammit, Jeb,' the drunk said, turning to the bartender. Jeb stopped wiping out a glass. 'There's no point calling it a *Leather* bar if yuppie pricks like this can just'— he gestured to my scrubs— 'waltz around like it's the goddamn Sizzler.'

'I wasn't aware that it was called a Leather bar,' I said to the man, and I pushed my money toward the bartender. 'It said *Comstock Lode* on the sign outside.'

Jeb, behind the bar, waved my money away. 'Ernest is going to buy your drink. Isn't that right?' he said to the drunk. Two Ernests standing side-by-side couldn't have eclipsed Jeb's torso.

Ernest sucked his teeth and looked me over. 'Fine. But you should know there's plenty of dyke bars down the road.'

'If I see any dykes, I'll be sure to let them know that,' I said.

'Ernest, just leave him be,' the bartender said.

Just that little acknowledgment, that pronoun, it felt like a victory. In my periphery, I could still see Ernest staring over at me, shaking his head.

'Maybe your balls haven't dropped yet.' He chuckled and picked up Magdalene's book. 'Or maybe just a pervert, huh?'

I snatched it back. He was mad I wasn't playing dress-up, afraid because one person not playing along might throw the whole hobby into light.

I wanted him to go away. 'Look,' I said, 'I'm a nurse. I wear a uniform all day. I don't want to wear another one just to get a drink, that's all.'

'This is *not* a uniform,' he said, rubbing his palms over his thighs.

I looked at everyone else in the room – the two men playing pool, the guys in the booth, still smoking their rolled-up doobie, the bartender, and the other dudes, like toads on the barstools, *all* wearing leather. 'Do you wear that all day?' I said, pointing to his chaps. 'Do you go to the grocery store in that outfit?'

'Shut up, dyke,' he said, but he was smiling now.

'When everyone's wearing the same outfit, it's a uniform.'

'I wear a tie to work,' Ernest said. 'This isn't a uniform. It's a second skin.'

He was smarter than he looked, or drunk-wise, which meant it was an accident.

'I understand that,' I said.

'You said you were a nurse?'

I nodded, and he lifted his boot up, started undoing the laces. 'I got this sore.'

I imagined beneath his sock nothing but rotten flesh, bloated and split open by subdermal gas, like the smell of my father's foot before his amputation, how it perfumed the house with a sweet putrid odor, how he kept the living-room fan right on it, like he wanted us all to live in the funk of his rotting flesh. 'I'm not sure I'm qualified to diagnose every, uh, little—' I said, but Ernest kept untying.

'C'mon, I'll buy you another drink,' he said, and before I could answer he'd pulled away his boot and sock and turned the sole of his foot toward me. In the middle, a blossom of white puffy skin surrounded an open sore.

'That's trench foot,' I said.

'Trench foot?' He curled his lip.

'Yep.' I tried humor. 'Been in any trenches lately?'

Ernest thought way too hard.

'Like that shit from Dubbya-Dubbya-One?'

'It's from not changing your wet socks.'

Ernest smiled and yelled to the bartender. 'Hey, Jeb. He said it's trench foot.'

Jeb looked from Ernest to me and back again. 'That's disgusting, E,' he said. 'Cover that shit up before the health inspector walks in.'

Ernest's ears flared bright red.

I tried to tell him how to treat it – sitz bath and dry socks – but I could tell he'd lost interest in help, or never had any and just wanted to complain, to be heard, listened to; some people just wanted their pain known. After he ordered me another beer, he reapplied his sock and shoe, stood up, and limped away.

Jeb set the beer in front of me. 'Where you from, kid?' he asked, which annoyed me. I wanted to say, *just because you're bigger doesn't mean I'm a kid*, but rational thinking still outweighed the beer.

'I live here,' I said.

'Don't fuck with me. I'm not Ernest. Where are you *actually* from?'

'Why?'

'Because you're acting like you've never been less comfortable in your whole life, and I don't think that's just my bar doing that to you. I think it's the city. So I'm guessing you're more country than you pretend. Aren't ya?'

'Kansas,' I told him.

'And how long have you been in the Emerald City, Dorothy?'

'A few weeks.'

'That makes sense,' he said.

'Look. I just wanted a beer.'

'Lots of places serve beer.'

I looked down into the foam of mine.

'I have a hypothetical,' he said.

'Okay.'

'If I was in your hometown, would you recommend I just walk into your local bar dressed like this?'

He stepped back a little. He was shirtless and his crotch was covered by a thin pair of red underwear. There was a small gap of hairless skin between the satin over his crotch and the black leather chaps that covered his thighs. He looked like a rodeo clown on his wedding night.

'No. I wouldn't recommend that,' I said.

'Well, kid. When in Rome—' He smiled like he felt bad for me. Then his face got real serious. 'Look I stuck up for you, but Ernest is right. You can come back, but not dressed like that. This is my main source of income, these guys. And I won't have anyone making fun of them.'

'I wasn't making fun of anyone.' But I knew what he meant. I definitely knew.

'If you come back dressed like you stepped out of a Sears catalogue,' he said, 'I'll assume you want war. You understand?' His biceps could wear D-cups.

I sniffed. 'I've got some chaps,' I said, and I did, buried in a closet at my mother's house, back from when I rode in juvenile rodeo.

'Finish your beer,' Jeb said, and he went to help someone else.

I felt small suddenly, unwanted everywhere. Everyone had their own fucking club, except me. I felt like a leper. Like full-body trench foot. I swallowed my second beer quickly and left.

Gwen and Flora were in the room when I got home, adjusting rabbit ears on a television I'd never seen before. I tossed my keys onto the desk, and Gwen looked over. 'Look what we found out by the curb,' she said.

I looked to Flora. 'What happened to *your* TV?'

'Nothing,' Gwen said.

'So does that mean you two are going to be watching shows over here now?'

They both stopped adjusting the rabbit ears to look at me.

'You just watch a lot of TV,' I said.

Gwen's eyes left me for Flora. 'I told you Sam hates me,' she said, and went to flipping the channel knob until some kind of picture came up on the screen: lions fucking, the male biting the female's back. I noticed the female wasn't crying or getting pissed or rolling her eyes, and I wanted to observe these things out loud but I thought about Trench-foot Ernest and his impulse to bitch. It was enough motivation for silence.

I put Magdalene's book on the desk, and Gwen eyed it. 'What's that?'

'It's called a book.'

She snatched it up. 'For me?' She smiled until she started flipping through the pages. 'A used book?'

'Not used. Owned. Someone left it at the clinic.'

'Should prolly disinfect?' Flora said, and Gwen let the book fall.

'Jesus, what is wrong with you?' I stooped to pick it up.

Gwen wiped her hands against her shirt. 'Why'd you bring it here?' she said. She wiped like she'd stuck her fingers in a dog turd. I held the book out and pretended like I was going to rub it – virus, death – all over her face, and she ran behind Flora and shouted for me to leave her alone.

Flora cursed and slapped the box: lions sharing gazelle guts, their mouths pink with blood. 'Ve going to party,' Flora said to me. 'You come?'

I imagined another houseful of strippers asking me what I did, *like, for a job*, and I told Flora I'd rather clean a blister, but that I hoped they had a 'super' time. It wasn't that I didn't like the party scene, but that I found myself more captivated by Magdalene, and having her book felt to me like having an open window to her brain. The only thing better would be her sitting right there in the flesh, outside of the pressure and constant morbid reminder of the study, but that wasn't something I'd worked up the nerve to ask for just yet.

Gwen started wiping her hands all over Flora. 'Don't be nice,' Gwen said, looking over at me. 'I don't want Sam to come.'

'That's fine,' I told them. 'I'd rather stay home with my nasty pages anyway.' I raised the book and herded them around the room until they ran out, and I was relieved to be rid of them for the night.

I reasoned, as I sat down and opened the cover of *Lolita*, that having Magdalene's words unfiltered, no performances, just her naked reactions to a book (one that had been used to label me a pervert no less) was an opportunity I could not deny mining. What kind of pervert was *she*? That was the question I most wanted answered. How did she think when she thought her words were totally private? And would she be interested in someone like me?

I flipped to the first page and began reading, stumbling over word after unknown word, things like *sibilant* and *poltroon* and *fructuate*, trudging through long blocks of writing with no breaks for my mind to put it all together, but still I read more. I wondered who she most identified with in the story; the girl would be the obvious choice. But no, the more I read, the clearer it became. She resented the girl. She was a *beast*, an *airhead*, a *tease*. She liked the yearning, the devious, the sex-crazed, and filthy Humbert Humbert, and she wrote to him directly. *I'd wiggle my knees loose for you, Humbert... Just drown your wife already... I would never call you Hummy...* In a way, it felt like I was reading Magdalene's diary and getting a glimpse of a secret side of her, a sexuality that had, until then, seemed repressed, and I found myself increasingly intrigued. Who was this girl? I started skimming the words, hungry for her next comment, and ignoring the story, but to my disappointment only halfway through the book Magdalene's comments disappeared. I read a page of the story there and gathered the girl and the man were riding in a car, but I didn't read further.

I wanted to know more, though. Not about the book, but about Magdalene. I wanted to know everything about her, which came as a surprise. I had a crush, I realized. Something about the way she underlined every little sexual detail and how she had her own private conversation with a character in a book, it made her seem so goddamn lonely, like maybe she'd resigned herself to only ever having that kind of man, a paper man, and that idea just tore me up because I thought maybe she deserved more. I couldn't justify having that emotion, really, seeing as I'd only spent a total of an hour with her up until that point, but I felt it already, a gravity she had, pulling me closer and closer every time I got her to smile.

12

The alarm barked at seven in the morning. It was Friday and I stumbled across the room to kill the noise. Gwen laid there like a lump of hair while I put on my scrubs and got ready for work. It had taken forever, but I'd found a leather outfit – pants, shirt, combat boots – after scouring five thrift stores and a bargain bin at The Emporium. Each item was a different shade of black, and when I wore them all at once, I looked like a sloppy ninja, but I hoped it would look, at least to Jeb, like a big white flag of surrender.

I had been thinking about him, or more, I'd been thinking about Magdalene, and how Jeb could help *me* impress her. If being friends with Marcus had taught me anything, it was how to be delicate when it came to asking for drugs.

So I packed the leather and Magdalene's book in my backpack, wearing the boots with my scrubs, and I took the stuff to work and did my job.

No one said a thing about the boots until Magdalene came in and started laughing. 'You join the Army?' she asked.

'Just trying something new.' I put one foot on the table.

'New!' She picked a fleck of dry leather. 'These look about a hundred years old.'

I let my foot drop to the floor. 'Aren't you missing something?'

'Like existentially?'

'No. Like a book.'

She perked. 'Did I leave it here? I thought maybe I'd left it at the laundromat.'

I handed over the paperback and she hugged it close. 'Did you snoop?'

'I glanced,' I said as I wrapped a tourniquet around her arm. 'What's it about?'

Her features slid in disbelief. 'Humbert Humbert,' she said, 'the pedophile.'

The clock on the wall ticked the seconds behind us. I felt slightly sour in my gut, remembering some of her written comments, because it was obvious, from the pages I'd skimmed, that the girl was young, but a child? No. And, clearly, the pervert turned her on, and her being turned on had, in turn, turned *me* on, leaving me to wonder, not for the first time, what the fuck was wrong with me.

Magdalene opened and closed her fist. 'My arm's going to fall off,' she said, and I realized I was still gripping the tourniquet.

As I drew her blood, I noticed another purple-red rash on her bicep, but when I asked about it, she said it was a birthmark. It didn't look like a birthmark. It was puffy and bruised-looking, and I wondered if someone had been pushing her around. When I finished the blood draw, I tapped the book cover and asked her who Humberto was. I said it all stupid, too. No silent H, like Hum-bur-toe. She gave me that smile again.

'You *were* snooping,' she said and pulled her sleeve down.

'I told you I glanced.'

She started to blush.

'Is he your boyfriend?' I asked, and she laughed out loud, but it wasn't the laugh I had expected, not pretty or girly, but big like thunder, and I got the feeling she might be laughing at me. Right at my stupid question-asking face.

'He's not my boyfriend,' she said. 'I mean, not really. I haven't seen him for a while.'

'Does he live here?'

'No.'

'Oh. So where is he?'

'The same place I'm going when I'm done here,' she said.

'So you're still talking then?'

She shook her head. 'No. You're misunderstanding. I mean, after this.' She thumped her knuckles against my clipboard. 'After the study.'

I didn't want to admit I wasn't following, but before I could say anything at all, she leaned forward and said, 'You want to know how I know you're giving me sugar pills?'

A lump the size of a child's fist found its way into my throat, and I tried to say yes but only managed a nod.

'Sugar gives me gas,' she said. 'And guess what I've had for four straight days?'

I finally swallowed and answered stupidly, 'Gas?'

'You,' she said, pointing, 'are very intuitive.'

I took a deep breath. 'At least you don't have diarrhea,' I said, and I lifted the Polaroid to take her photo without warning.

She snatched the square as it whirred out the front of the camera like a boxy white tongue and watched her face appear out of the cloud. 'How many patients have diarrhea?'

I shrugged, but I could tell that it was important to her, and that made me feel valuable. I told her I would check.

'A lot?' she asked. 'Most? Half?'

I didn't want her to worry, so I lied and said, 'Not many.'

She blinked, as if waiting for me to come clean with what I knew about the study, and then she looked back at the photo. 'I don't like it. My eyes look reptilian. Take another.'

I lifted the camera again, but she covered her face. 'No. Take one with me,' she said.

I wondered suddenly, stupidly, if Dinka counted the film inventory, but she'd already stood up from her chair, come around the table, and sat on my lap. Warmth spread up my legs and I knew it was unprofessional, but I let her stay. As I lifted the camera and pushed the button, she turned her face and pressed her lips against my cheek. The flash popped. The engine whirred. The heat of her lips lingered.

She seemed nervous as we waited for the photo to develop. 'I'm sorry,' she said, and I told her it was fine.

'Do you want to take another?' I asked. She said she did, and when I pushed the button, I meant to kiss her cheek this time, but she turned into me, and my wet lips pressed against her dry ones, and they stayed stuck together for a moment. I felt a jolt straight through my chest, a sharp and wonderful thrill.

Magdalene pulled away and started laughing. 'Wasn't it *my*

turn to kiss *your* cheek?' I said, and we both laughed. I realized the fuzzy ethics of what we were doing, that the table was there for a reason, but I discarded this concern because Magdalene looked happy, which made me happy, for the first time, really, in San Francisco. Happy.

We put the two pictures on the table, and I made a crack about filing them for Dinka's research. She asked what he wanted with the pictures anyway, and I told her I didn't know.

'I have a hard time believing that.'

'It's true. He doesn't tell me anything. He's like a robot, all business and no nonsense.'

'Oh, like a doctor?' Magdalene said, and we laughed again. 'Which one would you rather have?' she asked, holding both pictures up and putting her face between them like a third option.

I tapped the one with our faces lip-to-lip, and she nodded like I'd answered a difficult riddle. 'Very intuitive,' she said again, and she slipped the photo into my shirt pocket.

After she left, I changed in the men's room on the first floor of the building, over near the hair salon, because I'd never, not once, seen a man in their shop, all but ensuring I would be alone, though I still worried the whole time that Dinka or Magdalene might return and catch me dressed in head-to-toe cow skin.

Luckily I left unnoticed, but the bar was closed when I arrived, forcing me to sit on the curb while people passed, eye-judging. From then on, I decided, I would wait to change.

Down the street, I saw a wall of brown hair holding a grocery bag, and pure horror came over me. Magdalene. Same stem legs and big feet. What would I say if she saw me? 'Shhh. I'm undercover.' To my relief, the wind blew her hair back and I saw giant red glasses and a humped nose. Not Magdalene. A whole block behind the girl, Jeb stood out like a wildebeest trying to pass as a plain-clothes human.

'Kansas,' he said, holding the door after he unlocked it.

'Welcome back.'

I stood up, wiped the gravel from my ass, and went inside. Jeb took a few quarters from the register and told me to pick some songs on the jukebox while he changed clothes in the restroom. There was hardly anything I recognized, so I chose a bunch of Pink Floyd and Led Zeppelin, and I took a seat and had a good long look around the bar. In the dim dusty sunlight, the place seemed more like a basement or a warehouse, with concrete floors and cracked walls painted black and chipped away in big patches. Near the bar, an unframed poster of a naked man holding his giant veiny cock and wearing a leather mask with a zipper over his mouth hung like a warning. As I studied the poster, Jeb finally emerged from the bathroom, his plain clothes replaced with leather. He started moving shit around behind the bar – racks of clean glasses and kegs of beer – and his arm muscles twitched as if electrified. I realized I was admiring him. I realized this could be misread.

Without asking, Jeb poured me a beer.

'Why'd you move here, Kansas?'

'Needed a new job and thought what the hell, how 'bout some new scenery with it.'

'So you're not some undercover?'

'What? Undercover what?'

He shrugged casually.

'I'm a nurse.'

'You know, I never did see your ID.'

'If I was undercover, wouldn't the cops have come by now? I mean, seriously, I'm already drinking.' I lifted the beer to my lips.

'Just let me see your ID.'

'For what?'

'I want to see if it's from Kansas.'

'Why?'

'To see if your story is a load of horse shit,' he said, putting his hand out. 'Or I could throw you out. Your call.'

I considered the chances he'd even notice the F, that blemish in the periphery of my photo, so easy to miss in all the other numbers and letters. I figured I'd take the risk and handed it over.

He gave it a perfunctory glance, grunted, and handed it back. 'All right. So where do you work then?'

'A clinic. Sort of. It's actually a study.'

His eyebrows climbed his forehead. 'Not on lab rats, I hope.'

'No. They're all humans. It's for some new medication.'

'For what?'

I told him all I knew. AIDS.

He poked his tongue along the inside of his cheek. 'No kidding,' he said. 'I got a cousin. You think he could get in a study like that?'

'I could find out,' I said, excited that I'd gained some leverage, a service to offer in return for what I wanted from him.

'So I have another question,' Jeb said.

'Is it normal to interrogate new customers? I've never owned a business so I wouldn't know.'

'Oh, you're cute. Listen. My bar ain't exactly Club Med, get it? I want new customers, but I'm real protective of the ones I already got, so if that bothers you…'

'It doesn't. I get it. It's sweet, actually. Weirdly. You're like papa bear. Whatever question you have, I'll try to answer.'

'Are you just trying to figure things out or is *this* really your thing?'

'What do you mean?'

'I mean, why are you here and not some other bar?'

I asked him if he had time for a story.

'Make it short,' he said.

'Okay. So when I was seven I had this friend one summer, before her family moved to Arkansas or Minnesota or somewhere.'

'This doesn't sound like it's going to be short.'

'You asked. I'm telling you. So her family had these horses. Show horses. We rode them western. You know, with those big leather saddles?' I waited for Jeb to nod. 'And my friend rode a young horse name Schitzo – barely broke, and skittish as hell – and I always rode this bloated old horse because I was a shitty rider. Anyway, he had a good stride and could chase after Schitzo if I kicked him hard enough.'

As I was talking, Jeb emptied a rack of clean glasses. 'This story will eventually explain why you're at a Leather bar, yeah?'

'I'm getting there. So, all that bouncing around, and the jiggle of my friend's ass on that frothy beast, and one day I just came, like *came*. It was the first time that ever happened.'

Jeb stared at me blank-faced as he ran a cloth inside of a glass. 'It seems like you haven't really thought it through.'

'I've thought about it plenty. That,' I said, 'was a quality answer to your question. Leather and me; we go way back.' It was a lie, of course, but I needed to come at this from the side.

'So, was it the smell of the leather that got you off?'

I laughed. 'Does it matter?'

Jeb poured himself a beer. 'No, I guess I get where you're coming from,' he said. 'I got my first blow job in a brand new '74 Thunderbird. It had brown leather interior, and I still get a hard-on every time I get into a new car with leather seats.' He smiled, holding my gaze, and then he lifted his pint. 'To frothy animals,' he said, and we clinked glasses. 'May they all end up here.'

And slowly, slowly, they did. Coming in through the door in groups, their heavy boots scuffing the wood floor, a rowdy, ready smile on each of their faces. I sipped my beer as the bar filled up with men, some half-clothed, looking, in their animal-clad way, like mutations of centaurs, while others weren't wearing much of anything at all.

I scribbled on a napkin and tried to blend in, but they all left an open space around me, and I felt like the center of a bulls-eye.

Jeb slid into my periphery. 'How you handling this, Kansas?'

'I'm fine.' I shrugged.

He seemed bored and I could see my opportunity growing legs and running out the door. I knew if I didn't say something and soon, I might never.

'Hey, Jeb.' I paused and tried to remember the segue I'd prepared but my mind was void of any and all electrical connections, so I just blurted, 'If I could get your cousin in the study, do you think you could do something for me?'

He looked at me sideways. 'Sounds like you're about to say something that might get you hit.'

I forced the words to form in my mind before I pushed the air past my lips and the sound out into the air. 'I'm looking for some juice,' I said.

If he had an opinion about what I'd said, it didn't show. He just stood there, sucking on his toothpick. 'What you want it for?' he finally asked.

'Same as anyone else.'

Someone came over to order a drink, but Jeb put his finger up, indicating for him to wait.

'I think you might be undercover fuzz.'

'I already answered—'

'I'm not asking nothing. I'm telling.'

'I showed you my license.'

'Be easy for fuzz to get a fake. You here to bust me, Kansas? Shut us down?'

'I'm not a cop. I just want fucking steroids.'

'Can't help you. I suggest you finish that and go,' he said, and he started walking away.

'Wait,' I said, sounding desperate. I pulled the license out of my pocket and held it out. 'Just look.'

'I already saw that bullshit.'

'No, where my finger is. Look.' I pointed to the F and felt a revolting wave of shame. It had been so easy to accept people accepting me as a man, but going backwards, having to own up and admit to the murkiness of that fact, it felt like the waking version of a naked-in-school dream.

Jeb looked at the F, then he looked at me and rearranged his toothpick to the other side of his mouth but didn't say anything. The guy waiting for his drink slapped the counter and shouted,

'Dying of thirst here,' and Jeb went over to help him.

I figured I'd blown it, but just as I was getting up to leave, Jeb slipped me his phone number, which he'd written on a scrap of receipt paper, and he told me to try calling in the afternoon.

13

Gwen glared at me when I came through the door. She was sitting at the desk using a hand mirror to study her teased-up bangs. 'Where *were* you?'

I had already changed back into my work scrubs, but I tried to casually lay down my backpack, paranoid she might try to look inside. I walked over to the bed and collapsed. 'I had to help a patient home.'

'Flora's getting ready to leave,' she said. 'If you don't hurry, we're going to go without you.'

'I don't feel like dancing.'

'Who'd you help home?'

'My last patient.'

'A girl?'

I pressed the frown from between my eyebrows with my thumb and sat up. 'Are you seriously jealous of a girl with AIDS?' I tried my best to make this sound pathetic, absurd. It was unconvincing.

She lowered the mirror. 'Rachel called today, acting like some kind of go-between for Bobby. She wanted my address so she could "send me something," but I think Bobby just wanted it so he could come get me.'

I could see it already, this fuzzy image she had of herself as the damsel in the tower. *Come save me, Bobby.*

'You give it to her?'

She shook her head and went back to giving her hair all the attention. Then, 'She did tell me something very interesting.'

She was trying to bait me, I thought. She would say, 'I know this thing and I will tell you if you just do the thing I want.' I'd seen her do it a hundred times. I figured she'd say, 'Go dancing with us, and then I'll tell you,' but Gwen was not good at keeping real secrets hostage. She could keep gossip and hearsay and trifle details locked away fine, hoard them as collateral for her future transactions, but a real life-changing, earth-shifting secret was too much pressure. If it was worth hearing, all I had to do was wait. It didn't take long.

'Sally's having a baby,' she said.

I felt confused. 'A what?' A baby. What baby? What's a baby?

She snapped her mirror closed. 'You're going to be an aunt.'

The world wobbled on its axis, and I repeated the word 'baby' over and over to myself, but it sounded wrong. Sally the bean, Sally and her Snoopy pillowcase, the little bed-wetter, *that* Sally had a person inside her.

'Since when?'

She shrugged. 'I don't know. I wasn't there?' Gwen started aerosoling her hair and her head disappeared in a white fog. I empathized.

I lit a joint and turned on the TV and stared at the screen, but I watched nothing. I was wondering what Sally would do next. What my mother would do. Poor kid, I kept thinking, unsure if I meant Sally or her baby or both.

After Gwen left, I went down to the payphone to call Sally, but each time I checked, some junked-out twerp was on the phone and he'd turn his back to me, paranoid like I'd come just to hear his twitchy-ass yammer, so finally I gave up and went to bed.

Just as I was falling into a cold and shapeless sleep, an image of Eddie flashed against my closed lids. He was smiling, holding out two fingers. *Go on, smell her,* he said. I must have stayed that way, lying in the same position all night, because I woke up in the morning with a terrible pinch in my neck. Gwen lay asleep next to me, still wearing her club clothes, her makeup pasty and slid askew. I tried to remember her coming back, but couldn't.

Calling Jeb was the only thing on my mind.

At noon I went down to the payphone and tried Sally first, just to see if I could get an answer, but the line was busy. I pulled Jeb's number from my wallet and imagined myself as cool and calm before slipping a quarter in the slot and punching seven buttons. I listened hard to the ring, practicing what I'd say, rehearsing the smooth delivery of my words; three times I did this before a girl picked up. I worried I'd wasted my last quarter. 'Uh, Jeb?' I asked like an idiot. She told me to wait and she shouted, his full name – Jebediah – driving her voice like a spike deep into my ear. He answered.

'We still on?' I asked.

He smacked the sleep out of his lips. 'On. Yeah, sure, Kansas. We're on. Where you living at?'

I gave him my address and said I'd be waiting outside in an hour. He described his car – a black Camaro – but I pictured a hearse coming to take the old body of Rosie Gavin away.

Gwen – typical – was unhappy when she woke up and learned that I had plans that didn't involve her. 'Since when did you make a friend?'

I told her I met him at work, that we were going out to watch a game and share a pitcher.

'What game?'

'The… uh.' San Francisco had a dozen teams and under pressure I couldn't remember a single one. 'Baseball,' I said.

She folded her arms, and spoke in a baby voice. 'But I wanted to see a movie!'

'So go with Flora.'

'Flora has to work.' She kicked the covers from the bunk, and they fell in a soft pile on the floor.

'Then go by yourself.'

'People will think I don't have any friends.'

'Who cares what people think?'

'Um. Everyone.' She sat up. 'Let me come with you.'

'I'll be back soon,' I said.

'You don't *want* me to come,' she said, pouting some more.

She was right. Girls were so tuned in to not being wanted, it was like nature gave them radars for it, and she was hitting me with a full-frowning assault, not because she wanted to come – no one hated sports more than Gwen – but because she could not stand being unwanted.

'Jeb doesn't know you.'

'He can't know me if we don't meet.'

'What movie do you want to see?'

She folded her arms. '*Indiana Jones and the Last Crusade.*'

'Really?'

'What do you mean, *really*?'

'It's just a guy movie, that's all.'

'Fine, maybe I'll go with Brian then.'

'Brian?' I said.

She sat up straighter, encouraged by my pause. 'From the party.'

'Oh,' I said, 'that puny medium. I remember him. Yeah, you should go with him.' She was struggling for power, I knew, but her pouty bullshit wouldn't work on me, not anymore, and I think she realized it mid eye-roll because she folded her arms, defeated.

'Or maybe we'll go when you get back. Late movies are better anyway. Matinees are for geriatrics,' she said, finding a way to reel me in and make a commitment to time later served.

'I don't know when I'll be back,' I said.

She fell back on the bed and stretched her arms and legs like an irate child. 'But I'll be bored.'

'Stop being boring then.'

She threw a pillow at me. 'You're lying. You're going out with that girl, aren't you?'

I considered turning the table on her, letting her mope around while she thought I was out with Magdalene, but I knew it would only start trouble. 'Fine. You want to meet Jeb?'

It was gray and drizzling, and we stood beneath the awning, me smoking, Gwen whining about the cold, her arms tucked inside her T-shirt so she looked like an amputee. She said she wished we were back in Kansas in a couple of lawn chairs by the pool.

I told Gwen that people talked about the weather when it

was the only thing they had in common. Before she could get at my subtext, Jeb pulled up to the curb in a shiny black two-door.

He shouted 'hey' through the open passenger window but eyed Gwen with some trepidation, making me wonder briefly if 'hey' was a greeting or admonishment.

I introduced them through the window, and Gwen seemed more than satisfied; she seemed infatuated. Jeb's hand on the wheel, the angle of his arm, made his bicep look like it might rip his sleeves in half, Lou-Ferrigno style.

Jeb told me I looked like a drowned rat. I told him to stand in the freezing rain and see how he looked.

'When my shirt gets wet, the ladies do too,' he said, and Gwen giggled. I could tell she was considering a sudden affection for America's pastime.

'Down girl,' I said.

I got in the car, which was (no surprise) all black leather and oiled. Gwen waved goodbye, but didn't turn to go back into the building until we pulled away from the curb.

'You in a hurry?' he asked.

I looked in the backseat, which was impossibly small. As he accelerated a green satchel slumped to the floorboard, and I wondered if the drugs were in there. 'No,' I told him.

'Good,' he said, 'we're going to Oakland,' and I could tell he wasn't feeling particularly chipper – his eyes were tired, his tone, curt – so I kept quiet as we headed out of the city. I recognized the road as the same one I'd come in on from Denver. We approached the Bay Bridge and entered the dark mouth of its lower half. I tried focusing on landmarks, but my eyes were pulled down to the blue water of the bay, slapping itself out to the horizon. I closed my eyes and gripped the seat. 'I hate this bridge,' I said.

Jeb's hand brushed my thigh and he settled it there, and I told him it wasn't the bridge, necessarily, that scared me nearly to fucking tears, but being encapsulated as we were, strapped in a speeding coffin, dangled over water on a bridge built by entirely fallible people.

Jeb said he also hated driving across that particular stretch of asphalt, knowing that the San Andreas Fault was down below, deep beneath the weight of the bay, moaning and shifting, aching to stretch open and swallow us all.

He kept his hand on my leg and I let him because in truth, ashamed as I was to admit it, his hand was a comfort.

'You're fine, Kansas. Just fine.'

'Bridges aren't natural.'

'Keep in mind, death's about as natural as it gets.'

I didn't respond.

'I believe I've just convinced you to love the bridge.'

'You're so full of shit,' I said.

He told me how he studied geology at Stanford and that it wasn't just here we should worry about disaster, but everywhere. Every state did its own dance with apocalypse – California had its fault line, Washington and Wyoming had volcanoes, the Midwest had their tornadoes and drought, not to mention all the other catastrophes in the world: hurricanes, floods, famine, blizzards, ice storms. 'Don't even get me started on Asia with its tsunamis, and the Pacific Ring of Fire—'

'I'd rather get vaporized by an atomic bomb than fall off this bridge. I don't care if a million people had to die with me. I don't care.'

'You're dark, Kansas,' he said, grinning like maybe he liked that. Then he flipped on the radio, letting loose a rap song.

We made it off the bridge and past several giant steel buildings, smoke squirming from their stacks. Ten minutes later, we pulled over in front of a white stucco house, made dingy from years of sea spray and muffler exhaust. The address was stenciled between the doorframe and a single front window covered with flaking steel bars.

Jeb filled his lungs before saying, 'So this is my Nana's house, and my Nana is a nice lady, you know, like most grandmas are nice ladies, and I would really hate for her to get upset. She's fragile, get me? Tough in some ways, but old-fashioned and fragile. Especially seeing as my cousin Eli, you know, is sick in the hospital with all that shit in his lungs, so I can't have her knowing about things like *The Comstock*, or the leather, and especially the fact that I fuck around with men. Get me?' He licked his lips and I could see his blood pressure climbing. Home was not a place he could really be himself. Jeb seemed so invincible. It was good to know we had this weakness in common.

'No problem. Easy. Yeah?' I made the motion of zipping my lips and immediately regretted it.

'This ain't a joke. You tell her anything about my life, and you'll have bigger problems than being a squirrelly runt. You get me? There'll be nothing left of you. Not a tooth or a bone or a piece of hair. I'll flatten you, Kansas.'

I didn't mention that Kansas was already flat. Obnoxiously flat and square and stop calling me fucking Kansas. 'I get it. You don't have to threaten.'

'And if she asks whether you're a girl or not, what are you going to tell her?'

'What do you mean?'

He narrowed his eyes. 'You're not the first tranny I've met.'

'Don't call me that. I want muscles. That's all.'

He put the car in gear.

'Wait. I just. I. Why do I have to tell her anything?'

He smiled. 'That's all I wanted to hear. Some people are proud. Insistent on telling everyone their business. You're all right, though, Kansas.'

We got out and Jeb shook the chain-link fence, whistling a few high notes as if he needed to herald his arrival. A dog started barking from inside the house, and its boxy brown face appeared behind the barred window. Jeb opened the gate and we stepped through the yard, past a toppled tricycle and a knotted jump rope and several dry piles of dog shit.

A fat woman with sweat-stained pits answered the door and stretched her arms to embrace him. Jeb lifted her without effort and the dog spun excited circles, its claws digging at the carpet. The dog's excitement ceased when it caught a whiff of me and it barked until the woman pulled it into the kitchen, locking it behind a child's gate.

I don't know why dogs distrust me, but I've noticed a pattern. Maybe they can tell I'm nervous about them and they don't understand why I'm nervous, so they bark which ruins any calm I had not only with them but with the next dog I meet.

The old woman herded us over to a floral velvet loveseat where Jeb and I sat so close our thighs were touching. I felt out-of-place in that moldy house with their family portraits hanging all over the walls, some depicting Jeb as a skinny twerp, maybe fourteen, and I could tell nothing had changed in the decor, nothing, for decades.

Jeb introduced me to her after she inched down into a loveseat. He told her we met at Stanford.

She nodded but didn't acknowledge me directly. Instead, she picked up a piece of lint from her polyester pants and, as she dropped it to the floor, she asked Jeb, 'How's Deborah doing? She sure is a pretty thing.'

'Deb moved to Chicago, remember?' Jeb said, and I could tell by his tone that he was uncomfortable, which entertained me some. Jeb seemed like a mountain to me and yet here was this old lady politely turning the screws on him.

Nana rocked in her chair, studying the television. 'Where that Oprah lives,' she said.

'Yeah, but she doesn't know Oprah, Nana...' Jeb looked around the room. 'So where's Nester?'

'Walked over to the pharmacy to get my medicine. I suspect he's getting Eli's too, if they aren't two hundred dollars this time.' She perked up now. 'He's getting out of the hospital Monday. At least that's what the doctor told us.'

'That's good, Nana,' Jeb said.

'What time are you taking us by the hospital?' she asked.

'Soon. Whenever Nester gets back.' Then he turned to me and said Nester didn't have his license, something about a DUI, and we were going to drive everybody over to see Eli.

The dog started barking from the other room again, louder

this time, so that it echoed off the walls, competing with the rerun of Bonanza playing in black-and-white on the television.

In my periphery, a giant man appeared in the kitchen doorway, as did the dog, and they looked like two giant monsters. The dude, Nester, opened the child's gate and the dog came straight back for me. He jammed his wet nose right into my crotch as if to say *I know what you are.* Nester snatched the dog by its scruff and he tossed the invasive animal toward the corner of the room where it cowered, glaring at me from the tops of its black eyeballs. Nester yelled in German at the dog and it finally sulked off into the kitchen. Then he turned to us with something expectant in his eyes – an explanation, probably, for why I was standing in his living room.

Jeb introduced us, and Nester gave me a nod but seemed to notice me as little as Nana had. He asked to speak to Jeb in the kitchen, and I sat back down on the sofa as a *Hair Club for Men* commercial began.

Nana picked up a magnifying glass from the table next to her recliner, and she looked at me through the lens, her cataract eye now cartoonishly large, and she said, 'So what did you study at Stanford?'

Shockingly, out came the truth. 'Nursing,' I said.

She clicked her dentures a few times and said, 'You didn't want to be a doctor?'

'Too much school.'

Jeb peeked out from the kitchen door and waved me over. I followed through the kitchen and out the back door. 'I told Nester you were helping Eli, so he's cool with helping you,' he said as we crossed the back lawn to a small shed. The dog trailed along, and we went inside, where there was a weight bench and an assortment of free weights and dumbbells. A giant poster of Arnold Schwarzenegger hung on the wall next to a swimsuit calendar, creating an equation in my brain. Get muscles equals get primo pussy.

Nester went straight to business. He held up an opaque-brown vial, which I imagined as basically man-in-a-bottle, and

I wondered if this was all too fast, if I should think it over, weigh the consequences, take some time to look down each path – to juice or not to juice – and consider where I'd be in three months, a year, ten years, but I was impatient. I wanted to change how I looked, and I knew there was no alternative. Its permanency was not something I would regret. I was positive.

Nester explained how to use it. 'You'll have to keep it some place cool,' he said, 'but not the fridge.' He lifted a syringe and put his chewed-up fingernail to the 50 milliliter line. 'Fill it up to here,' he said, and he pulled the plunger back to the line. He stabbed the needle through the rubber top of the vial and filled the chamber with an amber liquid. Then he tapped the side of it – *releasing the air bubbles* – and he told me to pull my pants down.

'Right here?' I looked down at the dog who was panting from the heat. 'I haven't even paid yet.'

'The first one's on me,' Nester said, and I looked from him to Jeb.

'Is the needle clean?' I looked around, searching for a plastic wrapper and Nester pulled one from his pocket.

'Now. Drop 'em before Nana comes to see why we ain't left yet,' he said.

I lifted my shirt and unbuckled my belt. 'I'll do the injection,' I said, and he handed me the syringe.

I've always hated needles despite having used them on hundreds of other people. There was something crass and vaguely rapey about being penetrated, having skin split while something cold and foreign invaded. I pushed the plunger in and a fire branched up my spine and down my leg. The dog stopped his panting and looked over at me with an inquisitive tilt of the head, and I wondered if I suddenly smelled different. Nester gave me the whole vial, told me to shoot up once a week, said there were six or seven doses at least.

I buckled up my pants and Jeb grabbed hold of my arm as the room tilted and I wobbled. He guided me over to the weight bench and I sat there, riding out a wave of nausea. He and Nester got a good chuckle, remembering their first dose. 'Like getting the wind knocked out of you,' Jeb said. They had no sympathy. Jeb told me to man up, we needed to go, and we went back to the house and followed Nana's slow ass to Jeb's car.

Jeb reminded Nana that I was there to help Eli, and she gave me this long intense stare, like maybe she'd heard that line before and wasn't buying it. I rode in the backseat, crammed next to Nester, who looked a little like a bull stuffed into a clown car. Nana sat up front, complaining about what hacks the doctors at Highland General were, and Jeb nodded, but I could tell he was barely listening.

When we reached the hospital, I offered to wait outside to give them some privacy, but Jeb insisted I come in. 'How are you gonna know if you can treat him if you don't see him?' he said, and both Nana and Nester looked back into the car at me like, 'Yeah, how?' and I realized that, to some degree, they were all depending on me to do something. To save Eli. I felt the acid slosh around my stomach and up my throat, and I swallowed it down as I squeezed out of the back seat.

I was still feeling the nervous effects of the dose as we walked across the tilted parking lot and in through the sliding glass doors, but inside it smelled just like every medical facility I'd ever worked in – plastic everything wiped over with ammonia – and the overwhelming familiarity of the odor numbed my unease. Jeb grabbed Nana's hand, and we walked through the crowded ER waiting room and down to a row of elevators. Eli's room was up a floor and down a long hallway. A doctor was leaving the room as we approached, and he put a chart in a plastic bin outside the door. He smiled at Nana and Nester like he recognized them and said, 'He's resting, but you can say a quick hello.'

I stood outside by the door and watched them all enter soft and quiet like it was Mass. The man in the bed looked about eighty pounds, and his skin hung from his bones like a curtain. His nose was a sharp triangle jutting up between the valleys of his eye sockets. As I studied him the shaky feeling returned, and I wondered if I was really feeling the drug or if it was a placebo effect.

The man in the bed coughed and spit in a kidney-shaped plastic tray that Nester handed to him. I could see what they were choosing to ignore. For years, I held on to optimism, but once you've worked in a place where death is as common as breakfast, there comes a time when you have to let your optimism die and see things for real. There was no helping Eli. He was going to die. And soon, probably.

I pulled his chart from the bin on the door and I entered the room, flipping through the pages so I could avoid eye contact with Eli. Jeb spoke in a hushed voice, like he was speaking to an injured bird, and he introduced me as the 'man with the study.' I looked up from the chart and forced a smile, and I could see Eli weighing my sincerity. He put his hand out, and said, 'You think you can fix me, doc?'

I stuttered, 'I'm gonna try,' at the same time that Nana corrected, 'He ain't a doctor.'

I shook Eli's limp, boney hand and saw, all around his lips, the same purple sores that Magdalene had on her arm and I realized, fully, what I'd been trying to ignore. Soon it would be *her* in that bed. I could have crushed his bird-bone fingers. I could have crushed him in so many ways, most of all in spirit.

He asked what kind of drug it was, and I couldn't think of a better answer than the truth.

'It's confidential. I mean, it's a trial study. There are placebos—'

'Placebos?' Nester said.

'But *you* won't be getting the placebo.' It was hard to sound reassuring; there was so much desperation in that room. 'I just need to look through your prescriptions, you know, to see if there are any interactions. To make sure it's safe for you.' I opened the chart and thumbed through it like I was familiar with a hospital chart, but it was like looking through a foreign textbook.

I was just playing doctor here anyway. Eli was already dead, but I couldn't think of a reason why I should tell him this, so I feigned hopeful. I ripped a page free from the back of his chart and asked him to list his drugs.

'AZT,' he said, 'pentamidine, and whatever's in this happy sack.' He tugged at his IV cord. 'Morphine, probably.'

'Uh, nurse, could you make that a double?' Jeb said, and we all laughed but it wasn't funny really. It was the kind of gallows humor any medical professional would recognize. Some people trembled like children when looking at death. Others got angry, belligerent, believing on impulse that their sour mood might scare the end away. Others, like Jeb, became comedians. I was none of these. Staring at death, I always felt like I was looking at a problem I could solve if only given more time, which of course, was the fucking problem to begin with. If they didn't know it was days until he'd be gone, they had a sense of it, a feeling. I looked at his sores again and I knew I was looking down a scope toward Magdalene's future and it tore me up.

Immediately, I thought of Eddie, and how maybe I could've changed everything if I had been more aware, more attuned to the facts, but I'd been so distracted. Busy with my own shit. There was no helping Eli. I could see clearly he was out the plane without a parachute and he knew it, and on some level Jeb knew it. I kept my face smiling, laughing at Jeb's jokes, but inside I wanted to run, I needed to get back, I needed to start work on solving Magdalene's problem, even if it meant putting myself and the study at risk.

14

I got to the clinic early Monday morning and started digging through the charts. I thought if I could find something in common, a shared symptom among some of the patients – say, half – I could figure out if Magdalene was getting the real pills or not. I wasn't entirely sure what I'd do with the information once I had it, but not knowing was worse, I thought, than knowing.

I had imagined it would only take a few minutes, an hour at the most, but that was before I had all the sheets spread out in front of me. The information did not sort into easy piles; there certainly was no way to divide them into just two. Individually, the patients' vitals changed day-to-day, so consistency was ruled out as a possible control, and while there was a group of patients who all had diarrhea, not *all* of them had a fever or nausea or trouble sleeping, and not all the patients who had a fever or nausea or trouble sleeping had diarrhea. There were patients with headaches, and some with dry mouth, or open sores, but there seemed to be no glaring side-effect, no pattern I could pull out of the mess of data, and when I glanced over at the clock, it was nearly time for Franklin to show up.

Panicked, I decided to spread out all the Polaroids on the floor. I started lining out each patient's pictures into a row of themselves, five photos per patient, one for each day they'd come in. I lined them up in sequence of the days, starting at the beginning of the study, and by their scheduled appointment time. I laid out Franklin's first, and below his, all of Larry's, and below that Mitchell's, and so on, until a montage of my first seven patients were all lined up on the floor. That's when I saw it – oh sweet, merciful pattern – in the white square, the flash that bounced off the slick foreheads of every other patient from day three through day five. It seemed like a fluke at first, a trick of the light, but the closer I inspected, the more I realized each patient with a white square on their forehead was sweaty as hell.

I looked closer at Franklin's third through fifth photos (he, of course, had a shiny square on his forehead) and in each one, his upper lip was mustached with sweat. But Larry, the second patient, who had no square on his forehead, looked fine and dry those days. Mitchell, the third patient, was so sweaty his forehead was like a mirror to the flash, and his hair curled wet around his temples.

And so the pattern continued. Based on the time of their appointment, the patients were: sweaty, not sweaty, sweaty, not sweaty. Dinka clearly had no creativity and had patterned the study so that every other patient, based on their scheduled appointment, was getting the placebo.

I kept laying out the photos of the remaining patients, still ordering them by appointment time, until I finally got to Magdalene, and because Dusty, the patient before her, was gleaming with sweat I knew what I would find: a dry glow-worm against the white wall.

The filing cabinet shuddered from a change in air pressure, meaning Franklin had just come through the front door. I stood up and poked my head out into the lobby. He started walking toward me, but I put my hand up and told him I was running behind and would be out in just a few minutes. He checked his watch and I shut the door.

Quickly, I fumbled through the mess of forms, trying to shuffle them back in with their corresponding charts, because Dinka was liable to drop in at any minute of any day, and I'd be screwed if he saw what I was up to. Still, I wanted to double-check the pattern to see if the forms supported what I'd seen in the pictures, and, sure enough, for every sick and slimy face, a variety of the same three symptoms appeared on their form: nausea, headache, or diarrhea. The only thing that made sense, to have such a consistent pattern in that first week, was that the symptoms were a direct side-effect of the drug.

Magdalene was right. She was getting the placebo. She was

going to die.

Franklin coughed loudly, and he shouted through the wall. 'I got to be at work by nine-thirty.'

I decided it might be better to sort the charts at the end of the day, because it would raise all kinds of red flags if Dinka saw I was behind, so I threw the unsorted forms and the pile of Polaroids into the filing cabinet and put the empty folders on top to keep my tampering concealed.

I opened the fridge and, instead of getting out Franklin's pills, I pulled the cup from Magdalene's slot and went out to greet him.

I thought he'd be angry that I was behind but he was all smiles and jokes for his appointment, making me feel pretty terrible about handing over the chalky-brown sugar turds and watching him swallow them all. It conjured up memories of Eli in his hospital bed, emaciated and completely vulnerable. I imagined Franklin this way. I felt like a piece-of-shit no-good asshole until, on his way out, Franklin stopped in the doorway and turned around and it looked, it really looked, like he was concentrating hard to say something. I opened my mouth to ask him what was wrong, worried that on some small level he already knew what I'd done, when the sulfur smell of fart filled the room, and Franklin slapped his thigh and bellowed. He said, 'If you hadn't been running late, I would've been halfway down the block when that one slipped.'

I watched Franklin leave, trying hard to deny or ignore the fact that ultimately, if one were to boil it down, I *was* planning to kill him. Not with my hands or a gun or something direct, but I was responsible; I was taking his life, not that he'd earned the real medicine, but luck had favored him and I was saying no. I was also, I reasoned, saving a life and, ignoring my selfish reasons for doing so, I buried my guilt in arithmetic. A life for a life. A wash. My hands were clean if I really thought about it.

And any guilt that lingered faded into the ether as I took Magdalene's vitals and watched the mercury rise past one hundred degrees. I prayed, what little use it was praying to no one, that I was doing the right thing as I handed over the pills, identical in size and color to her original dose, and after she swallowed the first one, a feeling of peace settled over me, which I did not mistake as a message from the divine. I knew what it really was: a massive dump of dopamine, a pat-on-the-back from my brain, telling me I'd finally gained some measure of control. Maybe I couldn't keep death from getting Eddie so soon, but I thought maybe, just once, I could save someone I cared about.

After the second pill, Magdalene scrunched up her nose and asked for another glass of water. 'It's putting a funny taste in my mouth,' she said. 'Like metal or...' She looked off, searching some memory. '...or copper. Is there something wrong with them?'

Caught off guard I was a shitty liar, and I could hear my words come out all awkward. 'Well, they're definitely the same. I mean, maybe it's interacting with the residue of your toothpaste, or your fever is heightening your senses, making you taste the fillings in your teeth. Have you ever had a cavity?' I refilled her water and put it in front of her. She fished her finger around the paper cup, swirling the four remaining pills, and she lifted one up to her mouth. 'No,' she said. I watched the pill disappear between her two perfect lips, before she swallowed the entire glass of water and held it out for more.

'Perfect. Hydrate,' I told her.

She finished the last three pills together and let out a tiny burp. She looked embarrassed, so I swallowed some air and burped back at her.

She frowned like she wasn't embarrassed by her burp and that I didn't need to make her feel better, but all she said was, 'Do you have a girlfriend?'

'I live with a girl,' I said, 'but she's definitely not my girlfriend.'

'You're one of *those* guys.'

'She's my roommate.'

'Did she see the picture?'

The hairs on my forearms stood at full attention. I couldn't tell if she was prying because she really wanted to get to know me, or if she was just like Gwen, a dirt addict. 'Picture?' I said.

'Of our kissing.' Her lips perked. Her eyes were calm and chaos all at once, frenetic, meditative energy, like white noise embodied.

Every single blood cell rushed to the surface of my skin. I shook my head. She laughed and said I was fun to tease, that I had easy buttons she could push, some of which made me look like a ripe tomato.

'What are you doing later?' she asked.

I thought about the rest of my day. Returning to the apartment with a bag of fast food, and Gwen coming down the hall from Flora's to talk about her day, but that conversation would last about five minutes, and since I couldn't go ten seconds without thinking about sex since I started the steroids, once we finished our food, I might try to take off her clothes and she'd probably grab a hold of my wrist and ask if I had washed my hands and I'd lie and say I had and she'd insist I wash them again, and after I did, I'd hold my hands up like I was a surgeon trying to keep sterile, and I'd make some joke to that effect and she'd probably get pissed or cry or roll her eyes and say she wasn't really in the mood anymore, and we'd fight and she'd leave to go watch *Entertainment Tonight* with Flora again, and I'd be stuck with two sparkling clean and totally depressing hands to jerk myself off with.

I said, 'Something with you, I hope.'

She had a favorite place up in North Beach, a bookstore, City Lights, which was totally out of the way, but was cozy and had better choices, and she wondered if maybe I would want to come with her.

I didn't want to confess that I hardly ever read or that the last book I *did* read was assigned to me in eleventh grade, and I couldn't even remember the name, because it didn't matter. We could be going to Mars for all I cared. Any free moment she gave me, I wanted. I felt my attraction to her launching out from some lonely place inside of me, and I couldn't explain it, other than to say it felt beyond me. Conflicting as it was, I knew there would be no immediate foreseeable reason for her to see my naked body and, by extension, I would not have to explain it to her, making the idea of getting to know her infinitely easier to maneuver. It seemed ideal. 'That sounds like the best thing I could possibly be doing,' I said.

She touched my arm and it radiated through me. I told her to wait in the lobby while I threw the charts in the cabinet, and wiped down my instruments, and locked up the office.

As we walked to the bus stop, I considered some topics we could cover on the trip in order to avoid a forty-minute silence, or worse, questions about my past, but it was obvious as the doors to the M-line parted and a ribbon of armpit stench spooled out that it was standing room only. It's pretty difficult to have a conversation beneath the tricep of a stranger and your crotch in some child's face, so we stayed quiet, and I enjoyed the excuse for her hips to bump into mine every time we stopped to pick up more people. She smiled each time it happened, and I imagined the pills all piled in her stomach, breaking down and spreading out through her body, mending her white blood cells and making her stronger. I tried to picture my world forking off in two directions – one with Gwen, and the other with Magdalene – but the image would only go so far before the thought turned blank. It felt impossible for there to be *any* future. I felt, for once, completely engulfed by the present.

The bookstore was stuffed with hippies, stick-straight suits, women with babies, and college kids working the counter. It had a pleasant smell, like sweet dusty skin. While we were browsing through the fiction section, Magdalene asked me what I liked to read. I told her *Playboy*, which wasn't a complete lie. She gave me a look of pity.

'What do you read?' I asked, and she shrugged.

'Depends on my mood, usually. Baldwin... Plath...

Marquez.'

I had no fucking clue who any of them were, but I smiled and nodded like I got it and agreed, and I tried to think of an equally impressive response. I started looking for one of Bill's books and found a whole shelf of them. I pulled out *Naked Lunch*, one of the few I'd ever really heard of. 'No shit,' I said, pointing to his name on the cover. 'This is my mom's neighbor.'

'Sure, right.'

'Seriously. I grew up right next to him.'

Magdalene folded her arms.

I walked over to the store clerk and asked him where Burroughs lived.

'Gosh. You know what? Let me just pull out my address book here,' the kid said.

'Lawrence, Kansas,' I said, turning back to Magdalene. 'I'm not lying.'

'No. Totally. Sure,' she said. 'The icon-next-door story. Why would I question that?'

'Well, I don't know about him being an icon or whatever. He's just old Bill.'

'So old people can't be icons?' she teased.

'He's not an icon. He's just my neighbor. You don't think he has neighbors?'

She grabbed the book, flipped through the pages. 'Have you even read his books?'

'I tried. Once.'

Her grin was incredulous. 'You're a big fat liar, Sam Gavin.'

'Let's make a bet.'

'Do I get to set the stakes?'

'Whatever you want,' I said, certain of my victory.

'You get this signed…' She bit her lip, looked out the tops of her eyes. 'Or you tell me your deepest darkest secret.'

I wondered if she was testing me, if she could already see my secrets and was using this as a sonar, sending out a signal to see what bounced back.

'And when I get it signed, what do I get?'

She put the book back in my hand. 'When, huh? Okay, okay. What do you want?'

I tried to ignore every single sexual thought I had, but I couldn't. It was reflexive.

'Same thing,' I said. 'Deepest darkest whatever.' I didn't care about the details. I only wanted to impress her.

'I'll call my friend Marcus. He'll get it signed.' I bought the book and we went out to a payphone. I put the coins in and dialed, but he didn't answer.

'Looks like I'm winning our bet,' she said.

'We never agreed on a deadline,' I said. But we both knew there absolutely was one.

The next day, once Magdalene's appointment was done, I took her to the office and tried calling Marcus from there (free long distance and all). It was a stupid idea, letting Magdalene back in the office, considering Dinka would be coming to replenish the pills, but it was early and that provided some cushion, so we sauntered easy down the hall and she followed me in. As I picked up the phone and dialed, Magdalene wandered around the room, inspecting. She separated the slats of the window shades and peered outside. She jostled the file cabinet and opened a drawer.

The phone rang in my ear, and I reached over and took a chart from Magdalene's hand. She stuck her tongue out at me as Marcus answered.

'Hey, it's Sam,' I said, and I turned away from Magdalene, feeling a strong and irrational fear that if she heard me speak to someone back home, my past would become glaringly apparent.

'What the fuck, Gavin?' Marcus barked. No hey, no hello. 'You just leave the Dump out on the road like a piece of trash?' I felt gut-punched. I tried to say something, but it came out as air. I thought he'd be pissed I'd come here with Gwen, but leaving the Dump? He knew it was a piece of shit. But it was also more than that and I knew it.

'It *was* called the fucking Dump, Marcus,' I finally said, and

Magdalene looked up from the open fridge.

'They sold it already. It's gone. Probably in some junkyard somewhere.'

'Look, dude. I'm sor—'

'Fuck your sorry.'

I heard a throat clear behind me, and I turned around to see Dinka standing in the doorway, staring straight at Magdalene. She looked over at him and then rushed to shut the refrigerator door.

'You.' Dinka pointed at her. 'Out.' Then he looked at me. I hung up the phone.

A lie quickly bounced off my tongue. 'I was just trying to call her a cab—'

'What was she doing in here, looking in the fridge?' He was livid. I watched his shoulders heave.

'I don't know. I turned around for a second.'

'I'm sorry,' she said from the hallway. Her voice was smaller, more fragile than I'd ever heard it. 'I was thirsty. I didn't even think to ask him. I just looked inside.'

Something about that was bothersome, not just the way she was speaking for me like I couldn't fend for myself, but that she had such a talent to lie quickly, so utterly, and still sound authentic. Was she only flirting with me to find out more about the study? It seemed a valid suspicion. All that talk about sugar pills.

'It's not your fault dear; it's not your responsibility to maintain the rules.' Then he looked at me and pulled the door shut. 'Whose responsibility is it, do you think?' He was carrying the cooler, and he walked over and set it on the desk next to the telephone. 'I want you to dial the number again.' He pushed the phone toward me. 'Call the cab company again.'

I looked at the rotary holes and I tried to remember the number painted on the sides of the cabs zipping down Market. When I couldn't, I said, 'Magdalene gave me the number,' and I gestured to the closed door.

Dinka grunted, went back to the door. Magdalene stood on

the other side, rigid as a scarecrow.

'Could you come in just a moment, dear?'

'I thought it wasn't allowed.'

'It's all right if I'm here.' He was talking to her as if she were a kindergartener.

He was out to humiliate me. His tone was creepy-father, but his goal was to establish that his was the only swinging dick in the room. I did not enjoy being a prop in someone's power display, but what could I do?

I was sure I was going to lose my job or Magdalene would get kicked out of the study or, worse, both would happen.

Dinka gestured to me. 'Give him the number.'

I wasn't certain she'd been listening through the door. His demand for a number could mean anything, and she might blurt out something like thirty-two or three billion, instead of a phone number, so I lifted the receiver to give her a clue.

She said a string of numbers and I dialed them out. As the connection started to ring, Dinka put his hand out. 'Give me the phone,' he said. I did, and he pressed it to his ear.

I heard a voice come through the other end, and Magdalene and I met eyes. She gave me a soft wink, and I looked back at Dinka.

'Yes. We're, um, I'm calling for a cab.' He covered the phone with his hand and asked Magdalene where she needed to go. She gave him the address, and Dinka repeated it. He hung up and told Magdalene she should wait down in the main lobby, that they would be there shortly.

She left without looking at me, and before Dinka said anything he waited for the door to shudder in the frame, signaling that Magdalene had indeed gone. I wondered if she was worried about me. I wondered if she was worried about herself. All this time spent getting cozy with her pill person just to see him fired. Would she still go to bookstores with me? Was the bet still on?

Without speaking, Dinka snatched the cooler, flipped the lid open, and pulled out two big bottles – one red and one blue

– and an empty vial holder for the next blood draw. He set everything on the desk and went to the fridge. Inside, he took the vials of blood from the bottom shelf, and came back over, slowly lowering them into the cooler. He put the new empty container on the bottom shelf of the fridge and slammed the door shut.

He finally looked at me. 'I should fire you,' he said, and I could tell he meant it, wanted to, even. Still, there was something about his tone that reminded me of my father in his final year, lying there with his stump propped on the recliner, his belly spilled on all sides of him – *I should've flushed you when you were still small enough*. But I was too big to flush; Dinka *needed* me.

He was funding this himself – he'd already admitted that much – and he couldn't just leave his practice to dispense pills all day. He was hardly paying me anything at all, and I knew he'd have a hard time finding a replacement by Monday who was willing to draw blood for such pathetic pay. I knew he knew that. He knew it, too. All I had to do was keep my mouth shut, look unhappy with myself, and not make this into a choice between his money and his pride.

Maybe if I apologized, really sold it, we'd move on, so I did. I told him I was sorry. I said it had never happened before, and that it wouldn't again, and we stared at each other. Finally, he snapped free of his paralysis and told me to get out, he couldn't sort the pills in front of me. 'Or did you forget that too?' he said. So I rushed to put the charts away, a good little reprimanded employee, contrite and obedient, but the power had clearly shifted. I think he was hoping I hadn't noticed, but I had. Dinka needed me. The study needed me. I hung my head, but I felt untouchable.

I looked for Magdalene in the main lobby downstairs, but she was already gone. The sound of a blow dryer rumbled like a jet turbine from the salon down the hall, and through the window I saw a woman pause at a bus stop bench to replace her high heels with some sandals from her purse, and beyond her, a yellow cab was parked at the curb, and the driver's eyes came to life when we made contact. I stepped outside. The wind blew cold and constant from the west. I looked up and down the road for a flurry of long brown hair, but she was gone. I owed her a cab fare. I at least owed her that.

It was the third straight day of clouds and my mood curdled. I felt blurred in atmosphere, heavy as I ran over to the bus stop just as the woman crammed her heels in her purse and scurried away. I lit up a cigarette, and seeing me sit, waiting presumably for a bus, the cab drove off. I was convinced that if Magdalene had only stayed and said goodbye, I would've felt better, but I knew that wasn't all the reason I was annoyed. Marcus was mad. I knew I should do like I did with Dinka: just apologize. But for what? Eddie's parents gave me the car. If Marcus wanted it, he should've gotten his shit together and paid the insurance. Fuck Marcus, I decided. I understood that, to him, the car represented Eddie, and for a long time it had for me too, but was I supposed to be the perpetual pallbearer, lugging Eddie's one-ton, four-cylinder corpse around with me for the rest of my life? Marcus held on to grudges the way my mom held on to pounds: always complaining, never doing a damn thing different.

'Fuck him,' I said, out loud, as if making it real. Fuck him, because as long as my position was to be mad at him, it was impossible to feel like a betrayer.

'Yeah, fuck him,' a voice behind me said. I turned and saw Magdalene standing there. I wasn't sure where she came from or how she snuck up on me. 'Are you fired?' she asked.

'Got promoted, actually.'

'How's that work?'

'I'm just that special, I guess.'

'Well, c'mon, special Sam. I want to show you something fun.'

We rode the F-line up Market to 6th, got off, and started walking toward an adult video store. My stomach did a little flip, but my mouth stayed shut, and to my disappointment, we walked right past the store and into a place with a goofy sign above the doorway: PLAY FASCINATION. Inside was dimly lit and smelled like cigarettes and beer, and I could hear voices, mostly men's, hollering and the thunderous sound of rubber rolling against wood. As my eyes adjusted to the room, I saw a collection of tables, each the size of a pinball machine but with the look of a miniature bowling alley. There were thirty or forty of them, all lined up in rows, with a person at nearly all of them, occupying the stool at one end and playing what appeared to be a more complicated version of skeeball. I followed Magdalene over to two empty lanes, and she taught me how to play – the objective was to roll the ball down into any one of the twenty-four holes at the other end and light up a grid of lights above into rows, just like with bingo – but after a few games, I realized it didn't matter what kind of game we played; what made it fun was the gambling. Winning money for a skill I had barely learned was intoxicating. 'How'd you find this place?' I asked her.

'My foster mom, Debbie, used to bring me here.'

I started to roll the ball, but I stopped and looked at her. She kept playing and told me I'd better hurry or else I was going to lose.

'You lived in a foster home?'

'I lived in nine. Debbie was my second to last.'

A buzzer went off above Magdalene's lane – she'd won – and the dealer slid a payout toward her. We put our money down for the next game.

'Nine?' I said. 'How is that even possible?'

She held back a smile. 'I was a trouble-maker. The cute puppy everyone picks but always returns.'

'So, no family at all?'

'Nope,' she said and started chucking her balls down the chute again. I played along, but not with the same tenacity. My focus had shifted. These new details gave shape to a part of her I hadn't realized was missing, making me want to hear more, to know more.

'What happened to your parents?'

'My mom died when I was five.'

'And your dad?'

I saw her hesitate, like maybe she didn't want to share everything yet, but she answered, 'A few months after my mom died, he said he was going to get some ice cream and never came back. I finally told my teacher after a week.'

'You still went to school?'

She nodded. 'They had food.'

'I'm sorry.'

'He was an ass.'

But I meant for all of it. Life wasn't fair and I wanted her to know that I knew it. 'I'm just sorry,' I said again.

'Stop saying that.'

'But don't you have a grandma or an aunt or something? You really have no one?'

She shook her head. 'I have myself.'

Her independence struck me as a shield, but one made of gold, one that required only the smallest of fires to melt down and reshape, and I wanted to be that fire. I wanted to be her light.

'What about you?' she asked.

'What about me?'

'What kind of family do you have?'

I shrugged. 'Typical. Mom, dad, sister.'

'And they all live in Kansas?'

'Yeah, except my dad. He's still there. Just not living.'

She smiled, avoiding the typical I'm-so-sorry look, which I appreciated, and immediately I felt ashamed of my previous apology. But I didn't want to keep talking about me, so I asked her, 'How can you be so much trouble that nine families would all take you back?'

She won another game and put more money on the table but I stopped playing to listen.

'They didn't take me back,' she said as she stuffed some bills in her pocket. 'I ran away.'

'Every time?'

'They all had this hopeful look on their face when they first picked me up. But then I'd mess up or say something wrong, and I could see it fade, their attachment to me, and soon it was all rote with them, a way to get a check from the government, and I didn't want that. So I left.'

'Where to?'

She bit her lip. 'Wouldn't you like to know?'

Her evasion was enough to know that maybe it wasn't P.G. which, I guess, was her intent.

'Especially now,' I said.

'Win my deepest darkest secret and maybe I'll tell you.'

'Wow. It's *that* serious. It was a guy, wasn't it?'

She kept a poker face. 'Well, I was six when I first started running away, so that would be weird.'

'Oh,' I said, feeling stupid.

She laughed. 'But I didn't run to the same place all the time.'

I couldn't decide whether I should pry further. Did she want me to? It was hard to know; some girls left out a nugget on purpose – a test to see how hard you'd work – and others left it out by accident, failing to sweep up the entire trail. In a way, I figured she was doing both, that maybe she wanted to share her story with me, but that she worried if she gave it away too easily I might get bored, just like her foster families, and so I tried to hone in on what she really wanted: unabated attention.

'Oh, I'm gonna win that bet,' I said. 'And you're going to tell me your deepest darkest secret, and I'm gonna love it the whole time.'

'Sure, Sam. Sure,' she said, focusing on the game again.

She had a beautiful profile.

'Can I buy you dinner?' I said.

Magdalene grinned. 'Can you cook?'

'Maybe.' A total lie. I could make toast and macaroni with powdered cheese, but real food? I was completely useless. 'I make perfect Chinese noodles. Don't let the to-go boxes fool you.'

She started gathering her money. 'I like Chinese.'

'I can make rice, too.'

'So you know how to boil water.'

'Not only boil, but put things in.'

'Impressive.'

'You're not the first one to notice.'

She stood like she was ready to leave, and I gathered my money and stood too.

'How about Friday?' she said.

Immediately, I prepared to cancel any prior plans.

'My place,' she said and called it a date.

I walked home, strutting as if to my own soundtrack of self-satisfaction, erupting like a dork with dopey sunshine. The city was bird songs and sweet smells. I thought this must be how happy people feel all the time.

15

Dinka was already in the office Friday morning when I arrived, and I was certain his intuition had led him to come and beat the truth out of me.

He asked me to sit down.

'I didn't want to tell you over the phone.'

Gulp.

'I thought I should come down and tell you face to face. Though there's no reason you, or anyone, should really be surprised by this…'

Out with it, you old fuck. I'm guilty. I'm under arrest.

Dinka sucked on his front teeth and said, 'Patient 23 died last night.'

'Dusty?'

Dinka nodded.

It took a moment to process. I suddenly remembered every interaction I'd had with Dusty, every unscripted exchange, like a video montage: his crooked teeth, the way he drummed his fingers, how he stuck out his tongue after swallowing his pills, things I didn't even notice I'd noticed.

'Oh?' I said. If my assumptions were correct, Dusty was on the medication and not the placebo, and if he was on the medication, what had killed him? Selfishly, I hoped he got in an accident or offed himself like Eddie, anything other than the virus, because that would mean the meds weren't working, or worse, that they had killed him.

Dinka removed his glasses and pinched the bridge of his nose. 'We need to keep this quiet. If the other patients know, we'll lose more, believe me. And we can't afford to start losing our variables. One or two, maybe. But more than that and none of this will be worth a damn.'

We both heard Franklin come in, and Dinka rose up from

the chair. I poked my head out of the door and told Franklin I'd be right there. Dinka was already gathering himself to leave, but he waited for me to get Franklin's pills and chart ready, watching me closely in a way I couldn't help but take personally. I had no choice but to get Franklin's real pills from the fridge.

Dinka walked out with me and hurried by Franklin, not looking at him, not saying a word.

'He's a stiff one, ain't he?' Franklin said.

I took Franklin's vitals. He said he felt great, better than ever. 'Took my kid out skating even.'

I didn't know Franklin had a kid, but I refused to register that information as something good or bad. After all, I had been taking his medicine and giving it to a girl I liked for reasons that were, if I let myself think about them, nothing but selfish. Then I worried that I'd actually taken Magdalene off the real medication and put her on the placebo.

As the day went on, I tried to study each patient in a new way. Was their fever worse last week or today? What sort of rashes or nightmares or sore throats were they experiencing? Had they had their T cells checked and what were their levels? But nothing useful came from their comments. Linda had a dream her legs were paperclips, and Virgil said they weren't allowed to have their T cells checked for the duration of the study, and Peter said he thought he had a rash, but it was just herpes. I used the twenty minutes of Dusty's conspicuous absence to look through his chart. I thought maybe there'd be a clue, some sort of flashing neon arrow pointing to why he died, but he'd seemed fine the day before, chipper even – I remembered him saying something about a boat trip, and then I wondered if maybe he had drowned. I thought about him, somewhere out there, in a morgue or a mortuary, or already in an urn. Could they even embalm the body of an AIDS patient? I didn't know, but I felt sorry for him, for his mom.

By Magdalene's appointment, I could find no data to swing me one way or the other, though I had to make a decision:

change course or continue on. I debated for a while, standing in the chill of the open refrigerator, if I should give her Dusty's dose, considering I'd already given Franklin (and all the other patients) their assigned pills. I stood there for so long, the whole front of me started to feel numb, and finally, I pulled Dusty's pills from the shelf and brought them to the exam room.

Immediately, I could tell that something was wrong. A layer of slime covered her forehead, the scent of vomit rolled from her mouth.

'Are you okay?' I asked her.

'I've got diarrhea,' she mumbled.

I felt like dancing around the room, and I told her she should be happy it wasn't gas, a little clue I thought she'd get, but she laid her head on the table between us, and I could hear her intestines bubble.

'This is worse,' she said.

I pushed her pills toward her hand. 'This isn't worse,' I said. 'Trust me.'

She tilted her head up and we locked eyes, but she kept her cheek against her forearms and her forearms against the table. We stayed that way for a while, just looking at each other, and I wondered if she understood, and finally she pushed herself up, opened her mouth and slid her tongue out like a lizard. I stared at those fleshy buds for a moment, until she closed her eyes and I knew what she was asking for. I placed a pill gently on her tongue, and she swallowed it down with some water.

'Maybe we should take a rain check,' I said. 'And get together Monday?'

She pulled out another pill. 'You're probably right,' she said. 'Unless fun, for you, is taking care of sick people.'

'Of course. It's my job,' I said.

She pointed at me. 'No. See? That word exactly,' she said. 'Your *job*. I can take care of myself.' She swallowed the pill and reached for another. I felt relieved. She looked miserable, and yet I knew I wasn't ready to take care of her; trained as I was, there were conflicting emotions now. I had more than a crush,

I realized, and I was scared, honestly. Scared of caring too much and then losing her. Scared of getting close and having to own up. Scared, also, of the immediate, of knowing yet not really knowing if the pill switch was making her feel like she did, and I was responsible. There was worry from all angles. It was inescapable.

I offered to walk her home, which she accepted. After she finished her pills, she waited in the front area of the office while I filed the charts and gathered my things, just in case Dinka were to pop in again.

And good thing, too, I thought, because just as I was hanging up my stethoscope, I heard the front door to the office open. I came around the corner, expecting to see Dinka, but there stood Gwen and Flora, both wearing way too much makeup, their hair all done up like they were going to the prom. Gwen had on a short black dress pulled down low, highlighting an inch or two of quality cleavage. She looked like a high-end prostitute, and she smiled vindictively. 'Well, hello there, stranger.'

'What are you doing?'

She looked from me to Magdalene and back again. 'We were in the neighborhood and thought maybe you'd want to go to the party together. You're almost done, aren't you?'

Party? I had no idea what she was talking about.

Magdalene stood up, but in heels Gwen towered over her a good six inches. They looked like exact opposites. Magdalene's hair was big and long and wavy. She wore high-top tennis shoes and a pair of tight-rolled jeans and an orange Hypercolor T-shirt untucked. Without makeup, she looked about thirteen instead of twenty.

'I'm Magdalene,' she said, sounding like a first-grader, putting her hand out to Gwen. Gwen looked down at Magdalene's palm for a full second before she offered just her fingers in a half-assed handshake.

'You hardly look sick,' Gwen said in her most condescending tone. 'You're so pretty.'

Magdalene's ears turned red, but her wit was sharp. 'And you hardly look cheap. Great shoes.'

Gwen wiped her hand on the side of her thigh in a way that was supposed to appear absent, but I knew what she was communicating. She wanted to make Magdalene feel small. 'Thanks. I bought them at Macy's.'

'Then I'm sure they were way more affordable than they look.'

Gwen folded her arms. 'They cost plenty.'

'Very flattering ze long legs,' Flora said.

Something about the fluorescent lights in the room, and the bland eggshell color of the walls and the floor and the light coming in from the one window, and the three of them standing there together, I felt like I was being filmed before a studio audience. I was light-headed. Every sentence was ripe with possible pronouns and I knew I had to get her gone and fast. 'Look, Gwen, I'm working, so you really need to go.'

She shifted her weight, and Flora gave me a death glare. 'Are you going to ze porno-party or no?'

Before I could respond, Magdalene said, 'Oh, you two are actresses. That makes so much sense. All the makeup.'

'We're not participating,' Gwen said.

Flora tsked. 'Maybe not you.'

'You have to go.' I started to herd them toward the door. 'You can't just talk about my personal life—'

'You're almost done.' She checked her stupid sparkly wristwatch.

I didn't know why, but I laughed. I understood, suddenly, why Gwen cracked up when she was uncomfortable, but all empathy was lost in that moment. My brain was buzzing with possible ways she could fuck with my life, and I needed her to disappear. 'Write down the address. I'll meet you there. Okay?'

She could tell her plan to make me uncomfortable was working, and she reveled in it. 'Aww. You *like* her.' She pointed at me like she'd just had an epiphany. 'You do! What do you think, Magdalene?' Gwen turned her finger to Magdalene, who shrugged.

'He likes me as a friend, I hope.'

There it was. *He.* It hung in the air between us like a foul fart, and I felt the room bend in and out of focus, certain all I'd built would come crashing down around me in one big shameful pile of girl glares. Gwen gave me a scary maniacal grin, and I could tell she immediately knew what I'd been doing. Spiteful as she'd always been, I prayed she wouldn't rat me out, but I couldn't let this register in my expression because I knew if she knew how much I didn't want her to say something, she'd do just the opposite. 'Oh. I bet he's your friend, all right,' she said to Magdalene, but she was looking directly at me. I could tell there was more she wanted to say, but I stopped her.

'Gwen. Please. Just go,' I said, putting my hands on her body and she shook me off.

'Whatever. Sam.' She emphasized my name like it was a derogatory word, and then she looked at Flora and said, 'Let's go,' and they both whipped their hair and left.

'But the address,' Magdalene fake-shouted, seeming oblivious to any tension the pronoun had caused. 'You forgot to leave it.'

'Sorry about that,' I said. My knees felt like they were holding up a thousand pounds.

Magdalene grinned. 'Your roommate?'

I nodded.

'How do you know her?

I said it was complicated.

She reminded me, if I was walking her home, she'd be captive for six blocks. Her stomach rumbled again, and she steadied herself against the wall, but her face told me not to coddle.

'Okay, just give me a second,' I said, and I went to turn off all the lights. As I locked up the office, she walked down to the elevator and held the door open. When I stepped into the cold metal box with her and the door slid closed, I could tell she was still waiting for an answer, so I said, 'Gwen used to date my best friend, Eddie.'

'So, you grew up together?' There was obvious disappointment in her tone, like maybe she thought that history meant attachment, one that she could not possibly compete against.

'More like outgrew, really,' I said. 'I actually grew up with Eddie, and Gwen came in around ninth grade and immediately started twisting us up.'

We walked through the lobby, past the hair salon, and out into open air. 'Who'd she twist more?' she asked.

'Eddie,' I said without hesitation. There was no debating this. 'Eddie was always looking for a girl to define him. It was weird. Really weird. He'd date a girl and start turning into her. I know that sounds crazy, and I don't mean like dressing in dresses, but inside. Whatever music they liked, that was, like, his new favorite music, or whatever movies, or sports. Gwen was real big into church and God and Christ's forgiveness, so that's what Eddie cared about for a while. He stopped hanging out with me as much because I didn't care about that shit. Nothing can turn me off to God like kneeling on a wood beam every Sunday.'

She laughed and said she used to believe in a god, like a white-bearded man in the sky, and heaven, and sometimes she still wanted to believe, but she just couldn't anymore.

I asked her why and she shrugged.

'I heard once, that all the atoms that make up your body are as old as the universe. You, your skin and meat and bones, old as the sun. Older. That's much more interesting to think about than some grandpa in the sky, watching me, getting mad when I masturbate, sending down lightning bolts, crucifying progeny. That's really strange, don't you think?'

I was about to answer, but she kept talking.

'Anyway,' she said, 'I want to know what Eddie thinks about you and Gwen living together. Is he mad?'

'Eddie's dead,' I blurted.

'Oh,' she said. I thought she'd probe, but maybe she'd

seen enough death in her short life, making the hows and the whys irrelevant, because she didn't ask. Death was death to her, a consequence of being alive, a contract we'd all signed unknowingly, but signed nonetheless. 'You seem mad at him for that.'

'I am a little.'

'Well, that's not really fair.' I knew she was thinking more of herself than Eddie, but I felt the need to defend myself.

I told her I wasn't going to argue about fair. Fair was deceptive. An abstraction we'd layered upon another abstraction: deserve. It was all subjective and I didn't want to argue about it.

'Was he buried or cremated?' she asked.

'Buried. Why?'

'Just curious. Me, I want to be cremated. If I'm buried whole and in a box, I will come back to haunt the entire world. I mean it. I'll go fucking poltergeist. What about you?'

'My father bought a family plot. I already have a headstone.'

'No one actually does that, do they?'

'He thought it would be nice, all of us planted nearby.'

We crossed an intersection.

'You didn't ask me what I wanted after,' she said.

'You said you wanted to be cremated.'

'And then I want to be spilled from the back of the ferry going out to Alcatraz.' She stared off into the future, at her ashes churning in the propeller's wake.

'Why?'

'Think of it. Becoming a billion ashy particles swirling out there, filling up the bay. Becoming a small part of every fish and plant. I'd be enormous.' She spread her arms like she wanted to hug everything she saw.

I knew I loved her then. I knew because I suddenly envied the fish, the plants, anything that Magdalene would become part of.

The wind whipped strands of hair from the tether of her ear, and I put them back again. Her skin was cool and she leaned into me. I wondered how long it had been since she'd been touched, like really touched.

'If you could be anything you wanted, what would it be?'

'A sandpiper,' she said with no hesitation.

'Okay, not *anything*. Career-wise. What would you do?'

'It's too embarrassing,' she said.

'I wanted to be a ringmaster,' I said. 'Ever since my first circus, but I was too afraid of elephants and the noise they make.'

She smiled politely, but kept her lips shut.

'Come on,' I said. 'I literally wanted to run away with the circus. Yours can't be that bad.'

'I wanted to be a singer,' she said, looking a little scared, like I might laugh at her or ask her to sing something a cappella right then and there.

'See? That's not embarrassing.'

'I wanted to be Stevie Nicks. I wanted to be good, but I was awful.'

I tried to imagine her tiny body belting out 'Just Like The White-Winged Dove', but it seemed impossible. 'How much are lessons?' I asked.

'It doesn't matter anymore,' she said, and her meaning was unmistakable.

We stopped in front of her apartment building, an old distillery that had been converted into apartments, and I hugged her goodbye on the sidewalk in front of her door, careful to keep her arms over my shoulders to avoid her touching the compression shirt.

'Do you smoke pot?' I whispered in her ear.

She grinned. 'Maybe.'

'Monday,' I said, touching her face. 'I'll bring some Monday.'

16

I knew eventually I would have to face Gwen and her judgement, but I had expected her to be gone at the porn party when I got home. Instead she was up on the top bunk, chewing a piece of sandwich bread, pretending to ignore me but already perched in a fighting stance. Her hair was still done up, but she was wearing a pajama shirt and a pair of shorts. I walked in and set my keys on the desk.

In an effort to mitigate the damage, I went to the edge of the top bunk, where she was leaned against the wall, and I took hold of one of her feet. She peeled the crust from another piece of bread and set it in a pile of crusts beside her on the blanket. I picked one up and put it in my mouth.

She wrinkled her nose. 'I farted there.'

I folded another into my mouth. 'I'd lick your asshole, so.'

She tried to kick me but I dodged it.

'What happened to your party?' I asked.

'What happened to your date?' She sounded indignant.

'That wasn't a date.'

'Did you tell the little sick girl that? Because she seemed confused.'

My irritation spiked. It felt good. I wanted to fight. 'I think she was confused about why you were being such a cunt.'

'You told her you were a boy,' she said, pushing me with her heel. 'Maybe that's what's got her confused. Sam the Man.' Her smile was one I'd seen before. Gwen with a secret was like a violent psychopath with a loaded weapon. Power-drunk and in a hurry to destroy someone's life. I tried to disarm her.

'Fine,' I said. 'Maybe she thinks I'm a boy. Are you jealous of some lonely AIDS patient?' Hard as it was to belittle Magdalene, I needed Gwen off my scent. I needed her to be unsure of how to hurt me, because I knew, at some point soon, she'd probably want to.

'How many people, exactly, are you lying to?'

'Zero.'

'Sure.'

'I'm not lying to anyone. If they want to believe something, that's not my business.'

'Fine. Whatever. How many people are believing this not-truth, then? What about that muscle freak? Does he think you're a fellow swinging dick?'

I felt lightheaded.

'Say something!' She threw a piece of bread at me.

'He knows exactly who I am.'

'Exactly, huh?' she repeated, more like a mother's judgment than a real question. 'So you can tell a stranger what you're doing, but not me?'

'You'd just say it was weird.'

'It is weird.'

'Okay, weird, sure. Driving a car is weird, totally unnatural. Bread is weird, fucking bizarre if you think about it.'

'You're tricking people. It's not right.'

'I'm not tricking anyone. Having long hair, wearing a dress; that would be a lie for me. This is honesty.'

'You got a boy's haircut so no one will think you have a vagina, which you do have,' she said. 'That's tricking. And it's strange. And, if I'm being honest, kinda gross.'

'So you're really a blonde?' I said, swatting some of her bleached hair.

She looked annoyed. 'I'm not lying about my genitals when I color my hair.'

'Fuck you. Neither am I.'

'Yes you are!'

At this point in the conversation, I stopped caring about Gwen's opinion, and I became aware that the argument was, in many ways, a test run for what I would say to Magdalene. 'Think of it this way. How many dicks have you seen?' I said. 'Just give me a rough estimate.'

She stopped picking at the bread. 'I don't know. Seven.'

The number was more than I would've guessed, and surprisingly I felt no urge to ask more questions about who and when and where. I didn't care. I had a point to prove.

'And how many men have you seen?' I asked.

'Seen? What do you mean?'

'I mean, how many men have you seen out just walking around, you know, with clothes on?'

She squeezed her eyebrows together. 'I don't know. Thousands, probably.'

'You've seen a hundred thousand since we've been here.'

She blinked slowly. 'I'm waiting patiently for your point.'

'Did you see all of their dicks?'

She pinched her lips and stared down at her fingers as she rolled the bits of crust into a ball. 'I'm just saying, and you can wiggle out of this all you want, but someone is going to feel tricked if they find out and maybe kick your ass.'

'That's not going to happen.'

'You don't know that.'

'I'll fuck someone up,' I said. 'I'm scrappy. Marcus showed me how to take someone's ears off or pluck a fucker's eyeball out or crush their windpipe—'

'Gross.' She studied her little ball of bread crust before she launched it at the trashcan. I could tell we were gaining no ground.

'So, what does this mean for me?' Gwen finally asked. I should've known this would become all about her. How did it affect *her*? How would it make *her* look?

'Maybe you should, I don't know, go visit your mom.' The only word I cared about in that sentence was 'go.' Her calling me a fraud made me feel like one and I didn't want to feel like that anymore. Twenty-three years was long enough.

'I'm not leaving,' she said, folding her arms and grounding her ass into the mattress like she thought I couldn't just pick her up and throw her out the door.

'Fine,' I said, figuring a little reverse psychology might

do the trick. I sat down on the bed, feeling shaky from the adrenaline. 'I mean, of course you wouldn't want to face your mom and Bobby and get married since your wedding is in, I don't know,' – I checked an invisible watch – 'like two months. Stay. Start dancing with Flora. You'll make a shit ton of money. And then you can carry your own fucking weight.'

Her chin started quivering, not because she wanted to cry, but because she wanted to destroy me. 'Whatever,' she finally said. She slid from the top bunk and started putting on the clothes she'd been wearing earlier. 'I'm going to that party with Flora.'

I imagined her fucking some Ron Jeremy type in front of a camera. I didn't care. 'Cool,' I told her. 'Let me call you a cab.'

I went down to the payphone, slipped in a quarter, and punched out the numbers. As the phone started ringing, I heard a knock on the front door of the lobby, and I saw Jeb outside, standing in the grey light. He waved through the window, and I opened the door.

'What's up?' I said, stepping into the wind. He looked shaken. I offered him a cigarette but he declined.

'Eli's dead,' he said, like he'd been crying. 'So, you know, you don't have to worry about the, uh, thing.'

Selfishly, I worried what that meant about our agreement.

'I just wanted you to know,' he said, 'in case you've been laying some groundwork, sticking your neck out. No point now.'

'Dude, I'm so sorry,' I said.

Gwen and Flora emerged from the staircase and into the lobby, their voices a faint chirp through the front window. Flora noticed me and waved. Gwen came stalking through the entrance, but slowed once she saw Jeb. Flora walked past her and folded her hands (the good hand over the missing finger) like she always did when preparing to flirt.

'Ver you find za hunka-hunka?' she said, her accent overemphasized.

I introduced Flora to Jeb. I lied and told her we worked together. Jeb smiled and added a layer. 'I just drive the really sick ones to their appointments,' he said. 'Kansas does all the dirty work.'

'Oooh, you have nickname,' Flora said. '*I* vant nickname.' She slithered her good hand down Jeb's forearm. 'Vill you come to party and give me nickname?'

'Jeb's pretty busy,' I said.

Though it took only the words pornography and powdered drugs, and Jeb's mood shifted. Sex was, he later told me, a common distraction, not because he was bisexual, not even because he had about a billion years of evolutionary impulse, but because he was totally confident and at ease with himself, which was, apparently, attractive to all types, making sex the simplest mind-numbing activity he'd ever found. 'Work's over,' he said to Flora. 'Play time now.'

His shoulders loosened; his jaw stopped clenching. He offered to drive us, so long as he could partake in every heathen thing we encountered. I didn't really love the idea of all of us going together, but seeing as Jeb was suddenly behaving like we were friends, I didn't want to mess it up.

On the drive, Jeb told us he had a brief career in pornography, back when he was still a student at Stanford. He and Deb, he said, used to do shoots in Pacific Heights, fetish stuff mostly – sub/dom or sometimes phony snuff or rape – though Deb didn't really like the rape scenes, and that's when she stopped, and that's when they stopped.

'Zat's terrible. So no girlfriend to keep varm?' Flora kept touching him. She told him they were shooting straight-up normal porn: sex for middle America. 'For people like Kansas,' she said and winked at me.

I wondered if Gwen was thinking how atypical, how unboring our last conversation was. I asked her if she planned to fuck on camera, and she looked like she wanted to shout at me again.

Flora answered instead. 'I tell her she vill make five hundred, easy, but she doesn't know.'

'I just don't want my dad to see it.'

'Honey, if your dad sees it,' Jeb said, looking at Gwen in the rearview, 'you'll never know. I think your daddy would keep that secret to the grave.'

The party started out just as boring and predictable as middle-American sex. When we first arrived, the house was full of people with dull wandering eyes and meandering voices – women in nylon dresses and paunch-bellied men with tinted glasses and permed hair. They were eating finger foods, and sipping wine and chilled cocktails, and the only thing that separated the party from one my mother might attend were the lights and tripods set up in the living room and a sad ungarnished mattress in the center. Was everyone pretending it wasn't there, or was it just such a blasé thing to these people that no one cared? I couldn't be sure.

No one acknowledged any one of us except Flora as we walked up to a table of food. I loaded up a plate with chunks of white and orange cheeses and a variety of crackers. There were some wiener sausages drowning in a Crockpot of barbecue sauce (which I thought hilarious considering the party's theme), and a woman in fantasy French maid garb was impaling each wiener with a toothpick and putting them on a doilied plate. She offered me one, and I took it.

Behind the bar, on a lower shelf, I found a decent bottle of scotch and dumped some into two glasses for me and Jeb. Gwen poured herself a goblet of white wine and we drank in silence, watching Flora move from one conversation to another. Occasionally, a group of people would look over at us three and give a lazy jerk of their chins. A few came over and asked if Jeb and I were going to participate – they were short on men apparently – and Gwen gave me an exaggerated thumbs-up, completely dissolving both the happy fantasy I'd conjured of fucking at least one new woman in my lifetime and the satisfying warmth of finally being treated normal.

Just then, the door to the kitchen flung open and a man wearing nothing but a black thong and a cowboy hat galloped through the opening. There was a cheer. He held a pair of reins that led down to a woman on all fours. She came scooting through the doorway after him, her tits swinging through a cup-less lacy bra like milk-heavy udders.

'Yee-haah!' the man sang.

Jeb reached over and plucked a wiener from my plate. 'Now that's entertaining,' he said.

'Doesn't really go with the French maid thing, does it?'

The woman reared up and clawed her fingers in the air as if she'd forgotten she was supposed to be a horse. The thematic dissolution continued. No one seemed to care.

'Welcome to our home,' the man shouted, and he plucked the cowboy hat from his head and waved it around.

The other guests clapped. Some raised their glasses.

'Have some libations,' he said, 'some crustaceans' – he pointed to the table – 'but steer clear of incarceration or procreation.' I assumed he must say that often because the group shouted the last words with him.

It wasn't long before the lights warmed up and the cameras turned on. Clothes started bunching on the floor and dicks and tits of all different sizes hit open air.

It wasn't just a porn shoot. It was an orgy.

A blonde-haired lady started blowing some dude on the couch, while another guy held a boom mike over them, and a camera guy moved all around – over, sideways, under – saying, 'Slob that knob, Nancy. Atta girl.'

Gwen watched with her hand over her mouth as if worried, with all the dicks flying around, one might find its way suddenly in. Flora asked her if she was ready for a little blow. Jeb and I laughed at the pun.

Jeb asked some people nearby what the rules were: could he just walk up and stick it in someone or was there some etiquette? Before they could answer, Flora pulled him away.

'Blow or blow,' Jeb said. 'Don't make me choose.'

'Come on. You von't regret it.'

'Promise?'

'Promise. Come on hunka. Let's get high as kike.'

'Kite, doll.'

'Come, come.'

We all three followed her upstairs to a tiny bedroom. Flora pulled a Shel Silverstein book from a shelf and sat down on the twin bed. She cut up four lines on the cover and we passed it around while we listened to the people downstairs – the moaning, the slapping of wet skin on skin, the director directing – and Jeb started getting all antsy on the floor. 'Listen to that.'

'You feel like you're missing something, big boy?'

'They're missing me,' he said. 'You want to go back down there?'

Gwen shook her head. 'It's too weird,' she said. 'All those people watching.'

The imbalance in her morals was really starting to piss me off. 'I don't get it,' I said. 'You're such a prude about sex, but you'll do coke in a kid's bedroom.'

'The kid's not here,' Gwen said. 'And, I'm not a prude. I just like doing things in private, that's all.'

'Show us,' Jeb said, and Flora's face brightened with a smile.

'Show you what?' Gwen said.

'That you're not a prude.'

I was beginning to love Jeb.

'Come on. Let's do dance, Gwennie,' Flora said.

Gwen looked into her wine glass and finished it in one long gulp. She tapped her foot to a phantom beat while Flora stood and started gyrating against the post of the bed. Gwen went red, covering her face, laughing in self-defense.

'See, *she's* not afraid,' Jeb said. '*She* can dance.'

Gwen was not the type to lose once things became competitive, so she stood and started doing the same moves, only they were far less fluid and sexy. She looked unpracticed but Jeb told her she looked fantastic – *keep going*, he said –

injecting confidence. Flora, not to be outdone, removed her top and panties, leaving Gwen to stand there, faced with a decision.

Finally, she removed her dress in one single sweep.

I clapped but I was bored as hell. Jeb gave a long whistle and started directing – *touch her waist, kiss her neck* – to which Gwen surprisingly complied, and Jeb, like a puppet master, soon had them both on the bed and Gwen's head between Flora's legs. *Give it a lick*, Jeb said, almost whispered, and she tried, but jerked back and a wet burp slid from her lips.

I busted up laughing.

'It's not funny,' Gwen said, and she covered her mouth, muffling another belch and then another. It was obvious she was gagging, and she fell to one side on the floor and wretched into one of the poor kid's dresser drawers. She blamed it on the alcohol.

Flora closed her legs, but Jeb, not one to let a pair of open legs go wasted, stood up and started unbuckling his pants. Flora looked at his metal belt buckle and her legs slacked open again. 'You want them to stay or go?' he said, gesturing to me and Gwen. Flora shook her head like she didn't care, and she pulled him close. They started kissing.

If there had been a camera, I could've watched, but being there alone with them, seeing them fuck right there in the privacy of a child's room, the smell of their mingling heavy breath humidifying the air, made me feel desperate to leave.

I gestured to the door with my chin, and Gwen threw on her dress as Jeb began to push into Flora. I doubt they even noticed us leaving; they were such a frenzy of hair and hands and spit by then. Gwen and I hauled ass down the stairs, past the other group of people – now in a full orgy, camera crew orbiting the bodies – and we ran outside into the clean breeze, the quiet street, and she said, before we even had time to reflect, that she didn't want to talk about any of it. Ever. Then she smacked her lips and said she really needed some gum, and I laughed and laughed, even after she asked me to stop.

17

That night I drifted off into a deep easy sleep, content for the first time, probably, since Eddie died. This was, of course, ruined around two in the morning. My eyes split open to a dull blue light and thick shadows along the wall. I heard music, elevator music, then *Ladies and gentlemen, The Price is Right*. The bed above me shifted. Gwen gave a little cough. 'What are you doing?' I said.

'I can't sleep.'

'Neither can I now.'

She jumped down and lowered the volume. 'Happy?' she said as she climbed back to the top bunk.

I didn't understand why she was being a bitch but then I remembered her head between Flora's legs, and I figured the humiliation had finally caught up to her and she resented me now, like I'd manipulated her somehow. It wasn't the first time she'd accused me of that.

'It's just common courtesy, don't you think?' I said.

She resettled herself on the bed above me. 'Yeah. Sure thing, Ro.'

The word flicked off her tongue like a dart, and I jerked out of bed and postured right up near her face. 'What the fuck is your deal?'

Very briefly she beamed fear and flinched, but just as suddenly, as if she'd considered my size and power and thought, *yeah, no*, she looked back to the television and acted unfazed. She opened her mouth. 'I said, *sure thing.*'

I walked over to the television and turned the volume all the way down. On the screen, a floppy-armed grandma was sprinting toward the stage. 'If you want to talk about something,' I said, 'fucking talk about it. Don't be all passive-aggressive, trying to wake me up in the middle of the night.'

'I wasn't trying to wake you. I was just trying to hear.'

'Then, Jesus, you're deaf.'

She changed positions from her belly to sitting and reached to the far corner of her bunk, where she kept a stuffed doll and some papers and her knitting supplies. 'Should I be more pioneer-days? Should I read?' She held up Bill's book, then laid back down on her belly, and starting flipping through its pages as if she were just relaxing on the beach with a magazine. She was mocking me. 'Anal mucus and hard-ons and sex-machines,' she said. 'Who'd write about that? Who'd read it? Besides your new little girlfriend.'

'Where'd you get that?'

'No wonder she has AIDS if she's into that stuff.'

'Where'd you find it?' I said.

'Probably where you left it. That's a stupid question.'

Ever since I was a kid and Sally found the anatomy books I'd swiped from my school, I couldn't stand a snoop. Snoops, I'd decided, were shit human beings. Nosey and immoral, so bored in their own lives they looked to stir trouble in others.

I told Gwen to return the book and she laughed, sending a bolt of anger, real hot violent rage, through my chest and up through my face, a kind I'd never felt, or had, but never so potently. I grabbed and squeezed her wrist. She released the book to pry my hand away but couldn't unfasten my grip. I snatched the book with my free hand, but not before she clawed my arm.

She closed and opened her hand. 'You fucking hurt me,' she said, rubbing her wrist.

'Snoop again and I'll break your fucking arm.'

She glared. 'You'd go to jail. I'm tempted, seriously, just to see if you're that stupid.'

'Don't fucking do it, Gwen. I mean it.'

She examined her wrist. 'I think you did break it. What's wrong with you?'

'Nothing's wrong with me.' But something was. My anger was disproportionate and dug in like a tick.

Her eyes swelled red and started to cry, but I felt nothing. I knew then she'd try to hurt me, but I didn't know how or how soon it would be.

I needed to get away from her so I went to take a long shower.

When I returned, Gwen had reduced our apartment to shambles. My clothes and papers were scattered all over the floor and Gwen sat cross-legged in the middle of it, looking up at me with a greedy half-wild grin.

'You're twisted,' she said. 'You're evil and twisted in the head, and I hate you.'

She held out the Polaroid of Magdalene and me with our lips pressed together and she crushed it in her hand. I was speechless.

'I'm getting tested,' she said. 'I called Bobby and he said he'll kill you if you got me sick. And he will, Sam. He's on his way and you better pray—'

'Hold on,' I said.

I looked around at all the things she pulled out – everything was on the floor, my scrubs and T-shirts, my jeans, the leather. Behind her, my suitcase was unhinged and all the veins in my body pinched shut. My shots.

Gwen threw the picture at me. 'I know what you're thinking about. You. Sick. Junkie. Fuck. Did you shoot up with her? Did you share a needle?'

'It wasn't drugs, Gwen.'

'Right.'

'What'd you do with it?' I tried to step around her, but she got in my way.

'It's not in there anymore.'

'Don't fuck with me.'

'You're disgusting,' she said. 'You're a junkie-fucking-freak.' I tried to move past her, but she pushed me with all of her weight, and I staggered back. Manic, she laughed and moved to push me again.

So, I pushed her back and she stumbled over.

'Think you're a big man, huh?' she said, her voice rising.

'Does that make you feel big? Do you feel strong now?' She attacked me with a flurry of slaps. 'You killed me, didn't you? You killed me!' she shouted. I used my arms and hands to deflect most of her strikes, but she'd lost it. Gwen was gone and an angry hive of screaming wasps replaced her and I knew, in her mind, I deserved it, but I couldn't help it, I couldn't. I wound up and slapped her straight across the face. The sound was elastic. It stretched from my palm and to the walls and back to my ears again. My hand buzzed as the blood rushed back. Gwen gasped and fell into a weeping ball, holding her cheek. She glared up at me, her eyes two angry slivers.

'I want you to die,' she said.

'Just like Eddie, huh?'

She lunged at me again.

I grabbed her by the arm. 'If you don't leave,' I said, 'I don't know what I'll do.'

She shook her head. 'I'm not leaving without my stuff.'

I dragged her to the door, opened it, and shoved her through. 'Your shit will be in the hallway,' I said and locked the deadbolt.

She banged on the door until I heard Flora come and pull her away. I began throwing everything with her stain on it into a pile on the floor. I found the half-brick of pot, and what little bit of coke we still had, folded into a pair of her underwear, and I put them both in my pocket. It gave me precious hope that my steroids had survived her fit, so I searched my suitcase and the pile of clothes and every drawer in the room, until I finally found the vial shattered in the trashcan. Rage pressed at the seams of me. I had to break something. Had to. Her favorite thing. I tipped her television to the floor, but it didn't even crack, which infuriated me further, so I flung open the window, lifted the television, and pushed the fucking thing out. A few seconds later, my ears were met with a satisfying crash. But it wasn't enough. I wanted more. I wanted to crush Gwen. I wanted her to never find happiness again.

I heard her stupid voice repeating, *Bobby's coming to get me*, while I started throwing all her shit in her suitcase, and caught, in my periphery, a glimpse of something shiny fling through the air. A second later, I heard the soft ching as it hit the floor. Immediately, I knew what it was, and I started to crawl on my hands and knees like an animal, digging through the pile, until I found the gold ring under a red blouse. Excitement, delight, revenge churned deep within me. I pocketed the diamond and went to work stuffing her suitcase, which I put outside the door. Then I gathered a few things I thought I might need and left the building.

I stopped at *Frank's Fast Cash* down the road. The inside was cluttered with patio furniture, bicycles, hubcaps – shit junkies would steal to fund their fix – and I went up to the counter where a pock-faced man sat leaning into a baseball game on the radio.

I showed him the ring and he removed a pair of grease-smeared reading glasses and attached some sort of monocle thing to study the rock.

'So she said 'no', did she?'

'Huh?' I said, because I'd been thinking of how I could persuade Jeb to get more drugs for me by tomorrow.

The owner closed his wet mouth, and his lips looked like two shiny worms lying across his face. 'You steal this?' he said.

I put my hand out. 'Never mind. I'll go down the street.'

He closed his hand. 'I'll give you three hundred.'

Fucker thought I was stupid. I remembered how much Gwen said it was worth. 'I paid two grand for it.'

'Well, you're not gonna get what you paid for it,' he said, callously. Something about dealing with the desperate dredge of society all day gave this man super-powered apathy.

'Fifteen hundred.'

'Seven.'

'A thousand.'

His wormy lips sunk into his face. Finally, he put the ring on the counter, went to the back room, and returned with a receipt book, a paper sack, and a fat stack of twenties.

18

Gwen's suitcase was missing when I got back and I figured she was gone, really gone. The landlady came knocking later that afternoon, asking if the television was mine. I told her I didn't own one. She peeked over my shoulder, looking for some sign of disturbance, but I'd already picked up the place and put it back to order. Part of me wanted to tell her that Gwen had moved out, ask if maybe we could change the locks, because I didn't feel a hundred percent certain that Gwen wouldn't return just to trash the place all over again. But the television could've killed someone. It was grounds for eviction. I told her I hadn't heard anything but offered to help her clean it up, and we went into the alley, and I hurled the shattered thing into the dumpster.

It was satisfying to break Gwen's favorite thing twice.

Afterward, I called Jeb from a payphone and said I needed to see him. The desperation must've been detectable in my tone because he invited me right over. I pounded the pavement, thinking about the complicated umbilical that connected me to Gwen and how relieved I was to sever it. *Good riddance, dumb bitch*, I repeated until I found myself standing at Jeb's front door.

The place was not what I'd pictured. I'd expected some dingy, dungeon-like dwelling – a basement with slings and whips and handcuffs – but his apartment had lots of windows, and hardwood floors, and clean fancy furniture. He let me in and I sat on his white leather sofa while he poured me a glass of scotch.

I pulled the bag of coke from my pocket, scraped out three lines on his glass coffee table, and told him what I'd just been through: how Gwen had flipped and broken the vial of steroids, how I'd smacked her across the face, and how good that'd felt. Just talking about it got me riled up again. I did two lines and started pacing his living room.

Jeb handed me the drink and sat down to do the remaining line. 'I get it,' he said. 'She snipped your balls. I mean, literally. She smashed your manhood in the trash.' He leaned over and snorted the line. 'You know what helps when you're feeling that way?'

I had no idea. I didn't care, but still, I bit. 'What?'

He smiled. 'Life's a breeze when you can look down at a big fat cock in your hand.'

I blinked. 'Are you trying to make me laugh because that's an uphill battle.'

'No, seriously.'

'Yeah, well, I'm not into dick. Have I not been pretty clear about that?'

'C'mon. Not even when you were young and confused?'

'What? Held a dick?'

Jeb nodded.

'No. Never. And I mean never, as in future tense, too.'

'You a virgin, Kansas?'

I took a swig from my scotch and savored how it hurt. His window stared directly at his neighbor's curtained window just a few feet away. 'I've fucked around plenty,' I said.

'You ever been fucked?'

'Just stop, Jeb. I'm not one of those dumb bitches you can manipulate.'

'Look,' Jeb said, and I worried maybe he was going to make me look at his cock, but he opened a drawer in his side table and took out a sterile needle and a vial. He told me to shoot up and then we had somewhere to go.

He took me to a shop with a headless mannequin in the window, a gas mask slung over its shoulder, a pair of lacy underpants covering its nothing.

'In Lawrence,' I said. 'The only store that sold underwear was Wal-Mart'

'We're not here for underwear,' he said and hurried to the

far corner, where the wall was lined with a large assortment of rubber dicks. They hung from different pegs on the wall, organized by color and size. 'What you need is a cock that feels like yours,' he said, running his hand over a pink, vein-stuffed one. 'Don't go straight for the monsters. Your brain will reject it. It'll feel like a foreign object. How tall are you? Five six? I'd say seven inches is your max.'

'I don't understand what we're doing here.'

'We're confidence shopping.'

'I have confidence.'

Jeb turned and raised an eyebrow. 'Is that what you call it? Biting your nails, watching your girl eat another girl's snatch?'

'She didn't like it.'

'Exactly,' Jeb said. 'And all you could think about was how that revulsion related to you. Don't lie.' The testosterone was doing weird things to my psyche, and I felt weepy for a split second. Jeb picked up a floppy dick-and-balls set from the wall and held it over my crotch, casual, as if it were a pair of shorts. 'What do you think? Give it a grab.'

I looked down and my stomach cartwheeled. 'This is stupid.'

'Are you serious?'

'Of course, I'm serious. What am I supposed to do with that?' I flicked my finger against the tip and it bounced. 'It's all soft.'

'It's a packer. You wear it in your pants.'

I took it from his hand, and it felt fleshier than I imagined.

'Let's get it,' he said, taking it from me. 'And also one of these.' He grabbed a black hard dick from the wall and a box with a picture of some sort of underwear harness.

'I'm not black.'

'It doesn't matter.'

'But if I'm supposed to believe it's mine…'

'That's the spirit! Pick one. It should scream out, "I'm Sam's big dick. I make bitches scream."'

'So stupid,' I said but I laughed.

'Every knight needs a sword.'

I picked a pale circumcised cock, slightly bigger than the length he suggested and bulky in my hands. I tried to pay for both at the register, but Jeb insisted on buying them. 'Consider this the gift of enlightenment,' he said.

I should've known enlightenment wasn't free. When we got back to his apartment, Jeb wanted me to try them on, which I did, but only to satisfy my own curiosity.

I went into his bathroom, alone, and could hear him out there singing 'Rocket Man', dropping ice cubes into glasses, while I undressed and stared in the full-length mirror on the back of the door.

I decided to try the packer first.

Jeb rattled the doorknob, but it was locked.

'Hold on.' I reached for my clothes. 'Just let me get dressed.'

'No. I want to see it on.'

I looked at myself, scrawny and pale as a ghoul in the mirror, and my eye held on to it. The bulge. I looked from another angle. Reached down and clutched the lumpy plot beneath the fabric, feeling whole and fragmented all at once. I needed another opinion.

I unlatched the door, and Jeb practically fell in.

I dropped my arms to my thighs like, *well, here it is.*

He took one look at my crotch and let out a slow whistle.

'Looks good. Real good. Feels good too, don't it? I can tell. Your posture's better. You look taller. I swear.'

I wondered if I was supposed to say thanks or something.

'Okay, so now the other one.' Jeb tore open the box with the underwear harness. 'Let's see the soldier at full attention.'

'That's, uh,' I said.

'That's, uh, an order, private. Strap up.' He tossed it to me, playful, but something told me he wouldn't be smiling if I said no again.

'I need another line first.'

He gave me an oh-you're-so-pathetic look and said he'd get my line ready. He came back and emptied the rest of it on a vinyl Eric Clapton cover and scraped out four lines. I let Jeb do the first bump, and as I leaned over to do mine, he ran his hand along my compression shirt.

He tried to convince me to take it off, but I drew the line. I'd try on the cocks he bought me, but completely naked was completely out of the question. 'Fine, fine,' he said, and he went to work showing me how to attach the harness.

'So you just step into it like a pair of pants.'

I took the harness and hooked my leg through the hole.

'Take out the packer,' he said. 'You can't be hard and soft.'

'One thing at a time,' I said as I put the other leg through and pulled the whole apparatus up like some wacky pair of underwear over my regular underwear. I took out the packer and tossed it on the floor.

Jeb leaned in and deftly looped the straps through a metal hook. He was standing close enough I could feel his breath graze my neck, and a patch of goose pimples sprouted.

He made sure I understood how to fasten it myself and closed the door, showing me to myself in the full-length mirror.

There I was, all holstered and harnessed up.

'Grab it,' Jeb said over my shoulder. 'Own that dick.'

With my right hand, I gripped the base. I smiled.

Jeb's face brightened. 'You like it!'

'Maybe.' I took another long look. It almost seemed real, my phantom appendage.

'You want to fuck me with it?'

'Absolutely not.'

'Can I touch it, at least?' he asked, already reaching.

I thought about denying him this but didn't.

'No one's ever treated you like a man before, have they?'

'Not like this.'

'I would.'

Jeb grazed his lips against my neck and suddenly I felt all sorts of conflicted.

Our eyes met in the mirror. I could only shake my head.

He started stroking. 'Do you mind this?'

I shook my head again, watching the reflection. His pace was measured, practiced.

'Can I put my mouth around it?'

The idea made me queasy, and it showed.

'It's just practice,' Jeb said, calmly, like we were going to shoot some hoops. 'Just picture some long blonde hair on my head.'

'Brown,' I said.

Jeb took that as the go-ahead, and he knelt in front of me and opened his mouth. The whole thing disappeared into his face like a magic trick, and a feeling of power washed over me. I was invading his head.

He bobbed back and forth expertly while I watched in the mirror. I used my palm to cover his bald spot, and I squinted to minimize his muscles, to melt him down into something resembling a female. But it was hard to maintain, this image. I could only see his burly features, his wide back, his angled jaw, his giant hands, and soon I asked him to stop.

He gave it one last tug before he stood. The room seemed smaller than before, and I felt exposed and confined all at once. Jeb cleared his throat, and I moved out of the way so he could wash his hands in the sink. While he lathered, I busied myself by trying to unbuckle the strap-on. I couldn't even meet Jeb's eyes when he opened the door and said he'd give me some privacy.

When I came out of the bathroom, he was sprawled out on the couch, one arm behind his head, watching baseball on the television. He told me to take a seat, asked if I wanted a beer or water or something. The bag of body parts weighed heavy in my hand. I said I should probably go. He nodded to the two lines of coke still sitting on the vinyl cover. 'You gonna finish that first?' Maybe he wanted me to stay to smooth out the awkwardness, or maybe he didn't feel awkward and it was just me projecting, but I sat down and he reshaped the lines.

'You got any pimples on your ass yet?' he asked.

'From the juice?'

He snorted a line and nodded.

'Haven't checked. Should I? Is it a good sign or something?'

He handed over the straw and said, 'Felt like a thousand cactus needles were impaling my ass after my first few doses. I could barely sit.'

As we spoke, any weirdness evaporated, and I left with a new sense of purpose.

On the bus home, I searched the crowd and wondered why no one was looking at me or my brown paper bag, which seemed to radiate on the seat next to me. How could they not *see* what was inside? How could it all seem so normal? It probably looked like a sack lunch to them. I studied the man sitting across from me and wondered what was really in his briefcase: a severed hand, a bag of grass clippings, a million dollars. And the woman next to him with her big ugly purse; was she carrying around her taxidermied cat? Who knew? She wouldn't show me if she was, just like I wasn't going to tip over my sack and let those two dicks flop out. We were all handling bags, I realized. Normalcy was just an unmarked package.

19

That night, Gwen came pounding on the door, shouting about how she needed to get the rest of her things. I let her in and sat on the bed while she went through all of the drawers. When it was obvious she wouldn't find what she was looking for, she glared over at me. 'What'd you do with it?'

I leaned back on my forearms. 'With what?'

'Bobby's going to be here in one hour, and if you don't hand over my ring, I'm going to have him come up here and look for it himself.' She started rummaging through a drawer again. 'You're going to feel real stupid when you don't have front teeth anymore.'

'I don't have your ring, Gwen.'

She picked up my leather shirt and tried to rip the sleeve, but it wouldn't budge. A low growl came from her throat, and she threw it at me. 'I hope you die.'

I felt nothing. I laughed anyway, and she flipped me off and slammed the door.

I thought about leaving for a few hours, just in case her threat about Bobby was true, but I would look weak and I was tired of looking weak. So I smoked a joint and waited. An hour passed and I heard nothing. I paced the room, did a few push-ups, waited, until finally I heard Gwen's voice out in the hallway, and another voice, much lower than hers. Bobby, I guessed. I imagined our confrontation, him pounding on the door, my nervous voice. But nothing. They chatted for a good while. I leaned my ear against the door and I could hear their murmured argument.

'You don't give two shits.'

'I flew out here.'

'Big man. Sat on a plane.'

Suddenly I didn't want to punch Bobby. I had sympathy for

him.

Eventually, I heard Gwen shout out, 'Fuck you, Rosie!' and then she was gone for good.

The next day, I finally got a hold of Sally, who confirmed she was already six months pregnant, having hid her growing belly under baggy clothes, and our mother, while mad at first, was crocheting baby blankets and scouring Saturday morning garage sales for cribs and strollers and clothes. I let her tell me all about the doctor's appointments and the sonogram and the tiny apartment in Kansas City where she and Paul might set up a home. When she was finished, I told her Gwen was currently on her way back.

She seemed disappointed to not know this sooner.

I asked her then, gently, if she'd be willing to trade a favor for a favor.

'What kind of favor?'

'A fifty-dollar favor,' I said, knowing she was quick to work for a profit.

'I'm listening,' she said.

'So, I have this friend who really likes Bill's books.'

'Bill?'

'Neighbor Bill,' I said. Just then the payphone notified me that I needed to insert another quarter or it would disconnect in fifteen seconds, but I didn't have one. 'If I send a book, can you have him sign it?'

Her silence signaled her reluctance, and I knew it was because she didn't really like Bill, not since he'd yelled at her for picking his roses.

'Come on, Sally. Fifty dollars. It's so easy.'

'Fine. I'll go talk to Cat-lady Bill,' she said. 'But you're coming back home though, aren't you?' she said. 'I mean, you have to meet the baby at least.'

I tried to answer but the dial tone saved me.

I dropped Sally's money and Bill's book in the mail on the way to work on Monday. I planned to wait until she returned it to tell Magdalene I'd won the bet, but I was terrible at keeping a secret. When my father taught me poker as a kid, I couldn't keep the smile off my face every time I matched a pair, and a flush, forget it, I'd almost pee from excitement. So, I told her. I said, 'Soon, you're gonna have to spill it, Mag.'

'What does that mean?' she asked.

I put my hands gently on her shoulders. 'You,' I said, 'are gonna have to tell me where you went when you ran away.'

Her lips curled slightly and she shrugged and brushed a piece of hair from my forehead. 'Sure, Sam, sure,' she said. 'Let's just wait for the book to arrive before you go bouncing around the room.' The bet was still important to me, but I could tell she had lost interest, which should've been good news, considering my own secret was on the line.

I took Magdalene's temperature. 'One hundred and one,' I said. Too high.

'Please tell me you brought some pot.'

'Won't bring your fever down.'

'Says you,' she said.

I put the stethoscope to my ears and raised the disc. She pulled her shirt out from her waistband, and I warmed the metal with my breath before I slid my hand under her shirt. Inside, she was an orchestra of sounds, and I had to concentrate to hear each individually: the screen-door whine of her lungs; the galloping, never-ending relentless thump of her heart; the squish and whine of foods digesting; everything, all of it, working together like one mad, sticky clock slowly winding down. I moved the disc around, listening, touching. She sounded perfectly normal.

I pulled my hand free and told her not to worry. She cheered quietly as I produced a joint from my pocket.

'Let me see it,' she said, reaching.

'No. We can't smoke it here.'

'No. Just let me touch it.'

What if Dinka walked in? I thought, but I handed it over.

She started sniffing it.

The pills sat on the table and I pushed them toward her.

'Is it Kansas weed?'

'This weed, I shit you not, is some of the same weed old Bill Burroughs was smoking last month.'

'Now you're just showing off, you liar.'

'Cross my heart,' I said, tracing a crucifix over my layers of shirt. While she swallowed her pills, I stared at a poster of a kitten in a water pail that Gayla had hung the first week of the study. It read: *Positive Minds Yield Positive Results*.

20

We stopped for food on the way to Magdalene's and ordered pepper steak, wontons, and two giant fountain cokes. Before we'd even made it down the block, Magdalene reached into the bag and pulled out a cookie. She said she liked to have her fortune first. 'Good news,' she said, as if trying to conjure it. 'Good news.'

'Aren't they always good news?' I asked. Still feeling fatalist, I imagined the truest fortune cookie ever told: *You and everyone you know are going to die.*

She said, 'Some fortune cookies are bullshit proverbs. I don't need any more wisdom. I need good news.' While she crunched away, she read the note aloud: *Your days may be numbered, but your dreams are without measure.*

She barked a phony laugh, crumpled the paper, and threw it in the next trashcan we passed.

'So, what *are* your dreams?' I asked.

She put the other cookie-half in her mouth and mumbled around its edges. 'To get out of California.' She chuckled again but this time it sounded sad. 'It's ridiculous and depressing, but I've never actually been out of the state.'

That didn't seem possible – the way she spoke about the world, her breadth of knowledge of the cultures and peoples and problems of other countries (she once lectured me for an entire appointment for not knowing about the Ugandan genocide), so for a brief moment, I explored the possibility that Magdalene might be a plant in the study, sent in to look for inconsistencies in the distribution, or even worse, my god, maybe the researchers were researching me, a case study on morality and ethics, *does empathy trump research?*, *does a crush negate duty?*, but then we reached her apartment, and I saw her stacks and stacks of books all lined up against the wall.

I told her I'd only been to a few states other than Kansas.

'Is it like the Wizard of Oz out there?' she asked from the kitchen where she was getting us some plates.

'Fewer munchkins,' I said. I looked around her apartment, not much bigger than mine, but much cozier, lived in, full of something I didn't have and I tried to figure out what that could be.

Magdalene came around the corner with two plates. 'I mean tornadoes, smart-ass.'

I told her I'd heard of tornadoes in the area, but never a storm that picked up a whole house and dropped it, intact, in a brand new place.

She frowned, maybe thinking of those witch's legs poking out from beneath Dorothy's house, and she scooped some food onto her plate. She said she used to fantasize about that when she was a little girl, shuttling from one foster home to the next, that one day she would just be swept up and land in some magical world. She asked if I was going back to Kansas once I was done with the study.

I told her I'd have to go back to Kansas sometime. Not to live, but to see my family. Sally was pregnant. I'd have to meet the baby. 'Maybe when it's old enough to, you know, give a shit about meeting me.'

'Can I come with you?' she asked.

It took a deliberate effort not to contort my face into something like terror or disgust as I imagined all the awkward introductions, including the most awkward: Magdalene, Rosie. Rosie, Magdalene.

'You don't want to go there,' I said. 'It's the most boring place on Earth. I didn't leave Kansas, okay? I escaped. What about Disneyland? I'll take you to Disneyland.'

She put her fork down. 'Disneyland is in California.'

'Disney World, then. Florida. Let's go there.'

'Never mind. It was a stupid idea.'

'It's not stupid, I just… don't want you to be bored. It's so boring there.'

'I could meet Burroughs,' she said. 'And maybe see a tornado.' She stared into my eyes with a hunger that startled me. She was serious. Very serious.

Despite my efforts to look cool, she could tell I was bothered. 'Maybe we should just change the subject.'

'It's just, there aren't *that* many tornadoes.' I pulled the joint from my pocket and lit it without asking. Magdalene rushed over to the window and told me to exhale outside.

We sat near the windowsill and passed the joint between us while she told a story about how she watched *The Wizard of Oz* thirty-seven times in thirty-seven days when she was a kid. She was trying to get to one hundred, but one of her foster parents broke the tape.

'He just came in the room and snapped it over his knee and said "I can't stand anymore of this off-to-see-the-wizard shit."' She said the last part in a lowered voice, mocking the man. 'That's when I started reading,' she said. 'My tornado: books. I could be sitting in the same room as my teacher or my foster mom or my social worker and reading about people killing or falling in love or fucking.' She blushed. 'And no one had any idea. It felt good, like I was doing wrong right there in front of everyone and getting away with it.'

'Is that why Humberto gave you that book?'

She spread a smile and looked away. '*Lolita* was my first book. I mean, not the first book I ever read, but the first book I ever owned.'

'It's hard to believe you ever didn't own a book,' I said, looking at her massive collection, like a sideways pillar of wall-to-wall paper, mostly classics I'd never heard of, stories about rich privileged folks, and sad little orphan kids, and wars I'd never known of and places I'd never go. I took the final puff from the joint and tossed it out the window. 'He got you sick, didn't he?'

'Maybe that's part of my secret and you, sir, have not won the bet. In fact, last I checked, you were losing.'

'I'm not losing,' I said. 'I'm leading your ass, you just don't know it.'

'Isn't part of an ass-kicking the *knowing* about it?'

'My foot is in the process of swinging. When it lands, you'll know it.'

She ignored my provocation, so I asked her again in a different way: 'Why aren't you mad at him?'

'Because it's like getting mad at the tide for destroying your sand castle.'

'It's not like he was a force of nature, Magdalene. The tide doesn't make a decision. A conscious choice. It just does what it does. He was a person. He got you sick.' I sounded jealous and immediately I felt ridiculous because I knew, in a way, I was competing with a dead guy all over again.

'He didn't know he was sick until we both were.'

Oh, I guess *that's* forgivable, I wanted to say, so he didn't know the gun was loaded. Oh well. C'est la vie. But I could tell I had just pressed against a tender spot. 'How could he not know?'

'He was a user,' she said. 'With bad luck.'

'The worst luck.'

'You know what I miss?' she said as she laid back and closed her eyes, her face serene in a pot fog. 'I miss fucking.'

It was like Magdalene was two different people: this dour little girl and this hungry beast. I took the moment to run my eyes down her body and study her ribs through her shirt, her breasts, her skinny neck. She's a siren, I thought. Yet, I still wanted to slide my hand inside her shorts, bury a finger in her slit.

She groaned and covered her face. 'You're not saying anything,' she said.

I took a deep breath, trying to smother those thoughts. 'I think it's normal to still feel like fucking.'

She sat up and brushed a hair from her face.

'When's the last time you did?'

She wouldn't look at me. 'A long time ago. See, I know I'm sick, so to fuck someone, I'd have to kill them in my head first and I don't hate anyone that much.'

'There's ways to be careful.'

'Eh.' She shrugged.

'What about kissed?'

'Not counting you in the office, a long time ago.'

I went over the couch and touched her face before leaning in to kiss her.

Our contact was charged, as if every atom in her body was a magnet to mine.

She finally pulled away. 'Why do you like me?' she asked.

Her question surprised me. 'What do you mean? Boys like girls. Simple.'

'I mean, I'm going to die.'

'We're all going to die.'

'Soon, Sam. I am dying. As we speak.'

'Technically,' I said, stupidly, 'so am I.'

She glowered. 'I'll never have a wrinkle.'

'I'll make you smile more.'

'Take me to Kansas and I'll smile non-stop.'

'You'll have to sleep sometime.'

She pouted some more.

I touched her arm. Her skin was warm and it seemed impossible that it ever wouldn't be. 'You're funny,' I said. 'And smart. And you laugh easy, which makes me laugh. That's why I like you. People die every day. Healthy people who thought they'd live to be a hundred. People who took their vitamins and rode their bikes and never did a drug, they get hit by cars or drown or get murdered or kill themselves or their heart explodes. It's not safe to love anyone, but what the fuck else am I gonna do?'

'You said love.'

'I know what I said.'

'You don't mean it.'

'Don't tell me what I mean.'

'You just met me. You don't really know me.'

'I know what I see, and I know there's a lot more I don't see, not all of it good, but I do care about you, and I want to learn everything I can while I can.'

She looked up at me with those mossy eyes. 'Let me see where you're from.'

I told her maybe, but internally, I was leaning toward no. She said she only had a three-week window between our study and the next. Her case manager was working overtime or something. It was the only time she could go.

I probed. 'What kind of study?'

She tugged the sleeve of her shirt over her wrist and wiped her lips with it. 'Something. It doesn't matter.'

'In San Francisco?'

She looked at me differently. 'You are cute. I almost believe you love me.'

I was now profoundly aware she hadn't said it back, might never, and my proclamation might forever be suspended in air. My scalp started to itch. 'You don't even like me a little?' I asked, making a half-inch gap between my thumb and forefinger.

'Maybe,' she said with a flat smile, like payback.

I was sweating. I asked her if I could smoke a cigarette out the window, and she said she was pretty tired and let out a big exaggerated yawn. 'I can take a hint,' I said, and we went to part ways at her front door.

Before I left, I planted my feet in the hall looking at her, hopeful, pathetic, terrified she'd close the door and never open it again because I'd humiliated myself and, seeming to sense this, she did the best thing she could have done, because saying it back right then would have been reciprocation out of fear, hers or mine or both, and it wouldn't have meant anything other than as a token, like, 'Here you go, Sam, just in case I never see you again,' and it would have been cheap and I'd have regretted it forever. So she closed the door excruciatingly slow, like a ship leaving harbor, waving and singing off-key, 'You've got to hide your love away.'

I waved back and the door closed but I knew, just knew, with every fiber, that it would open again at some point, and I left feeling warm and full of fuzzy hope about the future.

21

Dinka dropped in most days, always unannounced and often when he was returning from a house call or a birth or whatever else he did in his private practice. He'd voice his concerns about my handwriting or the patients calling in sick or the state of the world, and I'd pretend to give a shit while my blood pressure rose and I worried my vena cava might burst open, waiting for him to call me out on the pill switch. I'd nod my head and smile and ask a question or two when there was a long pause so he'd think that I cared, but I didn't. My mind was lasered in on Magdalene's appointment, my favorite twenty minutes of the day.

She was starting to share things with me, too, little details of an earlier life: the horrors of high school, how she was forced to switch schools three times because her classmates discovered her serostatus and predictably tormented her, staging a walk-out to keep her from gym class, refusing to eat her cake in home economics, avoiding the toilet she used or the desk where she sat, and I wanted to tell her how I could relate. Not in the torment she felt, but in the need to keep a secret. It was a paradox: the reason I felt connected with Magdalene and the reason I couldn't declare it were one and the same.

I checked the mailbox each day until, eventually, I got a package from Sally. Inside, she'd crammed all my mail from the past five weeks, including a final notice from the Denver Police department stating they had sold the Dump and I no longer owed them a fine. It was a displaced sadness I felt, like hearing your favorite childhood teacher had died five years prior. The emotion was real, but I felt tardy to my own grief.

Inside the larger envelope there was a smaller envelope stuffed with the book, three Polaroids, and a note with a bullshit excuse about why she didn't get it signed. *He yelled at me. Come get it yourself when you meet the baby.* I looked at the photos: Sally in the bathroom, her belly a small globe in the vanity mirror; my mother asleep on the couch with a bag of chips; and David, the paraplegic neighbor with his everlasting boner, rolling down the street with a boom box strapped to the back of his wheelchair. I was pissed, but still I laughed. All those photos and no Bill.

That evening, Jeb and I met at Fascination to gamble a few bucks and have some brews. He told me how things with Flora were getting a little more serious without actually getting serious. They weren't dating, no – neither of them wanted a commitment – but they were fucking on a regular basis, and he'd seen her dance at work. She'd even told him how she'd lost her finger, something she hadn't revealed to me or Gwen.

'Apparently,' he said, 'it happened when she and her cousins were playing KGB in an old derelict tenement and they were "demanding" questions she couldn't answer and so one of them crushed her finger with a cinderblock.'

The moral of the story being that kids are shockingly cruel: here, Russia, no difference.

I told him I'd thought maybe the KGB had cut it off before she emigrated. We both agreed it would make a better story.

Before we left, he pulled a piece of paper from his back pocket and said he had something that might interest me. I thought for sure it would be some sort of leather thing, because he'd been grilling me on why I hadn't come back to the Comstock, but it was an address.

'I got a friend of a friend,' he said. 'He's trans—'

'Yeah?'

'And he and his friends meet every month to assemble a newsletter.'

'I'm not a writer.'

'Shit's already written. You'd just be putting it together. They need volunteers for folding and enveloping and licking.' He said the final word like a third-grader.

I looked at the card and told Jeb I wasn't interested.

'Just put it in your pocket,' he said.

I told myself it was a stupid idea, going to meet a bunch of strangers, but curiosity got the better of me, and I went despite the lingering worry I might discover some distortion of my future self.

I found the set-up at a booth in the back of Orphan Andy's, a tiny diner just a few blocks from Magdalene's place. At first I wasn't sure if they were the ones I was looking for – there were only four of them, and they all had mustaches or beards or balding hair – but there was one who looked a little softer, more like me than not, and I saw their stack of papers, their assembly line of stack, stack, stack, staple, fold.

I approached and said I was Jeb's friend and one of them, who introduced himself as Pancho, said, 'Yeah, yeah, he mentioned you might be coming,' and I stood there looking like a dork. The diner was impossibly small – four booths on one wall and one long line of red barstools on the other – and it was filled to capacity. Why they chose such a tiny venue to construct their newsletter was beyond me, but I didn't bother asking. The other guys all went around and said their names, but none of them stuck, except for the softer one, who was named Ed. They were calling him Eddie, and I had the sudden ridiculous urge to rip the name from all their mouths, tear it up like paper and confetti the room on my way out.

New Eddie slid closer to the man beside him, giving me a sliver of booth to use. I perched on one cheek while Pancho started telling me about their process. They were making newsletters, he said. Three hundred and fifty. It was aptly titled FTM. Pancho said they would leave the newsletters at businesses around the Castro and Mission districts. It wasn't a wide swath, he acknowledged, but it was a start. New Eddie leaned closer to me and asked how long I'd been taking hormones.

I asked him what business that was of his.

He raised his hands as a sign of apology. 'I just wondered if you'd started yet.'

'How long's it been for you?' Up close I could see he had a few sprouts of stubble on his chin.

'Eight months,' he said.

It was a disappointing answer. I'd hoped by eight months I'd at least have more facial hair. His voice was good and low, but it was the look I really wanted, and I wondered what his old name was and why anyone in their right mind would pick Eddie. It was a stupid name.

I started assembling a newsletter to avoid talking.

New Eddie leaned in close and said, 'At any rate, you should really shave.' He pointed to an article on page three of the flyer: THE ART OF SHAVING. 'The fuzz'll give you away faster than a nude beach. Until it's stubble, it's trouble. Dig?'

I folded another newsletter, ordered a beer, and listened to Pancho and a bald dude talk about someone they knew who got what they kept calling 'bottom surgery' and how now he could have a full-on erection (with help from an air pump), but sensation was a non-existent factor, like a numb finger hanging off the front of his body. 'Fuck,' Baldy said, 'I wouldn't trade my life's worth of orgasms for some floppy inflatable cock. Terrible decision. Terrible.'

One of the other guys actually looked offended. 'Not everyone can grow a five-inch clit, Rob.'

I was ready to leave.

I assembled a few stacks of newsletters and gave a half-assed offer to help again the following month, but I didn't plan on going back. They were nice guys, sure, but we didn't have much in common besides the obvious and I didn't want to discuss it endlessly. I wanted a world where I didn't think about it at all. It was the same reason Magdalene refused to go to any support groups, why she preferred to have friends who weren't positive: it was a drag, always being reminded.

When I got back to the apartment, I found one of Gwen's disposable razors and I filled an old jelly jar with water at the communal sink, and took it back to the room, where I wetted and ran the razor down my cheek. At first it felt like nothing, like one smooth surface running against another, and I thought about how, as a child, I'd watched my father shave on the rare occasions when he'd clean up for a wedding or a funeral or a job interview, and how he even let me do it once. He foamed my face like an old-man-beard and then, with a razor, I peeled the white away. I thought it might change the face underneath. I thought it might be how my dad (how all men) got that square jaw, like the razor was a block plane and faces could be worked like wood. But once I'd finished, once all the white was gone and washed, I was still a soft-featured child with screaming red skin. I cried because it burned. I cried because I was the same. He laughed, said, 'Pain's part of it.'

It.

He was smoking a cigarette at the time, and I, being the same height as the sink, watched his stubble and ash float atop the water like mosquito eggs.

It still hurt. I understood him then.

22

Days passed, weeks shed while the apartment turned into a den without Gwen and her inane TV shows and her long yellow hairs covering everything, though I barely did more than sleep there. Most of my free time was spent with Magdalene, renting movies or hanging out at her apartment or walking around the city, exploring parts of her hometown I never could've discovered on my own, places like the narrow alleyway between a pharmacy and a sandwich shop with a 19th-century mural of Dover Beach; and the sparse foliage in the north corner of the hedge fence surrounding the tea garden in Golden Gate park, where we snuck through after hours to have a picnic; and the basement tarot-card reader in Nob Hill with one green eye and one brown, who served us absinthe and told us we'd both live to be one hundred.

The sense of contentment remained, even as Magdalene's fever came and went again, even when she got another sore on her arm and she covered it with long sleeves. I thought the pills were working. I thought our trajectory was set.

I shot steroids in my ass each Friday. I shaved my face again. I worried I might be getting ready to bleed but the pain fluttered away and stayed gone. My voice started to crack and went sharp at awkward moments, times of stress or excitement mostly, and Magdalene laughed. 'What, a second puberty?' she'd joke. It was too slow for her to notice me changing the way that others would, people like my mom and Sally who didn't see me daily. It reminded me of how it had always seemed, to me, like my clothes were shrinking when I grew taller as a kid. Sooner or later, though, she would see it – the changes – and a new worry took root.

I exercised each morning, high weight, low reps, like Jeb advised. I started getting more muscles in my arms, and the soft edges of my face dissolved behind an emerging set of hard angles.

Jeb and I drank, got drunk, played pool, and acted like assholes pretty often, did coke, always at his apartment, but we kept our distance. We talked about baseball or Eli or weightlifting. I gave him the Mona Lisa acid stamp when I found it still in my suitcase. He had a bad trip; said he saw Eli doing aerobics with Richard Simmons, and he'd punched his television to free him, to free them both.

Flora dyed her hair crimson and said she was moving to Los Angeles. Some big-shot porn director saw her in a film and wanted to cast her as *Red, the Russian Spy,* in an upcoming flick. Jeb got choked-up when he heard about it. We both helped move her things out to a moving truck, and her apartment stayed empty.

Magdalene started talking about *after the study,* and I worried what that meant for her, even if she did have a new study to go to. But it wasn't her health she obsessed about, it was Kansas. 'I showed you my hometown,' she said. 'Now you show me yours.' I offered to buy her voice lessons – a paltry substitute, I know – but she refused. Instead, I bought us tickets to Alcatraz for the evening after the study's end, and we started counting the days.

The last week of the study, I skimmed a pill from each non-placebo-receiving patient, so that I would have a life raft to float Magdalene to the next study or drug. I feared Dinka would notice the changes in her photos, in her blood results, but he never did, and toward the end, I didn't care.

On the final day, I told the non-placebo patients it was only a lab-work day, and I drew their blood and asked the questions and took their pictures and hugged them goodbye before I put all their pills in the front pocket of my lab coat. It was surreal, knowing it would be the last time I saw them, especially when I packaged up their charts and photos and placed their folders in a box, and it felt a little like I was burying each one of them.

Magdalene and I agreed to meet up after I finished

packing the charts and cleaning the office, and when I was nearly finished, Dinka came in to congratulate me on a job well done. He'd been quite pleased with me actually – *Not one day of work missed* – and when we had discussed, earlier, my future employment, he had mentioned an old colleague in the ER at General, and Dinka reminded me of this fact while he unfolded a bright blue scrub jacket and said he'd gotten me a job. Apparently all the nurses at General wore that color.

'What's happening with the study?' I asked, feeling hopeful it was set for the next stage. National data.

Dinka tight-lipped a grin. 'No great patterns of importance, so far, unfortunately,' he said and shrugged. 'You win some, you lose some.' I knew it wasn't his first study, and it certainly wouldn't be his last, but behind his cool demeanor I saw pure disappointment, and I couldn't shake the terrifying possibility that I'd either muddled a study that had no real significance, thus making my pocketfull of pills irrelevant, or I'd just sank a study that maybe could have saved millions in order for me to save just one.

'I'm sorry,' I told him.

'Try it on,' Dinka said, shaking the shoulders of the coat, and I imagined my arms were in it, and he was shaking me. Carefully, I removed my own scrub jacket, while trying to think of excuses, should pills vomit from the pocket, but I had nothing. No excuse was good enough. Dinka shook the coat again. 'What's to think about?' he said, and I slipped my arms into the jacket.

I turned around and Dinka pulled the lapels and straightened the collar with satisfaction in his eyes like I'd just made rank. I'd never had a man look at me that way before, like he was proud of me, and a cold heavy guilt set in, but of course, by then, it was too late.

There was a note on my apartment door from the landlady when I got home. *Your mother called. Says it's urgent.* The phone number she'd written was unfamiliar to me, and my mind immediately went to worst-case scenarios. Sally in a car accident. Marcus ending himself like Eddie. Tornadoes.

Magdalene and I searched all over the apartment for some quarters, but we ended our search with a dime and three pennies. I had plenty of bills, so I went down to the deli around the corner, bought a bag of chips and a pop for Magdalene, and asked for change in quarters. The guy argued with me and showed me his till, explaining how he couldn't break change however I wanted. He wasn't a bank. He gave me twenty nickels and I fed them into the lobby's payphone back home.

A woman answered: *Providence Medical Center. How may I direct your call?*

I explained the situation and I could hear her shuffling through some papers. She transferred my call without any warning and, after two rings, my mother answered.

She sounded like she hadn't slept in ten years. 'Your sister's been admitted,' she said. 'Preterm labor. They're giving her drugs.'

I asked how many weeks along she was, but my mother didn't know. Twenty-nine? Thirty? She started crying and told me the baby might not survive. And Sally was in danger too. 'Hypertension,' she said. 'Or hyper-eclampsia something.' She sounded panicked.

I didn't know what to say. 'Sally can't hear you, can she?'

She blew her nose. 'No, she's doing a stress test or I don't know. I need my girls, Rosie. When can you be here?'

I thought about Magdalene upstairs, waiting for me.

I asked her what the doctors were saying. She said Sally was dilated two centimeters and having contractions every six minutes, but they were hoping to stop it.

I committed to nothing. Instead, I told my mother that I'd look into the details of flying and I would call her in the morning.

I went back upstairs where Magdalene was sitting on the bed, reading Bill's book.

'Is everything okay?' she asked.

I nodded. 'But we should scoot if we want to make the ferry.'

The open air from the bay was cold, and a misty drizzle hung around us, lighter than the sea, but only slightly less wet. We were the only people standing out on the back deck of the ferry, but Magdalene was so excited she wanted to see everything: the choppy water, the grey sky, the swirl of seagulls overhead.

'This is the first time I've left San Francisco in nine years,' she said.

I knew, in a way, she was trying to make me feel guilty. She wanted to see Kansas even more than she let on, and she knew I'd do almost anything to make her happy. Seeing as I *had* to go home and see Sally, there was no way around it, and I knew Magdalene would never forgive me if I went and didn't take her, I took the plunge. 'Let's do it,' I said. 'Let's just go.'

There was that lighthouse smile, that full-on teeth and no eyeballs smile. 'You mean it?' she asked. I nodded. My head felt like it weighed three thousand pounds.

She wrapped her arms around me.

Together, we watched the island enlarge until it looked like a monster crouching down, inspecting us. I felt miniscule and imagined what it must have been like to approach it as a prisoner.

On the island it was windy as fuck and the mist had coagulated into sharp, painful rain, forcing us to run for shelter as soon as the ferry docked. We puttered around the gift shop, and the main cell areas, looking at their vacant library and uncomfortable toilets and tiny living spaces while trying to dry off, but it was impossible; moisture was omnipresent, saturating every inch of air with ocean. I looked for a warm room, someplace where Magdalene could sit down and raise her body heat – her lips and fingertips had turned deep purple – but the place wasn't heated. I offered someone twenty dollars, then fifty, for their jacket, but they still said no. Magdalene insisted she was fine, but I could tell she was miserable.

I went back to the gift shop and bought the last windbreaker

– neon green, size XXL – and two hot chocolates, and we flew through the entire site until we found a fleeting patch of sunlight in a walled-in muddy field where inmates used to play baseball, and we stood there, looking out over the concrete wall at the city. The swells of land were more apparent from that angle, like waves of dirt, and it seemed a cruel torture for the inmates, day in and day out, to see such a beautiful city and all those free people eating and sleeping and fucking whenever they pleased. Magdalene settled on the steps near the field and the green windbreaker swallowed her entire body. I sat down next to her and she leaned into me while she finished her hot chocolate. She felt like an injured bird beneath my arms.

'If I was stuck here, I'd try to swim home,' she said, and I remembered how Gwen claimed she could swim out to the island and how I'd half-hoped she'd drown. Then I thought about the real island Magdalene was trapped on – her body – and how there was no swimming free. Not ever.

Magdalene slurped her hot chocolate. 'Do you really love me?' she asked.

I thought maybe she was going to say it back and so I nodded.

She bit her lower lip in contemplation. *Say it*, I thought. *My god, just say it.*

'I need you to do something for me,' she said. 'It's kind of a downer, but I don't have anyone else.'

Anything she said now would be a disappointment, I knew. *Why wouldn't she say it?* I kept my face cool. 'Sure, anything,' I said.

She fiddled with the lid of her cup before she finally asked, 'Will you make sure I don't end up in a box? I mean, a cardboard box for ashes is fine, but not a box box. Not a coffin.'

An electrifying pain zipped through me, cauterizing everything, making me feel numb from limb to limb. I managed a nod. 'That's it?' I said, like no big deal, like we were talking about a future that was far off and fuzzy, indefinite as the idea of heaven or heartache when you're healthy and under love's dumb spell.

She put her head on my shoulder. 'And then will you dump me in the bay?' she said.

The word 'dump' forced an image into my head of her body, whole and wrapped in a morgue bag, being plopped from the back of the Alcatraz ferry, and I wanted to say no, not because I wouldn't do it, but because I couldn't. But I knew I could. If I could help carry my best friend's coffin from the church to a hearse, I could open a box of ashes and throw it in the wind. I'd seen enough dead bodies to know that people weren't people once they were gone. But even then, sometimes a lump of thoughtless matter could invoke the worst thought possible: We are all winding down. All of us.

I lifted her hand and kissed the top. It felt like kissing ice. 'Of course,' was all I could say. We sat there for a while, watching the seagulls sail in the fleeting sunshine, until the clouds rolled back in and the temperature dropped and a zig-zag of lightning struck dangerously close to the rusty metal water tower nearby. I scooped up Magdalene and we ran for cover, back through the infirmary, and past the derelict officers' houses, and down to the next ferry home.

I held her shivering body on the way back, sanding my palms up and down her shoulders, rubbing her fingers between my hands like I was trying to ignite them. Halfway across the water, she asked me to take her out on the back deck, and she leaned over the railing for a while, watching the propeller churn the water as it kicked us toward the city. I figured she was thinking about herself as a bag of dust separating and swirling off into a million different directions, and it nearly ripped me in half.

When we got to her apartment, I ran her a bath and helped her undress. Each layer I peeled revealed another purple mark. They were raised and smooth-textured like moles. I kissed a cluster of sore skin on her ribs before I put her small naked body into the water, and she relaxed into an amniotic trance.

I counted twenty-seven sores all around her arms and torso and upper thighs. Most were the size of pencil erasers and crowded together in constellations. The largest was slightly bigger than a quarter and rested in the crescent hollow between her hipbone and her stomach. I dipped my hand into the water and ran my finger over it. She opened her eyes.

'You're a good person,' she said.

'Maybe.'

'Get in with me.'

'It's too small,' I said, but that wasn't the reason.

She curled up her legs to make room and grinned when she saw me look at the slit between her legs. She covered it with her hand. With the other, she made a wet grasp for my elbow and tugged, but I wouldn't budge.

'I have to tell you something,' I said. It seemed pointless to wait. The bet, my secret, none of it mattered in sight of this frail naked girl.

She stopped squeezing but her hand stayed on my arm.

I cleared my throat. I hadn't practiced how to say it. I wasn't ready.

'I know you switched the pills,' she said. 'That doesn't make you a bad person.'

I was caught by surprise. Selfishly, predictably, I hadn't been thinking about that. I was thinking about what she might think if I were to undress, if she were to see, really see, the all-and-everything I'd tried so desperately to hide. But switching the pills did make me a bad person. It made me a monster, honestly. Even if it was for her.

I reached back into the water and touched her hand. 'How did you figure it out?'

'I'm smarter than you think,' she said.

We locked eyes and I could tell she knew it wasn't going to happen, this mutual bath she wanted. I could feel her fingers start to move beneath my hand, stroking herself. I put my fingers over hers, trying to match the rhythm. She took a sharp breath, closed her eyes.

'I have more pills,' I said.

She stopped, opened her eyes again. 'How many?'

'About a hundred.'

She did the math in her head. 'A month.'

'Do you think they're working?'

She shrugged, closed her. 'Nothing works forever.'

After Magdalene fell asleep, I had a couple of beers and watched a game on her television, until the seventh inning when I finally had the balls to use her phone and call Marcus.

He answered and I told him it was me, prepared for another angry outburst.

His voice went serious, and he asked if my ears had been burning lately. 'Lotta gossip about you around here.'

'Yeah. Gwen might be a tad upset with me.'

Turned out, Gwen was telling the whole town I'd been sharing needles with an AIDS patient.

'It's bullshit.'

'Figured. Gwen's a bag of cunt. Besides, I know if you wanted to shoot up, you'd have come to your buddy Marcus.'

'So you're my buddy again?'

'It's just a fucking car, bro. Just a car.' The second time, I could tell he was saying it to himself.

'Well, I'm not sharing needles.'

'But you're doing junk?'

'No. It's not heroin. I wouldn't do that shit.'

'Good,' he said. 'Had me worried. So what is it then? Spill it, Gavin.'

I chewed on my lip and looked out the front window into the dark. 'Did Gwen say anything else?'

I heard Marcus light a cigarette and exhale. 'Like what?'

She hadn't spread the word that I was living as a man now. Of course she hadn't. Because effective as that information would be for smearing me, she thought it would reflect on her worse. She, after all, was the one who ran away with me.

'It was juice,' I said.

'What?' He elongated the word.

'Steroids—'

'Yeah, I know what it is. You want your bean to sprout like

a mushroom? Fuck, there are other ways to get buff. You're going to end up with a beard instead.'

'Maybe I want a beard.'

He started laughing and when he realized I wasn't, he went dead quiet. 'I mean, you're kidding, right?'

'I need you to help me change some documents.'

'Tell me your kidding, Gavin.'

'I'm serious.'

'You're out there pretending to be a guy?'

'Not pretending.'

'You're freaking me out, dude.'

'Yeah, well,' I finally said.

Marcus was thinking, I assumed, because he said nothing but I could still hear him breathing.

'Shit.'

More silence.

'Whatever,' he finally said. 'You're still *you*, though, right?'

'Yeah. Always,' I said and felt relieved. The divide had been erased. It would be okay.

He quickly changed the subject, said he'd won his last six fights by knockout and was no longer a journeyman but a bonafide amateur boxer. He'd even snagged the interest of a few managers, who had promised him some great fights and fat paydays in the future. One in California. He suggested we meet up if he did. I told him that sounded great, but that I'd be in Lawrence within hours and we should celebrate then.

'I... uh... we need somewhere to stay,' I said.

'Who's we?'

'I'm bringing a girl.'

'Fine,' he said, 'but I ain't cleaning.'

'Thanks,' I said, meaning a whole lot of things.

23

I tried to hide my apprehension as we climbed down the steps into the dark tomb-smelling mouth of the BART station. Aimed at the airport, we crammed in among the dull-eyed passengers off to jobs I assumed they loathed, and we found two seats just as the train screeched forward, and I had the sense we were riding a bullet through a very long barrel. The noise was a horror-show ghost wail or the way a human might sound stretching down a black hole, and it rattled my head so fierce I wanted to cover my ears but I didn't.

Magdalene asked me if I was okay.

'Fine,' I said, but I wasn't. I was pretty sure Gwen's wedding was in a few days, and I wondered how many people had heard the lie that she'd spread. Fifty? A hundred? I worried how Magdalene would feel if someone found out and reacted. It wouldn't be like the people in the Castro, or her foster parents, or even the bullies at school. It would be mid-western disgust. One of the most potent American strains.

When we got to the airport, we bought the cheapest round-trip tickets with the money from Gwen's pawned ring and went down to the terminal and onto the plane. Magdalene was so fascinated by the sight of the ground as we lifted up and it shrunk away that she didn't notice me white-knuckled, breathing like I was passing a stone. We were flying. I'd never flown before. Neither had she, but we were clearly having separate experiences.

'Holy shit,' she kept saying, perhaps a little too loud. 'Holy shit, holy shit. I'm flying, Sam.'

Right before we landed, agonized by doubt, I decided to come clean. 'So, there's something I need to warn you about.'

'Your roommate already told everyone about me. I'm

prepared. I'm used to people. They can say what they want.' She grinned. 'A scandal.'

'It's not just that.'

'I don't care,' she said. 'Whatever it is, I don't care. I'd rather deal with honest disdain than fake concern or whatever.'

I squeezed her hand and nodded. 'Of course.'

We both looked out the window at the view coming in. The fields spread out like geometric patchwork. Lines of road stretched between what appeared to be, at that height, nothing substantial.

I rented a cheap Buick with bench seats and shoddy power-steering. An agent pulled it around while a woman with orange hair and white roots took my money and gave me the legal speak. Magdalene leaned against me, feeling warm as noon sunshine, until she said she was freezing and went outside to escape the air conditioning. I thanked every god humans ever invented that she was gone when the clerk handed back my driver's license and said, 'Have a great trip, ma'am.'

The previous occupant must've had abysmal hygiene because it still smelled like armpit and a cloud of aerosol spray had settled over it in a film of baby-powder stink. Magdalene made a smiley face on her window. I could tell it had been a while since she'd been in a car because she started fiddling with the air-conditioner dials and the glove compartment and the window lever. She inspected herself in the side mirror before she flipped through the radio stations, looking for a weather report.

'Come on, tornado,' she said. 'Fuck all the towns and people and cows at risk.'

She wasn't quite kidding, either, and I loved her for it.

I reminded her that I lived in Lawrence almost all my life and I'd never, not once, seen a twister. Dust devils, sure, but never a town-swallowing cyclone.

Marcus answered his door, digging a goober from his eye.

'Dude, what's up,' he said before he gave Magdalene the up-and-down.

'Don't be a creep,' I said, pushing past him to put our luggage down.

The blinds were drawn, and the air was a confluence of body sweat and soggy trash. Marcus told us to sit anywhere while he scooped up a needle and dirty spoon from the counter and shoved them both in a kitchen drawer. He looked skinny and sallow. I could've kicked his junkie ass.

Magdalene sat on the edge of the couch as if afraid to commit herself fully to the cushion. Marcus came back from the kitchen holding three beer bottles between his fingers.

Magdalene opened her beer slowly and looked down into it. 'I don't think I can drink this,' she said and passed it to me. 'Actually, is there a place I can lie down?'

Worry punched me. 'Are you feeling sick?' I asked.

She sniffed. 'I think maybe I'm getting a cold. No big deal.'

I touched her head, which was bone dry and burning.

Marcus showed Magdalene to his room, where he cleared all the dirty clothes from the mattress to make a space for her. I didn't want to leave her side, but she said she wanted to be alone as she settled limp on the bed.

I tiptoed back out to the couch, where Marcus was packing a bowl.

'Guess who I saw last week?' he said.

'Ugh. Don't tell me.'

'With her lawyer boy. Did you know he has a perm?'

I laughed. Marcus patted a phantom afro on his head.

We smoked and talked about his last fight, how he got knocked out in the first round, an uppercut to the jaw, and he told me how he was trying to quit the junk so that he could win a few more matches and really crawl his way out of the journeyman shit, apparently forgetting he'd told me he already had.

'I thought about going to this methadone clinic up in KC,' he said, 'but I don't know. That shit gets put on your record.' As if his wasn't already shit-stained.

Just talking about junk got him itching. He went into the kitchen and I watched him cook his junk. The melting mess in his spoon was like lead he was fashioning into a bullet. I wanted to hit him square in the jaw, say *what the fuck are you doing?* But I didn't. Not yet.

'Sugar, bubble up for your baby boy,' Marcus said. He sucked it up and spit it into his arm. 'Sugar,' he said, a new droopy man. He seemed to melt beneath his clothes. 'Sweet, sweet. You wanna?' he asked, holding the needle out to me.

'Naw.'

'More for me,' he said, grinning. He fell open-legged and slack-jawed onto the couch, and we watched cartoons until he passed out snoring. It amazed me about junkies: the positions they could sleep in. Marcus was half on the couch, half on the end table, both arms above his head like stalks; his body looked like liquid trying to find a crack in the couch cushion.

I went back to his bedroom to check on Magdalene again. She was curled into a ball and her skin radiated fever. Concerned, I dug through the medicine cabinet in Marcus's bathroom. Behind the hair gel and a box of ribbed condoms was an expired bottle of pain killers: Ibuprofen, 200 milligram. I shook out three, went back to the bed with some tepid water, and tapped Magdalene awake.

She sat up, groggy. 'What are we doing?' she mumbled.

'Here, take these,' I said, and I put the Ibuprofen and five of Dinka's pills to her lips. She let me slot a few into her mouth, then I lifted the glass to her lips and told her to drink. We did that until all the pills were gone. She collapsed and fell back asleep. I went out into the kitchen and ate leftover pizza I found in the fridge, sniffing it thoroughly before nuking it, more for sanitation than a preference for temperature. I went in often to check on Magdalene, until, around 10 p.m., she'd kicked off the covers and her skin was slicked with sweat, indicating her fever had broken, and I finally fell asleep beside her.

When we woke the next morning she told me she'd had a terrible dream. 'You just kept shoveling pills in my mouth. Like literally with a shovel and I could taste the dirt.'

'And how do you feel now?' I put my hand to her cool forehead.

'Hungry.'

I made her some stale toast. Marcus too, once he woke up and slithered from the couch. He packed a bowl and I asked him if he had somewhere to be later.

He lifted the pipe and said he had a threesome planned with his couch and one Ms Nintendo.

'You ever played before?' he asked Magdalene. She said she didn't know what it was. Marcus slumped over to his TV stand and lifted up a grey plastic cartridge stickered with a cartoon of Mike Tyson.

He coached Magdalene through a few rounds with Glass Joe as we passed the pipe between us, but she quickly lost the fight, which Marcus said was almost impossible to do, and she handed the controller to me.

'Special bad is better than boring average,' she said.

Before I realized it, a whole hour had flown by and I was fighting some giant Russian for the second time, cussing, calling him a Ruskie-fuck. I noticed Magdalene's toe tapping against the floor, her arms crossed, her eyes zoned miles away.

'Let's get out of here,' I said, squeezing her knee.

She stretched her arms over her head. 'Okay.'

'You're too stoned to drive,' Marcus said.

'I'm a better driver stoned.'

'You believe this crap?'

'Yes,' Magdalene said with certainty.

I asked him if Bill was around, and Magdalene perked right out of her slump.

'You know him, too?' she asked.

Marcus pointed to a shitty piece of plywood that hung over his TV. It was splattered with red and black paint and looked a little like a Rorschach test. 'That's one of his. He gave it to me,' he said. 'We go out shooting sometimes. That's how he makes them.'

We all stared at the ugly painting for a while and debated what it looked like: a gargoyle, two ballerinas, a man on a sailboat. Magdalene said it was an old woman's vagina and there was a young woman, whole, inside it. That was the final word.

24

A month after Eddie had died, after I'd been questioned and cleared, after what felt like weeks of scrubbing every inch of my skin raw, my father lured me into daylight with a bottle of Jack. He drove me to the cemetery, over to our empty plots with the cold headstones and the sun-brittle grass, and he asked me if I really understood it, if I knew what dead was, if I *really* knew. He lectured about how a *real* man had to confront his problems; a real man didn't duck out. They weren't instructions for me, necessarily, but he wanted me to know the difference between a real man and Eddie. I felt dense as lead. I had to think hard to register the simplest things. *It is sunny, yes. It is warm, no. It is winter, yes. It is November. It has been two weeks. Three. Four.* I felt buried in my own body, having to claw my way out for even the simplest human interaction. We probably exchanged about a hundred sentences over the course of a year. I went mute at home and started college and watched my baby sister grow up into a lady, and was, essentially, just waiting to find a way to get free and move on, away from that stupid stone, that anchor that shouted out: you will *always* be Rosie. Like Billy Tipton, death would not let me choose. It was all down to biology, all of it. The fact that we're here in the first place, the fact that we all die in the end. Fair is just a word people invented.

I knew I was stalling. There were only so many miles of street and hours before we had to go by the hospital to see Sally, and everything would come unraveled. It was important that I told Magdalene before she found out another way. I didn't want to look like a weasel. But I felt like a fucking weasel, powerless and lame in all sorts of ways.

She commented on the size of Lawrence. How small it was. She said she lived in Monterey, once, in fifth grade. It was still bigger, but it seemed the same. No buses or subways or taxi cabs. I nodded like I was paying attention, but I could hardly stay focused on the road.

She asked when we were going by Bill's house. I told her to hold her horses, and I took her past the college campus and through the main drag, and we turned down Learnard Street, toward my childhood home. I figured the risk of swinging by Bill's was minimal; my mother would still be at the hospital with Sally, and even if she wasn't, I assumed she wouldn't recognize me in the rental car, but I'll be damned if my luck wasn't the worst.

As we rolled down the street, there was my mother helping Sally hobble from the house to the car. I tried to creep by, hoping I'd pass as just another stranger, but her eyes met mine as if pulled by some magnetic force, proving the existence of freakish mother instincts, recognizing her child's features from the shadow of an unfamiliar car. She opened her mouth enormous and shouted: 'Ro, you better stop!'

'I think that lady just yelled at us,' Magdalene said, giggling.

'You heard me! Pull over!'

I considered racing away, but, in the side mirror, I could see Sally holding her belly, her head hunched over in pain.

I assumed that the doctors had stopped the contractions – which was why she was home – but now they had started again. I pulled over to the curb in front of Bill's house and engaged the parking brake.

'I knew it!' I heard my mother say. 'I knew it!'

'Ms Gavin, I presume,' Magdalene said. She turned around to look over the backseat and out the rear window as my mother approached the passenger side.

In the rectangle of open window, my mother appeared. She leaned down with her hands against her knees. 'You didn't even leave town, did you? You've been hiding out this whole time. Have you been shooting up with that loser? I'll kill him. I'll kill you both.'

'I just got in last night,' I said.

'And you were gonna roll right by, not say a word. Why

haven't you called?'

'I missed the house is all.'

'Bull. Total bull.'

'What's wrong with Sally?'

'She's in labor again.' From the way she said it, I could tell there'd been several false alarms. She looked back toward Sally, who was in the car now, honking the horn. 'Look who, Sally. Look who graced us with her presence,' she shouted back.

Magdalene shriveled into her seat seeing as my mother was obviously speaking through her. 'I suspect you'll be wanting to stay in your room,' she said. 'Well, you can't. I've taken the bed out and I'm doing my workout tapes in there, but it looks like that ain't gonna be possible once Sally's had this baby. The sacrifices I make. Do you still have your key? Go in and get some food. Hamburger Helper's in the fridge. Stay close to the phone.'

The horn bellowed like a sick goose again, and my mother jerked her head away.

'Sally, don't you break my horn!' She turned back to us. 'You look different,' she said, 'Your face... you, are you sick?' She reached in and grabbed my chin. I jerked away.

'I'm not sick, Mom.'

She looked at me a second longer.

'Sally,' I said.

'Right. Right.' She turned and left. 'I'm coming, you honking goose.'

Magdalene looked over at me, bug-eyed. 'I still haven't actually met your mom, and strange, I've lost all interest in doing so.'

What could she have been thinking? I was in denial, hoping she missed it when my mother said 'her'. I nervously lit a cigarette and blew the smoke out the window. 'Where the fuck did I learn manners?'

Magdalene looked over at the house briefly, then back out the windshield. 'So where does Burroughs live?'

I put the car in gear and we started rolling. As we passed his tiny red house, I stuck my index finger out and pointed, and an eerie sensation crept over me, like I had been looking at myself all those years, sitting on the porch, watching those weirdoes drive by. What sort of person stalks an author? I'd wondered, but now I knew and I felt sorry for us both.

'It's sort of depressing,' she said. 'I mean, no offense, since he's your neighbor and all, but I thought it'd be bigger.'

'The house?'

She nodded. 'Everything.'

I worried that I'd disappoint her in a variety of similar ways.

I parked the car, and we went up to Bill's door, but he didn't answer. A cat appeared and threaded through Magdalene's legs while she tried to look through his dusty window. 'Nobody's home,' she said.

'This is his house.' I looked in his mailbox. Empty. 'I swear he lives here.'

'Correct me if I'm wrong, but the bet was getting the book signed. Not you showing me a house that could belong to anyone.'

She was right, and anyway, I knew I'd have to tell her my secret – hell, by then I *wanted* to tell her – regardless of whether or not the old man was home, so I took her hand and led her from the porch.

'So do I win?' she asked.

'I guess you win.'

'Don't take it so hard, big guy. You'll be back on your feet in no time.'

'Yeah, yeah.'

'Now where's my prize?'

I opened the car door and she slid in.

'I might as well show you it.'

She seemed satisfied and settled in for the ride.

We chugged toward Oakhill Cemetery and through the open gate. Growing up, the gates had not registered as a thing to keep people out, but seemed to me an actual opening, a portal from the burdens of the world. It was where they put Elijah, a boy from school who died of cancer in the first grade, and everyone said, *he's free now, free from pain*; and where I saw my father cry for the first time, over my grandmother's casket. He bought the plots, six of them, soon after that. When I was in middle school, I used to ride my bike out there and lie on the grass below the stone inscribed with my name, and stare up at the dome of blue sky, thinking: *this is it, my final view.* In high school, Eddie and I would smoke pot and drink beers over the empty plots, and make up stories about how I might end up buried there: a bullet from the Ruskies or a plane crash or old age. I told this all to Magdalene as I took one path and then another and we closed in on the section of earth I'd been avoiding for years.

I parked the car and we got out. I took her hand and tried to explain to her that I'd always been honest, but that sometimes honesty and fact did not agree. She looked nervous. I felt my world narrow down to this one single moment, and I knew, if we kept walking, we would reach a point of no return. An event horizon.

We approached the tombstones. My heart rate increased and I thought I might vomit. 'This is it,' I said when we were directly in front of them. She looked over at my father's stone. 'Bruno Gavin,' she said out loud. My mother's name was engraved on the other half of the stone, her birthday and a hyphen carved beneath it. Unfulfilled. She read Sally's stone next, noticed its empty half, which was meant for some future husband, and then she saw it, *Rosie Samantha Gavin*, but she didn't read it out loud. She just stood there, looking. A big gust of wind sent her hair flying. She knelt down and traced her finger in the letters. I finished my cigarette and ground it with my foot. She touched my birthday. 'You're a Cancer.'

'Ouch,' I joked.

She settled onto the ground. 'How come we never celebrated your birthday?'

'I don't like the attention.'

'Still, it's bad luck. Not celebrating birthdays.'

'Says who?'

'Says me.'

I couldn't even remember what I did on my birthday. Was I with Gwen? Or maybe I was at the movies, watching *Ghostbusters II*, getting a gut eating a whole bucket of buttered popcorn. Honestly, I didn't care.

Magdelene wove her fingers into mine and we both looked back down at the headstone, and I thought about my father's body, just a few feet away, and Eddie's, just a few hundred more, and the Dump, and Jeb's cousin Eli, and Dusty from the study, and just how heavy every single dead thing was. Literally, dead people were some of the heaviest things I'd ever moved, heavier than hay bales, heavier than fat living people, heavier than lead. But, metaphorically, their weight carried on. The dead left behind an invisible burden so intense no one ever seemed to talk about it. I knew I was setting myself up for that, loving Magdalene, loving anyone really, but I wasn't afraid anymore.

Magdalene started shivering, and I suggested we get her home, but she shook her head and sat next to the tombstone, using it to block the wind. 'Sit with me,' she said, patting the ground beside her. I settled down in the dry grass and wrapped my arms around her body. She looked up at the clouds. 'Not such a bad view,' she said.

The sky seemed within arm's reach.

'Play a game with me,' she said.

'Okay.'

She called it the ten-year-game, which was basically an exercise she'd learned in therapy, a way to trick the brain into dumping dopamine into the body, boosting the immune system by visualizing the future. 'Find a cloud that looks like something you'd want in ten years and make up a story about it.'

A plane flew over us. Time felt warpy and anchorless.

'I don't get it.'

'Okay, see that cloud over there?' She pointed to a blob of

white. 'That looks like a castle, and in ten years, I'll be on a tour of Europe, sleeping in fancy hotels and getting fat on Cornish hens and red wine and looking at all the loot those damn wars left behind. Now, your turn.'

I searched the different clouds, but my imagination failed me. 'I don't know.'

'Come on. Don't make me do this on my own.'

I scanned some more. 'Okay, fine.' I pointed to a fat shapeless cloud. 'See that there? That's a German shepherd. He'd be a good family dog.'

'You want to have a family?' She sounded surprised.

I nodded. 'And a house and kids, maybe. Vacations to Disneyland.'

'And a white picket fence and a barbecue grill?'

'I wouldn't object.'

She readjusted her body like she was thinking it over. 'I could do that,' she said. 'If you could do hostels in Hamburg first.'

I kissed her hand, realizing the real premise of the game was to completely submit to the make-believe world, to create this other world and live there for as long as we could.

'And our kids would have brown hair and green eyes,' she said. Her own eyes unfocused as if she were looking through a warm window, inspecting our kids, smoothing levitations of static hair, spit-cleaning smudged faces.

'You'd be a good mom,' I said.

That seemed to pull all the strings loose and shake her from the fantasy, probably because she'd lost her own mother so young and 'good mother' had no context at all. Her stomach growled. She said, 'I like your dirt home but now I want to see your home-home.' She put her hand out and I helped her up.

25

The familiar stink of my mother's house hit me as the door opened, before I had any view of furniture or the terrible portrait of Pope Paul VI, who I always thought looked like a bald pink goblin. It was a dusty smell, the odor of a dirt road before a good rain. I wondered if Magdalene noticed it too, walking in, her hand wrapped around my bicep. I shut the door behind us and we stood in the dim quiet living-room.

'It smells like books in here,' she finally said. 'Old books.'

I told her about the set of encyclopedias my father bought from a door-to-door salesman, which were shoved on the other side of the half-wall that divided the entry way, and Magdalene went to the bookshelf as I turned on a lamp.

'He didn't buy them all in order,' I told her. 'He just bought some randomly, when they were on sale – wasn't until the third time he'd bought *Wu* through *Ye* that he realized the sales weren't on all the sections, just the ones that didn't sell well. So all we have are the shit ones no one wants.'

Magdalene opened a book and buried her nose inside.

'You want the grand tour?'

She nodded and followed me around the small house. We started in the kitchen. I said, 'My dad croaked right here,' pointing to the floor. 'Doing his favorite thing. Eating.' She looked at the linoleum between her feet like he might still be lying there.

Sally's room was still a total mess, but there was a corner cleared of junk, where a white bassinet sat waiting. My mother's room looked like it always had, her king-sized waterbed taking up most of the floor space, but she had a new bedspread, some bright floral thing. I showed Magdalene our one bathroom, which hadn't changed a bit, and I described the time all four of us got food poisoning from a casserole, how my father couldn't wait and shat in the bushes in broad daylight. I showed her my old bedroom last, which was still extremely small but looked bigger than I remembered, probably because most of my stuff was gone. There was a new television on my old dresser, and an aerobics step and two five-pound dumbbells sitting on the middle of the floor where the bed used to be.

Magdalene walked all the way in the room and opened the closet. A few of my old button-up shirts still hung from the rod. She fingered one. 'Where are all your pictures?' she asked.

'Of what?'

She raised her eyebrows like *don't be dense.* 'Of you.'

The thought of her looking at Rosie, really inspecting and drawing conclusions, made me feel physically ill.

'I really don't want you to see the pictures.'

'Well, that sucks because that's the only thing in the world I want to do.'

'Those pictures aren't even of me. Not really.'

'Where you were is a big part of who you are now. Old pictures are like rings on a tree. You'd be hollow without your past.'

I wanted to lie and say they all burned up in a fire or that we never owned a camera, but I couldn't lie to her anymore. I didn't know how. I told her I used to have some old pictures in a box in my closet, but after my mother turned my room into her personal gym, who knew what she did with them. 'They might be out in the back shed. That's where she throws all the old shit.'

Without a word, Magdalene followed my pointing finger and went through the kitchen and out the back door. We trudged across the weeds, past the old bathtub my father buried in the ground years ago so that Sally and I could pretend we were bathing in the dirt. She pushed against the shut door and it opened halfway. Inside, the walls were bare wood, the beams totally exposed. In one corner, a window let in some sunlight, and a *Sports Illustrated* calendar hung on the far wall from a nail, forever suspended in October 1982. Before my father lost his foot to gangrene, he spent the majority of his time out in the shed, tooling around with one odd project or another, and, in a way, it hadn't changed since he croaked. My mother would throw in a new box of shit, sure, but there was still all his old stuff on the countertop – a half-built birdfeeder, a lacquered walking stick, all his goddamn tools – and there had always been boxes piled up, time capsules of magazines and T-shirts he'd saved and whatever-the-fuck else he hoarded, boxes everywhere, making the new ones almost impossible to tell from the old.

I was hopeful we'd never find a single picture of me, not in all that junk, but I saw a box, less damaged from exposure, sitting lopsided at the top of a nearby stack, like my mother had tossed it up there and hoped it wouldn't slide back down. I did my best to distract Magdalene from choosing it first.

'I'm just warning you,' I said as we walked in. 'This is the first place I kissed a girl.' I kicked a box that felt solid.

'Was she pretty?'

'She was eleven.'

'Perv.'

'I was ten.'

Magdalene kicked the same box and asked if she could open it. 'Sure,' I said. She unfolded the worn flaps and took out a T-shirt and stretched it wide. The front read: *If my fly's down, I'm looking for large mouth.* Below it was a screen print of a fish.

'What a gentleman, your dad, huh?'

I smiled.

She opened another box, found a stack of *Playboys*, and fingered through one.

After a few pages she said, 'So am I prettier?'

'Huh?'

'Than the eleven-year-old?'

'A million times.'

She stared at me. 'Then why aren't you trying to take advantage of me.'

'I didn't...' I was going to say 'care about that girl,' but I realized Magdalene wanted me to kiss her and I was being stupid. Too many words.

I leaned in and pressed my lips against hers. She tasted like salt and dust and when she pulled back, her breath came out in short bursts, hot as steam and void of scent. Her eyes had a hungry quality, like she'd been there before and she wouldn't turn around, not for anyone, and we started kissing again, fumbling over each other's clothes in the fray to get closer. I pressed her against a box and she shoved me into another, and we kept dancing around like two wild animals, moving our lips and hands with rabid devotion. I felt consumed by the moment, despite the small, nagging voice, Reason most likely, telling me we should probably stop soon. But I wouldn't listen. I lifted her shirt, kissed her stomach, her tits, her neck. She moaned. Begged me for more. But Reason (or total lack of Reason) had other plans, and annoyingly intervened when I tried to lift Magdalene up on a saw table (I don't know what the fuck I was thinking), and she caught her hand on the edge of the blade and cried out. Immediately, she put the wound up to her mouth and, when she pulled back, her lips were completely red. I could see the gash was long but not deep. She started to cry softly. I picked up one of my dad's T-shirts and wrapped it around her hand carefully. Blood got on my fingers and I tried to wipe it away.

It's just blood, I told myself. Just blood. But it wasn't, and we both knew it. A minor hangnail, an open scratch, one tiny breach in my skin, and I could be infected.

'Wash your hands,' Magdalene ordered. 'Hot water. Go now.'

I pretended I was without a single care. 'You're gonna need stitches,' I said.

'Nuh-uh. No way.'

I could've done them. I'd had the training. All I needed was thread, a needle, antiseptic. But we also needed Lidocaine and they didn't just sell that at the grocery store. She pulled the T-shirt away and inspected. The bleeding had slowed. She said she wasn't going to the hospital. She didn't feel well already, and she was not going to get admitted. No fucking way.

We hurried inside and over to the bathroom sink, and we argued about whether or not I should be wearing gloves, and I said there weren't any gloves, and she tried to stop me from helping, but I wouldn't. I told her to hold still, and I poured hydrogen peroxide over the wound and rinsed it clean while she bit into a washcloth. Then I dried the cut with a paper towel and asked her to hold it there. I went out to the kitchen and rummaged through the junk drawer until I found a tube of superglue, and I went back to the bathroom where Magdalene had peeled back the paper towel and was inspecting the gash. 'Right in my life crease,' she said, and she turned her hand toward me and, sure enough, the cut was bisecting the major line across her palm.

'You don't believe in that fortune bullshit, do you?'

'No,' she said, letting me take her hand. 'But it's fun to pretend. Kind of like ghost stories.'

I pushed the split skin back together and she winced. It had ragged edges, but it wasn't impossible to glue shut. 'Close your eyes,' I said.

She did it without question. 'If I was a ghost, I would come back to tell you.'

I opened the glue cap. 'I thought you said you wouldn't haunt me if I did what you wanted.'

'Not haunt you. Just tell you what it's like. Dying. Being dead.'

I dropped four dots of glue in the deepest section of her cut and squeezed the edges together. She tried to pull away. 'Shit,' she shouted. 'What the hell was that?'

'I know what I'm doing.'

'Yeah, well I want to know too.'

I lifted up the tube.

'I'm not a dish you can just glue back together, Sam. Jesus.'

'I did it to elderly patients all the time. Their skin is like paper. Stitches tore too easy. Besides, it's literally what this stuff was invented to do. Relax.'

She looked at the wound, sealed together like a dumb red

smile staring up at her. She closed and opened her fist. It stayed sealed. 'You glued me together like Humpty Dumpty.' She let me wrap some gauze around her hand. I taped it down and kissed her fingertips.

She told me to wash my hands. The soap lathered up pink and I watched remnants of her coil down the drain, but I didn't have one single worry. She knew the truth and she was still here.

Her stomach growled again and we both laughed. 'Feed me, Seymour,' she said, and I felt totally neglectful. I pulled her to the living room, turned on the TV, and sat her on the couch while I went in the kitchen to scrounge for food.

I found the pot of Hamburger Helper in the fridge. White beef-fat had congealed like Elmer's glue around the noodles. As a kid, I used to love that shit, but now it embarrassed me. There was no way I would feed it to Magdalene. I kept looking and found some cans of soup in the pantry.

My mother called while I was warming the soup on the stove. 'You're an aunt,' she shouted. 'Precious little five-pound boy popped out about twenty minutes ago. He's smaller than a squash and wrinkly as hell. So precious though. Goddamn, I'm tired.'

'What'd she name him?' I asked.

'Patrick, after your granddad.'

'And how's Sally?'

'She's taking a shower and then she's going to try to nurse.'

The thought of my sister's tits as things that actually existed and could be fed from made me squirm. 'Yeah, well, okay. I'll just give you a call in the morning then.'

'But we need fresh clothes.'

'You didn't pack clothes before you left?'

'You're going to come see the baby, aren't you?' It sounded like a question, but it wasn't.

'Of course.' I told her I would come up in the morning, and she gave me the phone number and an address before I hung up.

Magdalene was curled on the couch in the living room, half watching *Unsolved Mysteries*, half asleep. I went back into the kitchen and stirred the soup, which had boiled up and formed an iridescent foam, and I divided the liquid into two bowls and brought one out to her. She sat up but only barely.

'Are you feeling bad again?' I asked.

'Just tired.' She attempted a grin that sagged her pale tiny face.

I unfolded a TV-tray and moved her bowl from the side table to right in front of her.

'Eat something. You'll feel better.'

She took a few slurps. 'I'm not hungry anymore,' she said. 'I just want to know what happened to Barbara Jean.'

How those two sentences went together, I wasn't sure, but I assumed the second had something to do with the TV show, so I didn't ask anything else while she watched the screen with half-interest. I unfolded another tray and sat beside her.

'What if we never know what happened to Barbara Jean?' she asked, not to me, but quietly to herself. I put my hand on her arm. She was burning up. My immediate thought was God, don't let it be staph infection. I rushed to find a thermometer and something to bring her fever down. She was dozing again when I returned.

'Let me take your temp,' I said, placing the cold metal into the fold of her armpit, and I left her there while I went to start a cold bath.

When I came back, she had rolled fetal, the thermometer still, miraculously, wedged under her arm. One hundred and two, it read. Immediately, I made her take four aspirin and then I started to take off her clothes. She grinned and pretended to fight me off, which only made it harder.

'Mag, I need to cool you off, okay?'

'No. I don't want to be cold. I'm freezing already.'

'You'll feel better. I promise,' I said, and I undressed her quickly while she squirmed and cried, 'Don't, no,' and I wondered if maybe she'd done this before, had a fever bath, or maybe she was imagining something else all together, because I knew she wasn't all there. Not then. She was somewhere, deep down inside the fever, softly swaying in the lull. I reminded her of that and she finally relaxed and pulled her clothes free.

'I'm sorry,' I said, and I scooped her up and carried her to the bathroom. She weighed about as much as a bale of alfalfa and felt about as solid. She begged me all the way to the water, but I had to do it, and she didn't fight me when I set her down in the lukewarm bath.

'Please,' she begged with her arms up.

'Just for a minute. I know it's cold, but you have to.'

She looked at me like I was hurting her on purpose, and I felt the whole world fall away in two pieces – there was medicine and there was Magdalene – and I hated myself for having to bridge that divide.

'Five minutes,' I said. 'I'll make up the sofa bed.'

'No, stay here.'

'Let's get your hair wet, okay? Can I wash it?'

Her teeth chattered together. She nodded.

I'd done enough assisted baths in the nursing home to know not to dunk her, so I went to the kitchen and returned with a plastic cup that my mother used for 49-cent refills of soda.

'I just saw Sylvester Stallone,' she said as I knelt down by the tub. 'Really. He came crawling out of the toilet, and he told me, "You gotta lot of fight, kid," and then he dove back in, reached up, and flushed himself.'

I touched her head. She felt cooler but not by much.

'You don't believe me. Look. There's the puddle. See where he jumped in and water splashed out?'

She pointed, sending her own bathwater across the tile. I decided to play along, and I stood up and lifted the toilet lid and acted surprised. I hit the flusher and the water swirled away. 'Part of his jaw was stuck on the opening,' I said. 'He was glaring up at me.'

Magdalene smirked half-heartedly, closed her eyes, and rested her head against the tiled wall. I knelt back down beside the tub and turned the faucet to warm. 'Scoot forward and lean back,' I said, and she eased her head into my hand. For ten minutes, I poured warm water down her hair and she disappeared somewhere while I scrubbed her hair with Sally's strawberry-scented shampoo. Afterward, I pulled her to her feet and she swayed while I dried her limbs, squeezed the excess water from her long hair, and wrapped her in a towel.

'I had a dream about my mom,' she said. Her face registered an emotion I hadn't seen on her before. Nostalgia, maybe. 'She used to wash my hair,' she said. 'And sing a song. Something I almost remembered...' Magdalene hummed a few notes and then shook her head like they were wrong.

I re-bandaged her hand and took her out into the living room where she put on some clean clothes. She ate her cold soup and watched *Night Court* while I unfolded the sofa bed and covered it with sheets.

'Do you have any other friends besides Marcus?' she asked.

'I got Jeb.'

'I meant here.'

I shook my head. 'I used to have Eddie.'

'That's right. How'd he die?'

'He killed himself,' I said bluntly.

'Oh. Damn.' She looked down into her soup bowl. 'What happened?'

I'd shoved his death down into a dark damp corner in my brain, and I didn't want to go back there, not with her, not with anyone, so I gave her the short story: 'He got drunk, put a shotgun up to his chin, and pulled the trigger. No note. No see ya. That's the story.'

Magdalene covered her mouth.

I folded the sheet back so she would crawl in.

'How'd you find out?' she asked. It was an odd question, one I had never been asked before, I guess because everyone already knew, and so it came in like a curveball.

'What do you mean?' I knew exactly what she meant, but I didn't want to say it. I could smell it suddenly. Blood. I felt sick to my stomach.

'When I heard my mom was dead, I was eating a tomato. I can't eat them now. That gooey inside. It's sinister to me.'

'I used to go shooting, out with my dad, and I haven't shot a gun since. So, I understand.'

She slid beneath the blanket, and I turned out the lights but left the television on and settled in next to her.

'So you're really just going to ignore my question?' she said.

'What do you want me to say?'

She took a deep breath, like moving took some effort, and she sat back up to put an ice cube in her mouth. She spoke around its edges, 'You don't have to tell me anything.' But her tone painted two options. Either I talked about it or I was an asshole. Either I told her or I would be responsible for a loss of trust in our relationship. My father always used to say we could do it the easy way or the hard way, but I always saw it as two hard ways.

'How did I find out Eddie was dead. That was the question, yeah?'

She nodded.

'Pretty much all I had to do was open my eyes,' I said. I hadn't said it out loud before. Not even back then. It was just a given that people knew. Word spread quick.

'We'd been hunting pheasants. He was getting sloshy drunk and would not shut up about Gwen. *Trust is a lie, Gavin*, he kept saying. *It's a contract with one sucker's signature.* His whining was sad, kind of boring, really, since I heard it all the time. It never seemed serious. It wasn't even out of character for Eddie to drink too much and get mopey – he was always sour, always – but I would've never guessed he'd do what he did. So we went back to his parents' place. Drank more, played darts. I passed out.'

I paused for a long time, trying to form words for a memory I'd kept locked away for so long. Finally, I said, 'A gun going off in a concrete basement is like being inside a bomb. The sound can't escape anywhere so it just swells and I woke up hard, panicked. I fell off the couch, tangled up in a blanket, tripping, freaking the fuck out. It wasn't until his mother came running down the stairs and started screaming that I actually realized I was awake, and I hit the light and saw Eddie's face... wasn't Eddie's face anymore.'

'So while you were there sleeping?'

'Some friend, huh?'

We laid there quiet for a while, looking up at the ceiling, listening to Dan Fielding say something lewd on the television. The laugh track sounded like thunder.

'That's horrible,' Magdalene said finally. 'I get why you're mad.'

'Who said I was mad?'

'Your tone. You sound mad. I mean, who wouldn't be?'

An unexpected chuckle came out my throat, and I kissed her hair. No one had actually ever acknowledged that. How fucked up it was. I'd always felt blamed because I'd been feet away from him but unable to do anything.

'Have you forgiven him?'

I didn't want to answer the question, mostly because the answer was just another question, one I had asked over and over – why would he do that to me? – and still nothing actually seemed like a viable reason. Sure, I knew *why* he did it. Logically, he hadn't done it to me. He hadn't done anything to me at all. He'd done it to himself. Emotionally, though, psychologically, he'd fucking shattered me so bad that when it happened, I couldn't even feel the shards of my former self. I was dust. Glass dust that could never be repaired, that would have to be melted back down and reformed into something new or left in the wind to blow away and disappear from the inside out. I tried explaining this and she told me he couldn't have done it on purpose. I said it didn't matter. He was acting on impulse. He felt unnecessary, totally without cause or reason to live, and he flipped the programmed death-switch, messily removing himself from the gene and resource pool, and he went back to the earth to become a resource himself. I'd been combating the loss with cold logic and mostly felt like I'd won. Or understood. Fucking instinct was what it was. We all had it somewhere in there. But still the idea of taking my own life over something as small as a girl's betrayal with a pants-shitter, it seemed ludicrous. Even on my worst days, I didn't understand it. 'He was just so stupid,' I said.

'You can't stay mad forever,' she said. 'Anger is like replacing all your blood with acid. Who does it hurt?'

I didn't know how to respond. 'So, I'm just supposed to forgive him?'

'What an asshole,' Magdalene said. Not Eddie, but me. I was the asshole. 'How much pain does somebody have to be in to do that to themselves?'

'I'm the asshole?' I couldn't believe it.

'How many times have you gotten drunk and done something stupid?'

She knew none of those stories, but there were plenty. Not shoot-your-face-off stupid, but actions I was ashamed of. 'Yeah, but I never shot myself.'

'Well, lucky you,' she said sarcastically.

'Not everyone's as saintly as you. Maybe I can't just forgive him.'

She moved closer. 'It's not about being saintly. It's about accepting what is.'

The conversation was moving in a direction I did not wish to go, and it felt like some invisible hand was steering me there.

'You think hating Eddie will hurt him,' she said, 'but you're only hurting yourself.'

'Thanks, Oprah.'

'Make fun of me all you want, but I promise if you just decide *when* you should feel mad and when you shouldn't, you'll have a lot more time when you don't feel mad – you'll feel good – and that's a better way to live. Feeling good. Don't you think?'

I wondered if she was actually worried about herself. That I might get mad at her for dying too. All this time I'd wondered if she was using me to get better, but there was no getting better. I never once saw or overheard her lying to herself. She maintained no fantasies about her prognosis being anything but terminal which meant she must have been with me for another reason and I had a suspicion about what that might be. She wanted to be remembered. That was it. Unworthy vessel I knew myself to be, I wondered why she chose me. I rubbed her arm, which was clammy with sweat, and I felt relieved. Her fever had broken. 'How do you feel?' I said.

'Better, but tired.'

We both knew she needed to go to the doctor. Over-the-counter meds weren't keeping her fever down for long, and neither were Dinka's pills, and she'd already refused to see a doctor in town. I voiced my concerns and suggested we go back to San Francisco in the morning. She nodded like it was the right thing to do and she knew it.

'I'll go and you stay,' she said.

'No. I'm coming with you.'

'It'll cost too much to change the ticket.'

'I don't give a shit about money.'

'But you give a shit about your sister, don't you?''

She was right: What kind of person would I be if I just bailed on my family? Worse, what kind of person would *she* think I was? 'Fine,' I said. 'But you're going straight to the ward once you land.'

She nodded and gave a limp salute.

The image of her travelling all those miles, alone, sickened me. I tried my best to soften the reality. 'And, I'll be back next week. It'll go by like that—' I snapped my fingers '—and you'll hardly even miss me.'

She cuddled closer, smelling like my sister's shampoo and some faint kind of mold. 'You promise?' she asked.

I worried that I'd killed her with that cut, that maybe she had a serious infection and would die from sepsis.

'I promise.'

She sighed. 'I wanted to see a tornado.'

'It never happens.'

'It could've. Odds are like game show doors. Up to chance and conditions and whim.' She beamed up at me, said her brain felt fuzzy.

I kissed her nose and turned off the television and replaced the wet washcloth on her forehead with a colder one.

'What do you think dying's like?' she asked me.

'Are you scared?' I asked because I was. Not for me, but for her.

'I don't know. Not really. I mean, I don't believe in all that heaven and hell bullshit, but I wonder if maybe there's something else to it.'

'To dying?'

'To being here. Being part of the universe.'

I told her about Eddie's wild idea about an infinite universe with infinite planets and infinite yous, and how he thought maybe we would just die on one planet and wake up on another. 'You know how sleeping feels like no time passed?' I said. 'It's like that with death, maybe. A million years could pass, and it would feel like a good night's rest.'

'What makes you believe that you would be you and not something else? What if infinite yous just means you being infinitely different things? A spider? A cheetah? An alien?'

I didn't want to admit she might be right. I still thought of her as fragile, and so I lied and told her, 'No. I'm certain that when we die, we wake up in our new perfect bodies.'

'Even me?' she asked.

I touched the hollow in her neckline. She was sweating worse than before. 'Yes.'

I could barely see her face, but her teeth appeared out of the dark. She seemed to hesitate, like there was something she was going to say, but then she didn't say anything, and I'd like to think that maybe she was going to say, 'It's worse than you know,' just to give me some kind of warning, some little measure of compassion, because I was in complete denial. But instead, I guess, she gave me mercy.

She said, 'I want to see you naked.'

I put my hand on her waist and wondered if, on another planet, there was another Sam and another Magdalene lying together on my mother's fold-out sofa bed, and in that world, both our bodies were just as we wanted. I pretended we were in that world. I had the intense desire to squeeze her until my body consumed hers, as if we were only cells coalescing and not people with all of the problems that being people possessed. Instead, I kissed her.

26

I won't describe what we did after that. Not because it wasn't amazing. Not because I wasn't careful. Not because I'm in any way ashamed or regretful, but I won't. It's mine and I won't share.

27

The airport was on the other side of town, and I took the long way just so I could squeeze out a few extra minutes with Magdalene. Despite our conversation the previous day, when we made it to the check-in desk, I pleaded with the ticket agent, begged her to find a way we could switch my return ticket too, but there was only one seat, a six-hundred-dollar seat.

'I could get you on a flight tomorrow,' she said. 'One thousand for the both of you.'

Magdalene stood next to me, shivering, holding a folded blanket in her arms. I could tell all she wanted to do was unfold it, lie down, and wrap herself up.

'Just do the one today.'

We finished the transaction, and I gave her all of my money and asked if they had a wheelchair, but Magdalene refused to sit in it. She started walking toward the terminal. I threw her backpack in the seat and raced after her.

We reached her gate, and I gave her a pain killer I'd taken from my mom's stash. She swallowed it with tepid soda and finally conceded to sit in the chair when she realized there weren't any other open seats. The pill took effect quickly, and her eyes glazed and she gained a dull cheeriness she hadn't had just minutes before. The chair was for a much wider person, and she looked like a scrawny child on a throne. She nudged me with her shoe and said all she wanted was a warm bath with me in it.

I sat down on the floor next to her and I kissed her knee. I watched our minutes drain away as people walked past. Fat parents with their fat kids. Elderly couples in tracksuits. Hippie friends with ratted dreads. I wanted to ask her to tell me, once and for all, where she ran away to when she was a kid, but it felt like a heavy question and its answer was an anchor that I assumed, stupidly, would be there when I returned.

A flight attendant approached us and asked Magdalene if she wanted to board first, seeing as she was in a wheelchair.

I could see Magdalene charting out the rest of her long day – Plane, Taxi, Ward, Home – and she said, 'That would be lovely.' Then she looked at me with those big green eyes and said, 'Send me off?'

The attendant let me push Magdalene as far as the jet way. On the uneven floor, she stood and straightened my collar. 'Be good, Sam Gavin,' she said, and she kissed my cheek and disappeared into the plane.

I made it about fifty yards from the airport before a full-out weep tried to burp its way out. It came at me in waves, and I kept swallowing it down, pushing it back because it was stupid. Seven fucking days. I didn't want to be a pussy. But I was worried. I wanted her fever to be something easy, like a cold or some simple bacteria, one her weak blood cells could defeat, but I knew it was probably worse. Always, it was worse.

Sally's baby was down in the nursery in an incubator, lying in a giant diaper with an IV in his foot. He was screaming and writhing but we could barely hear him through the plastic. An overhead heat lamp beat down on him, and I thought, *shit, poor kid, what an introduction to the world.*

'It's like he's being cooked,' I said to my mother.

Sally was drugged-up in the other room, on Codeine or something, because they'd sliced her. Not a cesarean. Worse. 'Straight from one hole to the other,' she said. 'And they gave me stitches that'll just disappear! Just melt away. Did you know that they could do that?'

My mother tried to make a joke. 'I asked the doc if he could give me some of those. Tighten things up down there. Maybe I could get a date.' We pretended to laugh before she left to get more coffee.

I put my hand on the rail of the bed. 'Cute kid,' I told Sally. He wasn't cute. He looked like a fat worm, totally interchangeable with every other squirming baby. I pictured Mag as a newborn. Then Eddie. My dad. All fat purple worms. All screaming at the light.

'Isn't he? I just wish I could just hold him some more,' she said, and then she looked over my shoulder and smiled. I turned to see Rachel, Gwen's sister, standing in the doorway, holding a stuffed bear and a balloon. She looked right past me. Fine.

'Your mom called,' Rachel said.

I left them alone and went back to the nursery to stare at Sally's baby, wondering where and what he'd be doing when twenty-three years had passed. Probably thinking about some girl.

28

My mother followed me out to the rental center so I could drop off the piece of junk car and ride back with her. She was adjusting the radio when I got into the front seat, and she hardly acknowledged me until finally asking, 'So where's that girl you were with?'

'She went home,' I said, but didn't say where home was.

After a long silence, she opened her mouth again. 'Gwen's been telling people that girl has AIDS.' I could feel her trying to gauge my reaction. 'Is it true? Does she?' She said the word AIDS like she like was trying to hide how sinful she thought it was under a paper-thin layer of polite ignorance, like it might hear her and come looking to infect her.

'I don't want to talk about it.'

'I just want to know if I should be worried.'

'You shouldn't.'

'First your sister…and now you're doing drugs.' She started crying, which was unusual.

'Look. Here it is. Yes, I'm on drugs, but not for recreation. No, I don't have AIDS because I know how it transfers and I've been careful.'

'What kind of drugs?'

'Steroids,' I said and waited for her to freak. I could see her working it out on her face.

She gripped the steering wheel. 'But why?' she said calmly, as if she were asking, why *that* shirt?

I closed my eyes and listened to the hum of the wheels against the road. I thought about every time I wanted to tell her how I felt, and how I'd never had the nerve, not even then, but I forced myself to fake it. 'I want big muscles. I'm tired of these girl arms.'

'But why? Girls have girl arms.'

I looked at her. She watched the road. Her face looked old with concern and lack of sleep. I didn't know if what I was about to say would help her sleep or cause her to swerve off the road. 'I don't want to be a girl. I've never wanted to be a girl.'

'But you're such a pretty girl.'

'I don't want to be pretty.'

'Well, too bad. Because you are.'

I don't know what I expected her to say but her dismissal came as no surprise.

'Not anymore,' I said.

I tried calling Magdalene later that night, but the line just rang and rang. I assumed she'd been admitted to the hospital and would call me when she could. Though the time between 'when she could' and 'when she didn't' began to overlap and by mid-afternoon, the next day, I started to worry. I tried the ward, but the receptionist rudely reminded me that all patient records, as well as their comings and goings, were confidential.

'Why don't you just call and say you're a cousin or something,' Marcus said when we got together to smoke weed and play Nintendo.

'I tried that,' I said. 'I think she recognized my voice because she told me not to call again.'

'Well, you can't give up, right?'

'I'm not,' I said. 'I'm reassessing.'

'That sounds like pussy talk.'

I phoned the police stations, the hospitals, and got the same answer from each of them – nothing but a 'nope' in different words. Finally, I called Jeb and begged him to stop by her place and check for me. He called back three hours later and said that no one answered.

I pretended that she was ignoring me, that she hated my guts and wanted no more of me; anything to ignore the likelihood that she was really too ill to call, or worse, dead. No, I told myself. She was fine. All along. Fine. It was easier to trick the heart away from worry with anger than with love, and so I did.

But then I got a sore throat. Then my nose became a running snot faucet. Then my back ached and my skin slicked with fever. I had her cold. And, soon, so did Marcus. Maybe, in a way, I gave it to him on purpose. If her cold was still here, still in me, still in others, then she couldn't be gone, I bargained. She couldn't.

Five days passed before I finally got the phone call. It was early morning, chilly for the first day of September, and the weatherman said a front was coming through – *might stir up tornado conditions*, he said. I was pulling on my shoes when the phone rang. It was Marcus, I assumed, telling me he was on his way. We had planned on taking Bill out to shoot, off where me and Eddie used to hit bean cans and beer bottles as kids.

'Can you get that?' I yelled out to Sally, who was in the bathroom getting ready to go back to the hospital to check in on Patrick, who'd been growing in an incubator, trying to breathe on his own. She poked her head out into the hallway, pointing to her mouth, frothy with toothpaste, so I answered it myself, uneven in one shoe.

The doctor sounded strange, nervous like a kid explaining misbehavior, and full-body nausea gripped me. I braced against the doorframe and thought about Sally in the bathroom, spitting her toothpaste down the drain, seconds away from learning her little baby was nothing but a shell now – a husk of lost potential. Maybe it would be best. If the child was lost, maybe Sally's childhood could still be salvaged.

'What is it, doctor? What happened?'

The man said he wasn't exactly a doctor but a graduate student. 'Elswood,' he said.

'I don't care about that, just please, what's wrong with Patrick?' I said, and Sally came around the corner. I didn't meet her eyes but could see they'd gone buggy.

'Patrick?' Elswood said. 'I'm sorry. Is this Sam?'

'Yes.'

'Sam Gavin?'

'Yes. Yes, goddamnit. What is it?'

'Mister Gavin. I'm sorry. I'm calling on behalf of Magdalene Salas.'

And with that, the ball finally dropped. The disquiet I'd been juggling for days fell and shattered the Earth's mantle and I felt myself floating off, weightless, suspended, equalizing with the void around me, becoming nothing. There was a hand of bones tightening around my throat but I managed, 'No.' I knew the word was false. A fucking lie. 'Where… where is she? Can I talk to her?'

Sally reached for the phone and I slapped her away. 'No,' I said to her, to God, to Elswood. 'Can I?'

'I'm sorry,' he said. 'She asked me to call you. I've tried. I've tried twice. Magdalene passed on Friday morning.'

He said more but, being nothing as I was, I retained none of it. Something about peaceful. About Kaposi Sarcoma. Empty condolences. Empty condolences repeated.

I thanked him like a computer. I meant none of it. I meant nothing.

Everything went numb – my ears, my face, my legs – and I found myself on the floor, the phone thrown against the tile, Sally on her knees picking up pieces of beige plastic and putting them in the cup of her hand. My knuckles hurt. Blood. I sucked my wound. Was she in there, in my blood? Could I taste her? Could I keep her going?

'She's dead,' I told Sally, and the words sounded as if they'd come from another person's mouth. I tried again. 'She's gone.'

Marcus came by soon after to pick me up, and I said I wasn't going. I guess, by the look on my face, he could tell something was wrong and he asked what it was. Sally told him.

'Jesus Christ,' he said. 'What happened?

I went to lie down on the couch, and he followed me and asked me again what happened, and I told him I didn't want to talk. I couldn't.

He sat there for a while and then said he'd be going shooting again in a few weeks, once he got back from a fight. 'Why don't you come then?' he asked, but I didn't even bother to look away from the television. I'd stopped watching and was beginning to feel like I was the one being watched. Marcus sat with me but said nothing, experienced enough with grief to know what a minefield it was.

That night, a tornado ravaged a field near Salina, killing sixty cows. The owner, a broad-nosed old rancher, told the news reporter that he'd have to start from scratch. 'I don't know nothin' like I know them cows,' he said, and I imagined those mooing meteors. I would've done an impression and Magdalene would've laughed, and then reprimanded me. 'Have some fucking empathy.' Poor cows. Poor old farmer.

29

One day blended with the next while I drank all the liquor in my mother's cabinet. I missed my flight. I didn't bother calling the attending physician at General where I was supposed to report for work. The liquor restocked. Somewhere, a baby was screaming. One night, my mother stepped into my dark room and sat on the edge of the bed, rubbing her hand along my spine, and I closed my eyes and imagined being young again, imagined I didn't know anything about bodies – medically or otherwise – that I didn't know anything about how temporary every little beauty was.

'When your father died,' she started to say, but I stiffened.

'Don't,' I said, and she didn't go on.

Somewhere, a baby was cooing.

A box arrived later that week, courtesy of Elswood, and in it I found a smaller box with Magdalene's ashes, and her book, *Lolita*, which held the other picture of her and me, and a note on a folded sheet of yellow paper: *On another planet, in a different life, Sam Gavin, I will find you. Love, Magdalene.*

Love. It felt like a stab wound.

I laid in bed all day looking at that picture, the weight of her ashes held firmly against my chest. How could she be so small? How the hell could this be all that was left? And I thought about what we'd be doing if we were back in San Francisco, me working the night shift, and her in that Kodak study, and I did this daily. Weeks passed while I drifted around the house like an invalid, watching movies and eating junk food, smoking cigarettes until I felt nauseous, fattening up and softening like a goddamn olive.

I still hadn't cried, not until one night in early October when I was holding Patrick and he'd shit all over his clothes and I had to help Sally bathe him in the sink. Sally was holding him by the armpits, and I was spraying his backside clean with the hand-squirter when he pissed across the counter, right into an empty cup, and I laughed but only for a second. One blat and it was like a door opened, creating a breach in the gate I'd put between me and all emotion, and out of my laugh rushed every wet sobbing thing I'd locked up. I collapsed and Sally held me until Patrick, naked and cold on the floor with us, demanded her attention again.

The World Series began a few days later, between the Oakland Athletics and the San Francisco Giants, and Marcus and I watched the games at a bar with fifty-cent drafts. Before the third game of the series, as we were sitting there, watching the recap of game two, the picture strobed and went fuzzy while the voice of Al Michaels carried on like a static ghost – *I think...earthqua* – and a green screen replaced the picture. The bar went silent. Someone shouted, 'What the hell?' and threw a peanut at the screen. The bartender raised the volume on the television.

Michaels's voice continued over the green screen: 'I'm not sure if we're on the air at the moment, and I'm not sure if I *care...*' The crowd in the background sounded louder than before, like someone had scored. Commercials. Then, another reporter appeared and said they'd canceled the game. 'Bullshit,' someone shouted. We paid our tab and went somewhere else.

In the morning, when I came to, I saw the footage of the quake – the Golden Gate swaying, cars teetering from the upper deck of the Bay Bridge, cars crushed flat beneath, highways rippled and crumpled and cracked, dust and smoke elevating from the rubble, houses on fire, walls tumbling down.

I tried calling Jeb, but his phone was busy. Over and over. Busy.

Fifty people dead, the news said. *Dozens still missing. More to follow.*

'Whose idea was it,' Marcus said, 'to build a city on cracks in the earth?'

Jeb finally answered the next day, and he told me almost

every basic service was suspended. Electricity, garbage, water. A million people living atop one another, reduced to cavemen, and most of them acting accordingly. It seemed poetic, somehow. Jeb said I should come back, that I could crash on his couch if I wanted. Maybe he could get me a job at the bar. I thought about Magdalene in that box. I imagined the box in the bay.

Gwen came knocking on my window a few nights later, her round ugly face staring back at me like the past had never happened. I lifted up the window. 'What do you want?'

'I heard you were back.'

I waited for her to say something more. 'Well, for once the rumors are true.' She didn't seem to catch my full meaning.

She looked down at the ground, dug her shoe into a shriveled dandelion. 'I also heard about that girl.'

Locusts whined in the trees behind her. I didn't respond. I couldn't. How Gwen lingered in my life, while all the important people slipped into oblivion, still mystified me.

'I wanted to say I'm sorry,' she said.

'For what?'

'Aren't you even gonna come out here?'

'You're not worth walking to the door.'

'I *said* I was sorry.' She folded her arms.

'And now what? I don't even know what you're sorry for.'

'For your friend. For being a bitch. For just leaving you.'

'I *wanted* you to leave.'

'God. I'm trying to make up.'

I looked over at the digital clock. 'It's one in the morning, Gwen. Go home to Bobby.' A few weeks of marriage, I thought, and she couldn't be faithful.

'He's at the bar,' she said like a brat getting away with something.

'Then go to the bar.' I closed the window completely and waved. I figured she'd scream and go to the front door and start ringing the bell until I went out there and shooed her away, but she just swayed there briefly, staring off at the side of the house, and then she turned and started shuffling back toward her parents' house, her shoulders visibly heaving in the streetlight, looking about as fragile and pathetic as a newborn mammal. I finally understood what I hadn't all those years before: she was suffering too, struggling to make some sense of the world, just like the rest of us, just like me. As much as I wanted to villainize her, to make all of it her fault, it never was, not completely anyway, and what parts of it that were, she'd have to live with forever. She'd lost her hope the same way we all did, a little bit at a time until it was gone.

It made me think about Magdalene watching the *Wizard of Oz* on videotape as a kid, over and over, a merry-go-round of life switching from two-toned, to color, and back again. It depressed me. I couldn't keep pretending that Kansas would ever be enough. For years, I'd resented Eddie for so many things, most of all what he took. All that potential. Days he stole from us. Days we just wasted being sad and for what? I realized I'd been shedding bits of him – the guilt, the Dump, Gwen – since I first decided to leave Lawrence, and now all that remained was my grainy memory and a few things outside in a box.

I put on my shoes and went out the back door to get all my old shit, all the pictures and baby clothes and yearbooks and organized sports memorabilia my mother had saved and tried to give me when I graduated high school. 'Trust me, you'll want these someday,' she said, leaving the box in the corner of my closet until she threw it out there in the shed when I left town. I knew my mother would never pull it out again, that it would sit in there for years, a home to spiders and field mice and microbes, and then she would die or move into a nursing home and it would all get thrown in the dumpster, and it didn't seem right, all my old stuff just rotting in a landfill.

I grabbed a canister of lighter fluid and took it out to the bathtub in the dirt and poured some of the fuel inside, soaking the dead leaves and old scraps of litter that had settled there from the wind. I lit a match and threw it in. As the fire spread through the debris, I went back to the shed, grabbed the nearest box of my dad's shit blocking the way to where my stuff was perched, came back, and threw it into the fire. The flames wormed up the side of the box and inside, gnawing at the T-shirts, sending up a spiral of black smoke that smelled oddly like marshmallows.

My mother came out onto the back porch. 'You're going to burn down the whole neighborhood.'

'It's contained,' I said just as the fire spit up, sending sparks in her direction.

She came down off the back porch and looked from the glowing blob of cotton to the open illuminated shed. 'That better not be my romance novels.'

I shook my head. 'Dad's shirts.'

She put her hands out to warm over the fire. 'Oh, you mean the bed sheets?'

I smiled politely, lit a cigarette, went back to the shed. My mother followed close behind. 'You might as well burn things worth burning,' she said and went over to a box of porn. 'This. Use your big muscles and help me throw this in the fire.' I wanted to argue with her, *but there is so much quality tits and ass*, but I knew how much she'd always hated them, so I picked up the box and took it outside. She threw a few magazines down into the fire, and I watched the pages wilt up and wither to nothing.

While she emptied the box, I went back into the shed and started to move around stacks of other boxes until I found the one with my shit. Crunched in the middle, and somewhat smaller than I remembered, all of Rosie, everything from my past, was in that box. I opened it up. My first-communion dress sat folded on top of everything, the frills and satin mashed into a crispy square. Underneath, I found some old comics and maybe fifteen or twenty photos, most of them with Eddie. I shut the lid and carried the box out to the fire.

Sally came out the back door holding Patrick. 'What's happening?'

'We're making room!' my mother shouted. 'What do you

got, Sally? Go get it.'

'Not the baby,' I said, and Sally glared at me like *don't even.*

I tossed the communion dress into the tub and its synthetic fibers went up like tissue. Then I threw in the box of photos and my mother shouted out that I *shouldn't have done that*, which is what Magdalene would've shouted too, but it was too late. The box was already half-burnt and, seeing it all, every tangible memory, disintegrate into nothing, made me feel better than I had in a long time. Free finally to accept it all. I made a joke about how I'd crawl out of that tub of ashes like a phoenix, and my mother misunderstood and thought I said I was moving to Arizona.

I laughed. 'I'm moving back to San Francisco,' I said.

'When were you going to tell me,' she said, sounding both relieved and disappointed.

'I just decided.'

'Just now?'

'Yeah. Just now.'

30

Before I left, Marcus wanted to take me out shooting in the woods as a sort-of goodbye. I thought it was going to be just me and him, but guess who was sitting in the passenger seat like the butt of a goddamn joke? None other than Bill fucking Burroughs, dressed up like he was going to the granary: denim pants and a canvas jacket.

'I swear to god, Bill,' I said as I got in the car. 'I see you every single day I don't need a thing from you.'

Bill didn't even look up from his newspaper. 'That right?'

I shut the door. 'My girl was in town. She wanted you to sign her book.'

Bill just smiled that blow-me smile. 'I don't have time to sign books for every little girl who happens by my front door.' Marcus put the car in gear and said nothing.

We rode out to the country; Marcus driving, Bill up front wrestling with a newspaper, and me sharing the back with a paper bag full of spray paint cans, our targets. I wondered where Marcus got the guns, but thought better than to ask. I was nervous to be holding a gun, much less *the* gun. I turned my focus out the window to the sky: cloudless. The temperature was unusually warm. An Indian summer, my mother called it. I could smell the dirt road through the air vents and I rolled down the window.

I asked Marcus, who had been using methadone for exactly two weeks, what it felt like. He said it was like every single physical pain went away in an instant, every joint ache and sore muscle and pinched nerve. It wasn't the same euphoria as junk though, which erased all the mental pain too, making every sad thought and terrible memory, everything that could *not* be forgotten, feel somehow understood, or hammered down, smoothed out, so that all experiences were equal. None good and none bad. There only *was*. 'Nothing matters on junk,' he said, 'and it's fucking heaven. Methadone, it doesn't do that. It takes the edge away though.'

I wondered what it would be like to fully pack the wide and horrible wound Magdalene had left behind, but it seemed like a betrayal somehow. She deserved to have at least one person reel for her, to sleep horribly and forget upon waking that she was gone only to remember and feel wholly miserable all over again, at least for a while because someday, I knew, time would smooth out the edges on its own.

'Numb or not, there's still plenty of edge,' Bill said. 'I knew a man once, had some work done in his mouth, and the dentist told him not to eat until after the numbness wore off. Well, my friend had this thing about being told what to do, so when hunger came, he made himself a sandwich, and all seemed fine and good until the nerve block wore off and his lower lip throbbed like he'd face-fucked a chainsaw, and he looked in the mirror and found his once human-looking lip to be twice the size and shredded like brisket.'

'That's disgusting,' Marcus said.

'The less you pay attention, the less you have control,' Bill said.

My eyes followed a crow to an oak tree out in the field. Twenty or thirty other crows sat in the shade around it, and I wondered if the ones beside him were friends or just enough like him to tolerate the same branch for a few minutes.

Marcus parked the car in a brown field crowded with more trees, and we got out and set up three different colors of cans (orange, black, and green) on the ground directly in front of a piece of clean plywood that we'd propped against a tree trunk. Bill came over and lectured about the angle of entry and the can's orientation to the wood as he adjusted the board to lean less and then took the spray-paint cans and turned them with conviction, jamming them into the ground like that was the only way they could be.

We stepped away, stuffed our ears with rubber plugs, and

Bill took the shotgun and leveled it with his old arms. I braced myself for the sound, but the blast was so loud it shook the birds from tree branches and the core of my chest. I was transported to Eddie's basement by the smell of rotten eggs and campfire, the splash of color. I watched Bill aim again and hit the can farthest away, making it spin and explode in all directions, splattering orange onto the wood and everything else. 'Ho-a!' he hooted. 'Ho-a!' After he'd hit five or six cans, he turned to me. 'You're up.'

My body was buzzing. I thought about Eddie and how, for the first time in four years, I felt sorry, not for myself, but for him and all the things he'd miss, every single possibility he'd erased with one drunk and selfish decision.

Marcus ran out and traded Bill's plywood for a clean piece. While he did, I laid out Magdalene's favorite colors – green, blue, and yellow – on the ground, trying to jam them in, giving them a good twist just like Bill.

He handed me the shotgun, barrel up.

'No mercy, Gavin,' Marcus mumbled through the rubber in my ears.

I wasn't ready, and probably never would be, fully, but I brought the butt of the gun to my shoulder, leveled the heavy barrel, and put a can between the sights. I was shaking so hard from the weight, all the weight, that the can was bouncing left and right and Marcus said, 'Steady,' and Bill said, 'Shoot the damn thing,' and I squeezed the trigger and dirt kicked up, but the can remained intact. Pissed, I lifted the barrel, pulled, the second barrel bucked, and bright yellow erupted with a crack of fractured metal, thrilling me almost to tears, and in the splash of color I could see, like a Rorschach oracle, I could see the future, the plane touching down in the ruined city, the warped streets and smoke and piles of brick, and pull and pow, green overlapped the yellow but not completely and I owned it, the color, the random splatter; I had my brush, fucking finally, and the last can was trembling.

Acknowledgements

Many thanks to Rebecca Gorman O'Neill, one of the best writing instructors I've ever known. Also in this category: Wendy Brenner, Rebecca Lee, Robert Siegel, and Clyde Edgerton. Their careful insights gave me so much hope.

Thanks to the Ralph Brauer Fellowship for the opportunity to travel and research in San Francisco, and also to the UCSF Library for access to their extensive archives.

Thanks to the Department of Creative Writing at the University of North Carolina Wilmington where I met some extraordinarily talented and intelligent people, whose advice and friendship I will cherish for the rest of my life.

Thanks to those who read various drafts (Christine Hecktor, Kathryn Miller, and Leigh Huffine especially), whose feedback and encouragement were invaluable.

Thanks to Literary Dundee and the Dundee International Book prize for shining their bright light on my work, and to Freight Books and my editor, Iain Maloney, for so diligently bringing this book into the world.

Thanks to my family and friends, and especially to my son who's heard, 'Not now, I'm writing,' more than once and never complained. Thanks, also, to my mom, Cathy Heikes, who has always shown me that hard work and focus are easy when you love what you do; and to my sister, Megan Dvorak, who first taught me how to read and adore books.

And, above all, my endless love and gratitude goes to Mike Bull, who has read every word of every draft and who has always been fiercely supportive and, still more, fiercely honest with his red pen. *The Cure for Lonely* would never exist, not like this, without him.